Glynis Peters lives in the seaside town of Dovercourt. In 2014, she was shortlisted for the Festival of Romance New Talent Award.

When Glynis is not writing, she enjoys making greetings cards, Cross Stitch, fishing and looking after her gorgeous grandchildren.

Her debut novel, *The Secret Orphan*, was an international bestseller.

www.glynispetersauthor.co.uk

twitter.com/_GlynisPeters_
facebook.com/glynispetersauthor
instagram.com/glynispetersauthor
bookbub.com/authors/glynis-peters

Also by Glynis Peters

THE ORPHAN'S LETTERS

GLYNIS PETERS

One More Chapter
a division of HarperCollins*Publishers* Ltd
1 London Bridge Street
London SE1 9GF
www.harpercollins.co.uk
HarperCollins*Publishers*
1st Floor, Watermarque Building, Ringsend Road
Dublin 4, Ireland

This paperback edition 2022
First published in Great Britain in ebook format
by HarperCollins*Publishers* 2022

A catalogue record of this book is available from the British Library

PB ISBN: 978-0-00-849241-0
TPB ISBN: 978-0-00-855919-9

This novel is entirely a work of fiction. The names, characters and
incidents portrayed in it are the work of the author's imagination. Any
resemblance to actual persons, living or dead, events or localities is
entirely coincidental.

Printed and bound in the U.S.A.
by Lake Book Manufacturing, LLC

For the student nurses I trained and lived with at St. Margaret's, Epping during the '70's.
We worked hard and played harder. Thankfully we had no war to deal with, only Matron!

Chapter One

Kitty Pattison looked at the small group around her, then down at her blood-spattered apron. Her body trembled with cold from the snow, and shock. Her tongue struggled to move around her dry mouth as she tried to call for help. People lay everywhere and she struggled to understand what had happened. The screaming voices, and the rattling bells of the fire engines vibrated her eardrums, and she clamped her chilblained hands over her ears.

Exhausted from another night of heavy bombing, Kitty wondered how much more northern England could take – how much more she could endure; the deaths were getting to her, and her body ached less than her heart after the recent attack. Winter cold was another obstacle and she watched people struggling to keep warm as they headed in nightclothes towards the makeshift medical or tea marquees.

'Another night like this and we'll have nowhere to

work,' complained a doctor Kitty was seconded to work alongside.

'It's better than not having anywhere to live or parents to watch over you,' Kitty retorted. The man had done nothing but moan all evening. She appreciated he was tired and frustrated, but talking like a defeatist in front of frightened victims was not – in Kitty's opinion – the professional approach.

'We're sitting ducks, doesn't that scare you, Kitty?' asked one of the other Red Cross nurses working nearby.

'I think Hitler invading frightens me more, but yes, areas like this make those living around here easy targets,' Kitty replied and continued to assist the doctor attempting to stem the blood flow from a pregnant woman's leg. The woman looked exhausted and Kitty wondered what her life was like before the war. Going by the five children hanging around her skirts – faces black with soot and dust – not an easy one, but better than today, of that Kitty was certain. The woman was pulled from the wreckage of her home and refused to budge until all of her children were found. She said her husband was a stevedore on duty, but they feared he was crushed in the first wave of the bomb attack and her children were all she had left to remind her of the love they shared.

The British docks were large targets for Hitler, and he ensured his pilots kept up their endless attacks. Quite often the pilots would offload excess bombs when they headed home, and residential properties bore the brunt of their disposal. The latter part of 1941 was proving to be a nightmare with back-to-back rescue missions. Every spare minute was spent helping the injured and the duty rota at the hospital rolled into one long week of working nonstop, and brought about the same horrific duties for Kitty on a daily basis. Her dreams were now nightmares and she often only had two quiet hours per day, which were frequently disturbed by night sweats and the calling out of the other girls in the room, enduring their own horrors.

Kitty knew she was at the end of her tether with mopping up blood and seeing young men lose their limbs, or their bodies burned beyond recognition or help. She sobbed in private and smiled at those who needed someone strong and supportive in their lives. They deserved that much from her, but she was not sure how much longer she could paint on the smile. She had lost hope and it was a dangerous thing to lose during World War Two.

With a heavy heart, Kitty had sent a letter to Michael, expressing her feelings – in need of his guidance and the comfort of his wise words.

She gave up on his response when, after weeks, she had not received a reply. The silence haunted her. Would she ever know if he was still alive? Had he remembered to name her as next of kin when they got engaged? She had added him to her list alongside her aunt and uncle. In her last letter she asked if she was to be contacted should anything happen to him. When they spoke about being orphans, Kitty remembered he had never spoken about other living relatives in Canada. Would she ever become Mrs Michael McCarthy and visit the land of his birth? Questions pounded her each day and drained her emotional bank.

The more Canadian patients she met, the more curious she became about the country. With the recent bombing of Pearl Harbor, she took more notice of America and – along with the rest of Britain – waited for news of their forces also arriving on British soil for support against Hitler.

Life for a twenty-one-year-old was not what Kitty had imagined and she felt sure a lot of people her age felt the same. One of the biggest troubles rambling around her mind was that of finishing her nurse training. The positivity she felt at the start of it all had now dwindled, the more exhausted she became, but she knew something else nagged away at her and she had a decision to make which might alter her life path.

Her friends Stanley and Jenny Walker-Fell had a house full of local orphans and Jenny's health had declined during the winter months. Stanley had gone from strength to strength since leaving Kitty's ward in Shotley Bridge Hospital and his gait had now improved to no more than a minor limp. Allowing him back into the RAF was the best thing the force could have done, for him and for themselves. Kitty's friendship with his wife had grown into a strong one, and Kitty didn't hesitate to join them when invited to enjoy Christmas at Fell Hall with the children. In between festive activities, Kitty spent time encouraging those floundering in their new life to speak about their fears – telling them she understood. Their faces often showed a little more interest in life when she confided she too was orphaned at a very young age, and they could trust her to help where she could.

Two of Kitty's favourite orphans, the Gaskin brothers

Peter and David, were now living on a farm but joined them for Christmas dinner. They made the most of their day away from chores by hiding under the table tying Kitty's shoelaces together or sneaking extra pieces of ham, their gift to Jenny for the celebration table, to feed the dog. Kitty loved how the two orphans embraced life – how they handled the devastating loss of their parents. They met with Stanley on a regular basis, and he gave them school lessons inside his home, which gave them sanctuary when they needed it most. They were the first of Jenny's successes and they adored her.

The other children Kitty met all benefited from a newfound dose of affection. Some of them had never had any before they lost their parents, and often rebelled at hugs and regular bathing. Others climbed from the darkness into a bubble of awareness and possibilities. Kitty vowed she would visit whenever she could and help bring a little joy into their lives, much as she had with the Kindertransport children in her hometown. In her last call home, Aunt Lil said they still arrived via Holland into Harwich, and she volunteered to help the children along with the other ladies from her church. Kitty recalled the distressed, sad faces looking to her for comfort and how they triggered the carer inside of her, which led to her applying to the Red Cross for nurse training. The children of Fell Hall pulled her emotions in another direction – away from nursing adults.

When she left the hall on Boxing Day for night duty at the hospital, it was with a heavy heart.

At the end of her shift, Kitty yawned and stretched. Her body ached, and she needed sleep. She knew her mind needed clearing and release from the thoughts racing around inside. Rushing through her tasteless evening meal, and declining various invitations to join the other girls in her quarters, Kitty curled into a ball on her bed and fought the nightmares which threatened.

Chapter Two

1942

The harsh wind hissed through a rotten window ledge and Jo's voice echoed down the telephone line. 'Happy New Year! A week late, but what the heck, 1942, can you believe it? Let's hope it's the last one of this darn war.'

'We can only hope!' Kitty called back and sat shivering as she chatted with her friend in the old guard room. Her sympathies went out to the guard, who sat at the entrance of the hospital gates day after day. She'd taken him a warm cocoa and a cheese sandwich on Boxing Day and from then on he allowed her to use the telephone to call Jo, which meant she no longer had to wait in a long queue in the nurse quarters. 'Jo, I'm like a walking shadow. I can't eat properly, and I've realised I've given nursing everything I have. I knew it in November, and held off until now. I can't keep hiding from the truth.' Kitty leaned her forehead against the wall in front of her, desperately trying not to cry.

Jo had already made a switch from nursing to become a driver for the Red Cross and understood the sacrifices Kitty had made in the past year.

Before she could draw breath, Jo jumped in with a forthright response. Her voice was firm and steady. 'And then some, Kitty. You have gone above and beyond. I've seen you burned out but still jumping to the call for someone to crawl down dangerous holes, choking on gas. Rescue and orphans, that's your passion and you know my thoughts on leaving a placement you no longer feel you can give your all. You've done your duty in every hospital you've worked in, and it's time to change direction,' Jo said.

Jo's voice was a comfort and bold – reassuring, but Kitty still struggled with the idea of walking away from a nursing career.

'That's true, but why am I feeling guilty?' Kitty replied, untangling her fingers from the telephone cord. Her nerves were twitching with anxiety.

'Probably 'cos of the team you are in – you're a loyal soul, but another nurse will take your place and you'll soon be forgotten. Start thinking about yourself for a change. Listen, get some rest, I'll keep my fingers crossed for you. Speak soon and remember how happy I am now I've made the move.'

'Thanks, Jo. Not hearing from Michael isn't helping.'

'Take a break. I'll deal with it for you. Get yourself to Trix, she's our calming force. Regroup and, whatever happens, you will be stronger. No arguments, I'll get back to you. Speak soon.' Jo hung up and Kitty knew she couldn't argue against taking a break. She replaced the handset and took a moment to reflect on the conversation.

Relieved Jo had proved herself to be a loyal friend once again, Kitty managed to relax, eventually, and thought about her future.

It was New Year when Stanley and Jenny approached Kitty about a Red Cross project, under discussion with the Durham section, wanting her advice on who to employ in Jenny's place. Jenny no longer had the strength to help the two local volunteers and needed to step away from the more hectic side of housing the orphaned children. They were also the reason Kitty wanted to do more for the orphaned children in their area. The Walker-Fells deserved the support.

She telephoned Jo from the draughty guard room to seek out her advice. Once the general chit-chat was over, Kitty explained her quandary over the job opportunity.

'Listen, Kitty, what Fell Hall offers sounds the perfect job and, don't forget, not many would know what to say to an orphaned kiddy, but I've seen you in action – as I say, the job's perfect for you,' Jo said down the line. 'Apply for it. You can always return to nurse training if it doesn't work out – take the chance, Kitty. Darn it; I have to dash, speak again soon. Stay safe, my friend.' Disappointed their chat was cut short, Kitty returned her goodbyes and replaced the handset. Later, as she thought over her friend's response, Jo's positivity boosted her determination to make the necessary changes in her life.

The following day, another call for all staff to the ward after only one hour of leaving made up her mind. Kitty took in the fresh batch of horrors facing her and her colleagues and her knees buckled beneath her. She bent to regain her balance and courage, but knew this was no longer the path she could follow. It broke her heart, but if she was going to do any good during the battle against Hitler, it had to be done with a strong mind and hers was no longer of any use inside Shotley Bridge Hospital. It was time to face the facts and speak to Matron.

The matron of Shotley Bridge tore into Kitty for abandoning those in need and accused her of thinking only of herself. The accusation stung and Kitty drew upon the last source of energy left inside her war-torn body to remain calm; the actions and verbal reprimand of her elder angered and upset her. She removed her cap and bloodied apron, laid them both on her senior's desk and, despite trying to hold onto a smidgen of dignity, she caved in and broke down in tears. Once the tears subsided, she looked the matron directly in the eye and realised it was not the first time the woman had dealt with the same sort of situation.

'I'm sorry you feel I've let the side down, Matron. However, my inner desire to help orphan children during this war burns like an ache – it's a painful reminder of my own loss at such an early age and I can no longer ignore the calling. I've worked hard to complete my nurse training, but just know I can't continue. I've nothing left to give here anymore and if it makes me selfish, then you are right, I am. I'm just...'

Kitty drooped her head. She had chosen her words carefully between sniffles, still annoyed at herself for becoming tearful and out of control. She knew it was frustration created by the woman in front of her with a furrowed brow and dismissive manner relating to Kitty's desire to care for orphans.

'It's a passing fancy. You became too close to the Walker-Fells, and they've confused you. You have a lot to give us here.' Matron wagged her finger and scowled at Kitty.

With resentment that the woman wasn't taking her seriously, Kitty gave a vigorous shake of her head to emphasise her denial of the woman's words. 'No. It's not a fancy. It's something I did before signing up. I cared for children pulled away from their parents; Jewish little ones – bewildered and lost. I beg you to help me by writing to my Red Cross recruitment leader and explaining I *am* the right person to run Fell Hall – even for a brief time. The Walker-Fells have sent their recommendation, but your referral would have more influence. I'll be joining the emergency rescue team in Brancepeth, making use of my valuable skills learned here, too.'

Kitty watched as Matron stood listening; to her relief, she saw the hardened face gradually soften to a semi-friendly smile.

'I think I've heard enough, Nurse Pattison. Your loyalty to the Red Cross is commendable and your passion to help the orphaned amongst us is not something to be ignored. I see it now. I will telephone, not write, and offer my recommendation. If your mind is elsewhere, you will only perform half a job on my wards, and I need full commitment from my nurses. You are an asset to the rescue teams and have exceeded your assessment expectations. I'll let you know the outcome. I suggest you compose yourself and join your colleagues, but keep this between us for the time being.'

With a gush of thanks and gratitude that Matron understood the path Kitty laid out for herself was the best for her to follow, Kitty headed onto the wards, her heart lighter but her stomach in knots hoping for a favourable outcome. Her shift was another tough one, but with Matron's support, Kitty no longer felt the despair inside and worked solidly for over twelve hours with optimism, knowing she had made the right choice.

Chapter Three

'K itty. There's a telephone call for you.' One of the girls shook Kitty awake. She glanced around the room and realised she had slept a good hour past dawn and breakfast. It was a week since she expressed her need to leave and each day she hoped for positive news from the Red Cross.

As she jumped from her bed and ran down the corridor, hastily wiping away the sleep from her eyes, she suddenly felt lightheaded and put her hand to the wall to stop herself passing out. She cursed herself for missing supper and breakfast. She grabbed the perched handset and whispered a fearful hello.

'Miss Pattison?'

'Yes.'

'Good. I've had a call about the Fell Hall Orphan home we've taken over to help Mrs Walker-Fell. A most unusual event for us, but a necessary one from what I gather.'

Kitty recognised the voice of the woman she spoke to in

Harwich and drew comfort from a distant contact from her hometown.

'Mrs Deeks? Hello. Yes, it's a wonderful place set up by an ex-patient's wife. Sadly, she's ill, but they're so generous and have given over their home to the children.'

A slight cough from the other end of the telephone stopped Kitty from gushing out her praises for Jenny and Stanley.

'Your matron at Shotley Bridge has only good things to say about them, and you as a potential nurse, but has also given us enough evidence to show you are more than capable of undertaking the task of running the home on our behalf.'

'She did?' Kitty questioned in disbelief.

'She did, and she also hinted we'd be foolish to look only at your age and miss the opportunity to have an orphan with understanding as our lead on this trial project. We will review the situation after twelve weeks, then we will assess it. See how you are coping.'

'I see. Yes, thank you.' Kitty's heart thumped inside her chest. She had a lot to prove, and twelve weeks wasn't anywhere near long enough for her to help one orphan, let alone several, but she would do as much as she could to show them she was the person they needed on a permanent basis.

'As I understand it, you have accumulated a week of leave and need a break. Take the rest period, use it wisely. I'll send further details – but congratulations, the position is yours. When I took the call this morning from HQ, I can tell you I was so proud of you. Come and see me when you come home again.'

Kitty gripped the handset and stopped a loud scream of joy escaping her lips for fear of deafening Maureen Deeks.

'Thank you. Oh, that's wonderful news. My aunt and uncle don't know yet, but I'll write to them soon, so please don't mention it yet, if you see them. Oh, I'm so happy, thank you.'

'Get that rest and again, well done. You do us proud, Kitty.'

Kitty waited for the click announcing the telephone call had ended before taking a deep breath. The wait was over.

The following forty-eight hours moved so fast, Kitty barely caught her breath.

On her last day on the ward, she received a cool farewell from some of her colleagues, but others told her they knew exactly how she felt and envied her ability to deal with the situation.

Jo telephoned Kitty and kept her promise to oversee Kitty's wellbeing by buying her a train ticket to Cleveland for a visit with Trix. Kitty was to recuperate in the guest room of the cottage Trix's fiancé Smithy rented for his GP practice. Grateful for such caring and supportive friends, Kitty no longer felt guilty about not returning home for her break. She knew if she returned to Harwich, she would not find peace, and would only upset her guardians by resenting them fussing about her future and health. A good rest with a dear friend would set her up for working at the new Red Cross orphanage.

The train to Yorkshire trundled at a slower than normal pace through the heavy snow flurry which, to Kitty's relief, looked in no great hurry to settle into large drifts as in the previous year. The places where it did sit glistening under the flittering rays of sunshine, trying its best to brighten a dull sky, reminded Kitty of the icing on past Christmas cakes made by her aunt.

She could not recall any made by her mother, but if she had made them, Kitty would have only enjoyed a slice of one or two, before her mother's death. She remembered days of lifting soft peaks of icing with a fork, then her aunt giving her permission to lick the utensils after the baking sessions. She smiled out towards the pretty countryside of Yorkshire and marvelled at how a fleeting glimpse of snow could bring back such vivid memories – and the urge to have luxury items such as Christmas cake with dried fruit and icing once more. Rationing and shortages ensured none of the treats were available to them anymore. The want of a ceasefire and a return to a life she recognised threatened to dampen the excitement of seeing Trix again, so she pushed the thoughts to the back of her mind and picked up a newspaper left on the seat next to hers. The news did nothing to lift her spirits, each article recording the Japanese forces putting strain on the already battle-weary British allies. She shed a tear whilst reading of the invasion of Singapore and of Japan's attacks on northern Australia. She pushed the paper to one side and inhaled deeply.

At last, the hiss of steam, the slow dub-dub sound of the

wheels on the track and the appearance of the guard alerted Kitty they had arrived at her destination.

Any doubt of whether she was at the right place vanished within seconds of hearing Trixie's voice call out her name. From the other end of the platform, she waved wildly above the heads of other passengers heading for the exit.

'Kitty, over here!'

With a high wave in return, Kitty rushed towards her friend and the moment they were a few inches away from each other, she dropped her case gently to the floor and they hugged. A tight hug of reassurance from Trix and one of gratitude and relief from Kitty.

'Oh, it's so good to see you. And look at you, a proper picture of health,' Kitty exclaimed as she held Trix at arm's length. Her friend was no longer the pixie-haired girl, but a rosy-cheeked woman with her dark hair tied into a bun. Her skin was tanned and her smile wide.

'I'm happy and the air is good around here. Being able to work alongside Gordon is wonderful and we are grateful for a good life. Plus, when there is no money in a home, he is paid with vegetables in return for medical care. I'm an unofficial midwife, too. I've delivered four babies now – one in a barn – it was a calf! The vet was dealing with another too far away, and the farmhand decided I'd be the next best thing for advice. I made him do the dirty work, believe me! A far cry from life in Birmingham.'

Kitty gave a loud laugh. 'It conjures up so many images, Trix. I wish I'd been there.'

They chatted as they walked the short distance through

Pinchinthorpe village to Rosehome Cottage, the place Gordon Smith – otherwise known as Smithy – had set up his GP surgery. Kitty admired the pretty lanes lined with stone cottages, and smiled at the local people who greeted Trix with hearty waves or friendly shouts of 'Hello'. Everything settled over her like a blanket of comfort, easing a weight from her shoulders, and by the time Gordon Smith gave her a crushing hug of welcome, Kitty knew the week was the recipe for coping and acceptance.

After dropping off her bag, they collected eggs from chickens who scratched around the doctor's surgery garden. They walked a few yards to Trix's home, a small rented cottage at the end of the lane from the practice. Smithy lived in another around the corner with a doting housekeeper, ensuring gossip was kept from both doors. The pair only met at work or in public, never alone in Trix's one-up, one-down home. The cottage was tiny, but Trix had made it home and the thick walls retained the heat from the stove, giving it a cosy feel. Kitty felt the weight of the past few months ease from her shoulders as she sank into one of the two comfortable chairs either side of the front window. She took in the magnificent view of the rolling hills before the late afternoon bled into a cold, dark evening.

'I bet that's beautiful when spring comes,' she said, waving towards the hills with her fork as she and Trix ate their meal of scrambled eggs.

'It is glorious. It looks pretty in the snow, but it's not easy to walk to the next village when it lays heavy.' Trix rose from her chair and placed her dishes in the sink. 'They'll soak 'til morning. I'm done in.' She waved her hand at Kitty, who suppressed a yawn. 'You've had a long day, too. I've got an early start and I'm on stand-by for Mrs Richards and her first child. If you hear hammering on the door, it will be for me. Now, let's get you back to the surgery and settled down for the night.'

Trix handed Kitty her coat and they embraced the freezing air outside with gasps and giggles as they took the brief walk to Rosehome Cottage.

Trix gave Kitty a quick tour of the cottage and when they stepped inside the guest bedroom, Kitty was grateful to see a small coal fire.

'Precious coal, thank you, Trix. But don't burn it every night just for me.'

'The room needed airing and warming through. You deserve a bit of comfort. You've been through a lot, Kitty. I couldn't have coped with what you've dealt with since leaving the bombings when we started out in Birmingham. Scotland blitz rescue, Roker Beach bombing and then joining the rescue teams in towns and villages near the hospital – on top of your ward practice and studies. Not to mention the running back and forth for the orphan house.'

Kitty lowered her head, tiredness taking its toll on the last of her strength. She gave Trix a soft smile and stretched. 'I could sleep all week,' she said.

'I'm sorry my place isn't big enough for you to stay with me, but sleep and get some energy back. We'll talk more tomorrow. I'll head home and leave you to it – sweet dreams.' Trix turned back the covers and patted the bed. Kitty smiled her thanks. Once unpacked she checked herself in the mirror and saw what Trixie had seen. Lank chestnut hair, with curls struggling to find their place on her shoulders, grey-blue eyes set above dark circles of tired flesh. Her skin was paler than normal and Kitty was shocked at the image facing her. She could only hope the break would restore her to her usual healthy state. She teased the unruly curls around her ears and set about resting for the night, unsure she would be able to sleep through the nightmares always threatening to take away her precious rest.

Chapter Four

A cockerel crowing and the clip of horses' hooves on the cobbled street below alerted Kitty to the start of a new day. She reached over and peered at her watch. Six o'clock. Miraculously, she had managed to sleep with no interruptions.

Aware Smithy would arrive for work at some point, Kitty slipped on her dressing gown and headed for the small kitchen where Trix informed her there was milk, bread, an egg and a slice of bacon for her breakfast. The smell of the bacon sizzling in the pan soon filled the building, and Kitty enjoyed the small moment of domesticity. She never cooked for herself, nor had the pleasure of eating breakfast in peace. Even before she left home, breakfast with her aunt and uncle was always a time of chatter.

A mist rolled down the hills and a layer of pale gold formed across the horizon. A soft overnight snowfall melted under the early morning rays. The kitchen window steamed up as the room warmed through, and Kitty rubbed a small space to watch the sun struggle awake. Wiping her bread around the plate to catch the last delights of bacon grease and egg yolk, she gave a contented sigh. Only one thing could improve on the moment and that was if Michael sat opposite her at the table and they spent a few hours enjoying each other's company. Not wanting the melancholy of missing him to take over her improved mood, Kitty placed the dishes in the sink to soak and rushed upstairs to wash and change into a warm woollen skirt and jumper, with newly darned woollen stockings.

Rinsing away the last of the washing-up water, Kitty heard Smithy enter the front door to the surgery. She dried her hands and before she could call through that the kettle was still hot, and would he like a cup of tea, he poked his head around the door.

'Morning, old girl. My, it smells wonderful in here. Sleep well?'

Kitty smiled. She could never help smiling when Smithy was around. His sandy hair and freckles added warmth to an already friendly face. Like Trix, he looked the picture of health.

'I did! What a wonderful place you have here – it's bigger than it looks from outside. The garden is enormous. It seems a world away from the war – peaceful. I'm so happy for you both.'

Smithy placed his medical bag on the countertop, pulled his gloves from his hands and removed his coat and scarf. 'The village suits us, but we need more young blood around the place. Most of the residents are over fifty. Haemorrhoids and old age are my speciality. Trix will need to go elsewhere to deliver babies. The last of the younger mothers has now left.'

Kitty poured Smithy a tea and handed him a mug. She watched as he wrapped his hands around it for warmth and blew the rising vapour across the rim of the cup. Life was as fragile as the steam, scattered to the atmosphere with one act. His words were loaded with emotion. She knew he meant the last of the young men had gone to war, and the guilt he felt for an injury preventing him from signing up with Michael as a medic.

'You are needed here. People need assurance that their life is precious, too. They want to feel healthy in readiness for whatever comes their way. You are important, Smithy. Maybe it's time you and Trix considered bringing your own young blood to the place. Settle down. Make an honest woman of her. Live here and build a life of happiness.'

Smithy placed his empty mug in the sink. He turned back to her and shrugged his shoulders.

'She won't be able to practise as a nurse once married. I can't make that decision for her, I'll wait.'

Kitty gave a short nod. 'But she will still be able to help the practice and probably become an unofficial midwife once young folk settle here again – and they will. As a married woman, Trix can volunteer for many things. The war is changing our lives every day. Women are valued much more than before. Speak to her, tell her what you feel. Men need to tell us women, not leave us guessing.'

Smithy nodded.

'I know, we have to stop dallying.'

A shadow outside caught Kitty's eye.

'Oh, I think you have a patient walking up the path. I'll finish up here and venture down to meet with Trix. Have a good day and Smithy – remember your worth.'

Once he left the kitchen, Kitty got to thinking about her friends and of how divided within the village they were. In a few hours she'd realised that if they failed to move forward, they would struggle to forge a future together. Dreams and duty were not the same, but they could be combined to bring a positive outlook. Goodness knows, happiness was in short supply for all caught up in the political clamber for power around the world; it had to be found wherever possible, for sanity's sake. Death and fighting divided her and Michael through no choice of their own, and she could never take a guess on when he would return – if ever – but Smithy and Trix were a couple she could help see a way towards a future and bring hope to what Smithy described as a hopeless place.

During the morning with Trix they walked through drizzling sleet, greeting neighbours and friends. Another powerful sense of peace washed over Kitty and for a few hours her mind drank in the beauty around her, despite the dark clouds flitting across the sky at great speed. Occasionally the images in her nightmares flashed through her mind, but Kitty suppressed them. At first it felt disrespectful to those she had once nursed, but she knew her mind was in desperate need of light, just a chink, enough to see things clearly.

As they left the home of a woman who had received a telegram of loss, again Kitty experienced the warmth of friendship and welcome from a village in mourning. She was in awe of Trix and of how she comforted her neighbour, and admired Smithy as he ensured the wellbeing of a new widow was in hand.

'You are both good for this village, Trix,' Kitty said as they walked home. 'You are trusted, and I can see you have set your hearts here. I mentioned to Smithy this morning, it's about time he made an honest woman of you.'

Linking her arm through Kitty's, Trix gave a light laugh. 'He tries so hard to encourage me to become a midwife, and we discuss every option of me retaining the position after marriage, until it becomes a circle of conversation. A roundabout of words which never results in a conclusion. I've often considered leaving the Red Cross, marrying him and giving up on midwifery training, just helping with deliveries as and when, but I'm proud to be part of something so wonderful.'

Walking through the narrow streets and across fields over three days with her friend, Kitty became more convinced this was the place where Trix could do her best work. The villagers adored her. Who would not? She was gentle, firm, kind and loving. Her smile radiated from morning until she said goodnight. Stepping away from Pinchinthorpe would send her spinning into a world of bombed-out homes, shattered limbs and no Gordon Smith for her to dote upon each time they met during the day. It was a world Kitty feared would destroy her friend, no matter that she declared herself a strong woman. Both Jo and Kitty had exchanged concern about their friend's fragile mind.

On the last day of her visit, Kitty took Trix to one side. 'Listen. I know you have ambition and dreams, but make sure you also consider your future. I thought becoming a nurse was the dream job, until another opportunity opened my eyes – Jo's the same. Don't lose something precious over what you think might be the right path – I've seen enough here to know this is where you should stay. They need you. Bring your family up here, give the village hope.'

Unloading her shopping and folding her bag away, Trix pulled on her pinafore and gave Kitty a smile.

'You've made me do some serious thinking this week, Kitty. You've opened my eyes – and Gordon's – to what we have and how lucky we are. We spoke last night and have agreed I will support his practice as I do now, but as his wife. How do you feel about being my bridesmaid in a few months?'

With a loud whoop of joy, Kitty rushed to her friend and pulled her close.

'I'd be honoured. Oh, I'm so happy for you, but you let me bleat on and on, I must have sounded a right nag. I'm sorry.'

Trix patted a seat at the table and pushed a small pile of potatoes Kitty's way.

'Mash those as punishment,' she quipped.

A new light-hearted atmosphere filtered around the small cottage and by the time they had taken a meal to the surgery, both Kitty and Trix were wedding planning. Smithy interrupted with ideas and suggestions about adapting the surgery into a home and workplace, which would help them save money on rent. Kitty left them both discussing their future whilst she went to her room to pack for her journey home the following morning.

It was a refreshed and contented Kitty who sat on the train early the next day, after promising to return to help Trix with the wedding now set for the end of July.

Chapter Five

Fell Hall,
Brancepeth
2nd March 1942

Dearest Michael,

Another letter in the hope you receive it, and you are safe and well, my darling. After I wrote and told you about my stay with Trix and Smithy, I settled nicely into my new post at Fell Hall. I've a beautiful bedroom at the back of the house, facing the garden and Brancepeth Castle, and no snoring companions!

The army are active around the area and now live in the castle, much like when I lived in Buchanan Castle in Scotland. Ah, the memories of meeting you there again and rekindling our love. If only we could kiss like that again, hold hands and whisper our wishes – if only. Anyway, I mustn't look back, only forward. Life here is good and my nightmares are subsiding. It is odd not seeing Stanley limping around his home, and Jenny fussing over him, but it is good to be here and knowing I am helping them both ensure their war effort is fulfilled.

Jenny is weaker than when I arrived and, sadly, the doctor cannot help her any more than he already is, which is frustrating those around her, but Jenny is accepting of her cancer which means we don't fuss around her, just ensure she's comfortable each day.

Stanley is so busy; he has accommodation with his squadron and comes home when he can for short visits. It scares him – his future without Jenny – so he is forging a strong bond with the RAF once again. After nursing him and encouraging him to return, I feel it wrong of me to suggest he gives it all up to sit all day beside his wife and become the helpless husband. He depends on us, and we have a duty to him. He's the man who defended us and gave up his home to ensure children have a safe haven when they need it most.

Fortunately, Jenny has a woman from the village to tend to her needs, as I am busy with the children. I sit and read to her in the evening. They have a wonderful library of books.

We (my four staff – all Red Cross volunteers) care for ten children at a time and have managed to settle seven into new homes during the time I've been here. Five with relatives and two with potential adoptive parents.

I've been busy using my brain and nearly wore it out (I can hear you laughing and suggesting I don't have one – stop it, you tease). I've created a file of parental responsibilities and our requirements for those outside of families, going by my personal experience. It is under review, but I have been told to follow it here at Fell Hall. It's also to ensure the children are not taken as slave labour; it has been reported that some of the evacuee children have been used in this way. As if the kiddies haven't been through enough!

Jo visits when she can and she's great with the boys. She teaches them mechanics and takes no nonsense from them, which helps me when they play me up. A threat of no time with Driver Jo always gets the chores done.

The Gaskin brothers are regular visitors and are proving helpful with settling in some of the traumatised children by sharing their own experience. Life on the farm has helped them come through their own nightmares. They are still a pair of little devils, but lovable ones. They'll always have a place in my heart. As do you.

Trix has upset the applecart with her parents, but I understand her thoughts on getting married in the village she and Smithy are to live in, and not Somerset. The village needs something happy to lift their spirits. I must admit, a wedding will lift mine.

I miss you so much, my darling. I've still not received any letters from you, but am sure you write them – you promised me, and I trust you. I pray you are well and not captured – or worse.

On a positive note. I get to see the sea each time I visit the rescue team for briefings or to help roll bandages. The smell of salty seaweed reminds me of when you surprised me back home. What wonderful memories we made. What I'd give to go to Dovercourt and Durham with you again. Oh, Michael, come home to me safe and sound.

My love always – always

K x

Fell Hall,
Brancepeth.
2nd March 1942

Dear Aunt Lil and Uncle Frank,

I hope this letter finds you well. Since I last wrote to you, I've experienced a whirlwind of children coming and going. Their little faces filled with fear and confusion never fail to bring a lump to my throat. Thank you for the tips and advice you learned when taking me on after Mum and Dad died, they have been valuable. I give the children space and time alone, but not so much they feel lonely and afraid. I often wake in the night with a little one curled up at the end of the bed, and, as you suggested, I lift them back into their own despite the temptation to comfort them in mine. It's true, they must learn to deal with sleeping alone, but most are in a room of four, so they are not totally isolated from the comforting noises of others.

We have a little boy who insists on sitting upright to sleep. I think his fear is if he lies down, the nightmare he's lived through will return. One young girl of eight, Nancy, is embracing her new life. She's never had new clothes, a bath or the opportunity to speak with other children. She's in awe of everything she sees. Her family had very little money, and from what I gather from neighbours it wasn't an untroubled home. She's my shadow and wonderful with the little ones. A child with an aged head on her shoulders, she often has a way of making me feel like the child.

She is accepting of her mother's death, and, as I understand it, there is no father on the scene. I'll leave it there and share others with you another time, as for now I am recovering from cleaning boot polish spread across the kitchen flagstones. I tried to teach a few children to clean their own shoes. I'm not sure it was worth the effort. Tomorrow, I have the pleasure of combing for headlice. Oh, the joys!

Take care of yourselves,
   Much love,
   Kitty x

'I still itch.' Kitty scratched her head out of sight of the children. Daphne, the loyal cook to Jenny and Stanley, laughed. Kitty gave a theatrical shiver and cupped her hands to prevent more scratching.

'The bairns gave you a run for your money this morning, that's a fact. I've never seen a child squirm and squeal so much as young Nancy – but ee, she's a canny lass.'

Kitty agreed. Nancy had a cheeky wit and challenged the most patient person in her company, but was a loving child.

Fell Hall
Brancepeth
19th March 1942

33

Dearest Michael,

Oh, the joy of receiving your letter – and clever you, coming up with the idea of coding them. This is letter C, and I look forward to reading A and B if they ever arrive.

As you are still TS, I'll simply imagine you are on home turf – Great Britain, I mean, not Canada. If only you could tell me where you were, I'd be there in a flash. I pray you are safe from letter C onwards as you write of experiencing harrowing ordeals. I understand the toll it can take as I mentioned in my letters and plead with you to try and remain strong of mind.

My darling, I wish we could communicate with our minds when we are apart. I look at the moon every night it is visible and hope you are somewhere where you can see it too. Dreadful stories of prisoner camps are filtering in from RC support teams abroad and my stomach churns at the thought of you ever being captured.

I heard from Belle Farnsworth last week, it appears she is running the family pub in Cornwall and has returned to the Red Cross for part-time duties. She's helping the war effort by making visiting soldiers welcome. She'll be like a cat who got the cream with the hundreds of men she must come across.

Jo sends her love, as does Trix. Smithy sends a special request: 'Old man, please stand beside me when I marry Trix. Come home and be my best man.'

Obviously, he realises you might not be able, but isn't it lovely of him to ask?

I am writing this perched on a rock in semi-sunshine. The clouds keep threatening to drop a shower, but nothing happens. We had a bus ride to Roker Beach. The seaside smells are triggering fond memories of us together. I've enclosed a few pictures drawn by some of the children. Their chosen subject? Me! But I'm sure you will recognise me; tall, one arm longer than the other and stick thin with green curly hair. I can assure you though, since we last saw each other, I've not gone boss-eyed!

Take care of yourself, my darling, and come home to me soon.
  My love always,
  Your loving fiancé
  K X

Fell Hall
Brancepeth

Dear Sarah,

  Just dropping you a line to see how you are doing. How are things at Drymen? I bet the castle is cold! I hope you are still making friends and your gran is still sending you those precious parcels to cheer you up.

  I wanted to let you know I have a new assignment and you will notice a new address. It's a long story but basically I had an offer to remain in the Red Cross caring for orphan children. They are orphaned due to the local attacks from the German planes and are now housed with us until we can find them a new family. Thanks to the generosity of a wealthy pilot and his wife, they have a better chance than the many still out there floundering on the streets.

  I will keep you updated on their antics, as some are finding their feet again and put my patience through daily endurance tests!

Take care, my friend, and I look forward to hearing your news from Scotland soon.

Kitty x

Chapter Six

As the days grew longer and the evenings lighter, Kitty encouraged the children to work on the vegetable garden to grow more food to support the household. They grumbled and moaned, but always knuckled down, appreciating the end results on their plates.

To keep their minds occupied, she organised lessons in a room converted into a school room. The children needed easing out of their grief, although the care team agreed they were not to be mollycoddled. While the countries of the world battled hard against each other, the house became a place where they could laugh and enjoy some form of childhood during their wait for a new home. Quite often the smallest snippet of sad news could bring about a tearful panic amongst the more sensitive in the home, which prompted Kitty to move the radio into her bedroom. When the children were out of earshot, the staff would gather and express their upset out of view. With them all having contacts in various parts of the country and world, the news was often overwhelming. Two of the women fretted over news that their husbands, aged forty-three and forty-five, were called up as part of the new conscription act. Both were in jobs which meant there was no reason for them to remain at home, and the women asked Kitty for permission to bring their three children to work with them. Unsure as to how the orphans would feel seeing other children with their mothers, she made the decision to turn down their request. It was not an easy one as she knew they would want to talk her down, but Kitty had to think of the children in her care. The women brought their argument to the table that happier children might help the sad ones come through their bad days. However, Kitty explained she experienced long spells as a child early on in her grief, where she was jealous of children with parents. Losing a parent often meant there was still one remaining to help them mourn; when both are lost through tragic circumstances, it is hard not to be resentful.

Most problems were discussed and adapted to suit all, but on this topic, Kitty was not swayed. She braced herself for any problems to follow, but the women listened and eventually understood. Grateful for their support, Kitty pondered on how she could integrate their children without upsetting the orphans and hit on the idea of a night camping in the garden. Their mothers could keep their distance or even stay home, and she would try to rope Stanley into helping on his next visit. Whenever he came to see Jenny, he always found time to play with the children, or teach them something useful.

'Put Cat down, boys. She's frightened. She does not like

swinging. It's cruel, and you know it, now stop! Bring the poor thing here,' Kitty called out and strode over to the Gaskin brothers, David and Peter, also invited to stay over to show the young residents of Fell Hall that life can become brighter after such a terrible time. Kitty suspected their new parents embraced the peace. The boys worked hard on the farm where they now lived, but when left to their own devices it inevitably meant trouble for someone.

Eric, one of the recent arrivals, stood to one side of the two boys pushing the cat backwards and forwards in a box on the tree swing Jack had set up for them. Kitty waited for them to hand the cat to her, and she cradled it until it was ready to run back to the sanctuary of the shed.

'We thought Cat would have fun. We always have fun on the swing.' David's face fell with the realisation he had scared their precious pet.

Kitty smiled at him as she stroked the cat into a sense of safe calm.

'Animals like different things. Go off and play, show this one your sensible side, and just think next time.' She ruffled Eric's hair, and shooed him off to play with the brothers.

Looking at the three new friends now intent on seeking out the enemy from behind shadowed shrubs and trees reassured Kitty the camping idea was a good one. She checked on the other children, then joined Nancy, who was sitting alone making daisy chains and looping them around the pet rabbit's neck.

'Time to put Flop-Ear to bed, Nancy.'

Always a willing girl, Nancy made no argument. She lifted the rabbit into his box and carried him to the hutch and covered him up for the night, whispering her love for him and promising to find him a dandelion in the morning. Nancy adored the rabbit and Kitty had a feeling she would be given it as a gift when she went to her new family at the end of the week. When Kitty took on her role, she noticed how the animals had a soothing effect on the children and encouraged them to interact with them every day; now she made a mental note to ask Jack to seek out a replacement for Flop-Ear.

The evening peered around the corner, but the children showed no signs of feeling tired, or put off by the slight nip in the air. The Gaskin brothers raced around chasing Eric. Even if they weren't the best influence sometimes, the saddest of the children perked up when they were around. Eric idolised them.

'What are they like, those boys?' Stanley's laughing voice rang out across the garden as he joined Kitty. She joined in with his laughter and accepted the promised glass of brandy.

'They'll be the death of me, I can tell you. When I catch the brothers up to mischief, they make their accents harder to understand, so as to punish me in fun, and that's me done for the day, I spend hours trying to decipher what they've said. Eric is their adoring slave and they've done him the world of good.'

A chuckle rumbled as Stanley sipped his fine brandy. He waved Jack over to them.

'Join us, Jack. They'll be in bed soon and all will be well with the world.'

With a loud guffaw of a reply, Jack lumbered across the

lawn and joined them. 'I'll not say no, Stanley. Thank you. Where do they get the energy? Mind you, I suppose I was the same at their age.'

'You, Jack? I always thought of you as a good boy.' Stanley grinned and chinked his glass against Jack's.

One thing Kitty admired about Stanley was his ability to ensure his staff were on an equal footing with him and Jenny. There were no airs and graces around them, and he ensured everyone worked together as friends.

Kitty took a sip of her own brandy, set the glass aside, wanting to keep a clear head, then called over to the boys to wash up and get ready for bed.

Jack and Stanley had erected borrowed tents from HQ which were no longer of use due to tears and nicks, and Mrs Marston and Kitty had repaired them.

Tonight, Stanley, Jack and Kitty were camping out, but Daphne refused to lie under a damp sky; however she willingly packed enough food to keep the small troop happy. Kitty wore layers underneath her siren suit and ensured Nancy would be warm and comfortable in their tent. She hated to admit she had become quite fond of the girl, but made sure she spent time preparing her for the life ahead. How to handle boys, or how to dodge questions about her parents if they were upsetting and not relevant to the situation. Kitty made sure Nancy was as armed for the road ahead, much as her aunt had helped her. In some ways, Nancy reminded Kitty of herself.

'No lights in an hour. It's seven o'clock now, so make the most of your torches until blackout, but keep the torches low when you are playing, just to be on the safe side,' Kitty called out to the boys. She didn't want to scare the children, but they had to be made aware of the dangers of attracting the enemy.

Later, Kitty settled into her makeshift bed, and listened to the soft sounds of Nancy already deep in sleep. Occasionally she heard Stanley or Jack suggesting the boys might like to keep their voices down, and the odd cheeky retort, but, aside from that, the night was quiet. Even the droning sounds of the army trucks further across the fields were limited. Although Kitty would have preferred to spend time reading a book curled up on the sofa or in bed, the brandy had warmed her, and she soon gave in to the sleep she craved.

A dog barked in the distance and Kitty rolled over; she guessed she had slept for the best part of four hours. The nagging sensation of needing to use the toilet refused to leave, so she slipped quietly from the tent and ran to the house. The moon filtered across the lawn and the searchlights flickered across the sky, and Kitty thought back to Scotland and her evening walks with Michael. The nagging ache of missing him never left, but she put her mind into her daily routine; it helped keep the sad moments at bay. Unsure as to whether the brandy, combined with tiredness, had brought about the spell of sadness, Kitty struggled to suppress her feelings as she usually did, and a large tear trickled down her cheek and dropped onto the front of her dressing gown. A noise outside stopped her in her tracks. A cup rattled in its saucer. Kitty ran across the lawn just as the siren sounded and the noise surrounding the house ramped up several notches.

'I'll get Nancy. Daphne's now coming and she'll fetch Jenny!' she called out to Stanley as he and Jack were gathering the boys, still groggy with sleep. Kitty alerted Nancy and, as instructed by Stanley, ushered them towards the Anderson shelter; tucked under a small cluster of trees. Kitty knew Jack and Stanley were fetching Cat and Flop-Ear before the children became distressed.

Once inside, the adults sat in their favourite seats and Kitty pulled blankets over the children, encouraging them to settle down on their truckle beds. The shelter was well kitted out and every comfort thought of, even though the place felt damp and claustrophobic.

'The one night I have off,' Stanley muttered as he and Daphne made a weak and tired Jenny comfortable.

Before anyone could respond, the thudding vibrations of planes overhead became the main focus.

Nancy sniffled, and Kitty patted her head. The brothers and Eric sat in silence; fear etched across their little faces. The other members of staff rushed back and forth with extra blankets after ensuring the two toddlers and a baby were safe with Kitty. They cuddled the boys and Nancy along with their own children. It made her heart swell to see the mothers tend to the orphans back at the house as tenderly as they did their own and she knew she had to rethink their request that the children had more time together. It was time to admit she was overprotective. She recalled the neighbours in her own street, inviting her for tea and other family gatherings, slowly easing the pain she had inside as a child. She also realised those orphaned through enemy attacks needed protecting, but they also needed stability and to be shown the world was not a place to fear; that there were still people willing to comfort them. The war could not be allowed to add pressure to the way they coped with their losses. Other children, guided by mothers who cared, would bring friendship and light relief. Kitty would discuss play days with her team and try to ease the burden and fear of the orphans brought to Fell Hall. If the Germans hadn't decided to attack an unsuspecting port further afield, the evening would have been perfect for the children. At last, the all-clear sounded, and in the calm of her room Kitty sat listening out for the last of the children settling down. She heard the comforting whispers and giggles and smiled to herself. Tonight, the enemy lost a battle. They failed to weaken the spirit of the next generation.

Chapter Seven

Fell Hall
Brancepeth
May 1942

My dearest Michael,

I do hope this letter finds you well and not under too much pressure. I miss you so much and there are some days I ache inside. I try not to let others see my pain as there are several worse off than me.

Recently, we were reminded of Hitler's might, yet again. I hate to admit he has some, but cannot deny the atrocities his pilots heap upon us are taking their toll. I heard recently, via the Red Cross jungle drums, that he threatened gas attacks. I pray not. The horrors of the first war showed us the evil effect they have.

We had sad news for one of our volunteers whose husband was recently called up. His ship, Kitty's Brook, was sunk by a submarine in Nova Scotia. I expect you know where that is, and maybe you can describe something beautiful about the place for me to offer her something positive later down the line. She's left with two nine-year-olds, a boy and girl. They are heartbroken but the wonderful thing is, they are staying with us and the orphans are helping them. It is quite something to sit and listen to the comfort given by those who need comfort themselves. My heart is full of love for them all. It still has room for you, so never fear.

The countryside looks beautiful and some days it is hard to imagine we are living the horrors of war, but I am always brought back to earth when I'm on emergency duty in the surrounding villages. Families are ripped apart and news of extended family around Great Britain is dreadful.

In more positive news, I heard from Trix she delivered a nine pound two ounce boy in an Anderson shelter during a raid last week. It appears the sixteen-year-old granddaughter of one of the women turned up in disgrace after being thrown out by parents who no longer want anything to do with her. Apparently, she had managed to walk miles and was in labour by the time she got to the village. Her cries from the shelter were heard by a passer-by. Trix told me the locals embraced the girl as one of their own and supported her with gifts for the newborn. She is going to stay there and, with the help of her gran and Trix, will bring him up. The whole village celebrated the new life. Apparently, the grandmother is a good woman, and the story has ended well.

I've just read this through, and it comes across gloomy. I won't change anything as it is how life is at the moment. We've been apart far too long, but I'm still here, waiting. Always.

My aunt and uncle are still in good health and spirits. They work their allotment and feed the village. I'm so proud of them.

Jenny is still very frail, but the warmer weather enables her to sit outside and watch the children play. She reads to them, and they adore her. Stanley walks well now with a stick and has recently earned a promotion. Daphne is a dab hand at turning a carrot into something representing a treat. Jack keeps the grounds immaculate, and we tick along as best we can. I'm due to have the twelve-week assessment on June 3rd. It's a Wednesday, which means it is play day with the children whose mothers work here. A chaotic day of games with hidden lessons, so I hope it makes the right impression! I am nervous and can only hope I've done enough here to establish a permanent position. I've offered one of the rooms to a teacher to come and teach mathematics. The school closed in her village, and she has skills we need here. I cannot believe the decisions I make nowadays. If only I had the power to insist you were to return to me. My heart needs medical assistance in the form of a kiss from you, Michael.

Stay safe, my love.

Kx

Kitty laid down her pen and looked out of the window. Eight months of being apart from Michael felt like years. She missed his smile, his smell, his voice. She declared to Jenny she would give a month's worth of rations just to be held by him again. Jenny offered encouraging words and Kitty received them with good grace, but it never altered how she felt. Bereft. Cheated. Scared. Words which ran through her mind on a regular basis.

'That's everything. Now, you understand it will be

strange at first, but your cousin is a good person, and she wants the best for you. If you feel unhappy, you must tell her what is making you sad. Understand?'

Kitty sat facing Nancy on the bed. Her heart ached for the sad-faced little girl leaving their care.

'Can I visit Flop-Ear?' Nancy asked as she wiped away her tears.

'I'm sure something will be arranged for you to see him again. I promise, it will work out for the best going to your new home. Look at me, I'm doing well, don't you think?'

Nancy drooped her head. 'I'll miss you, Nurse Kitty.'

'And I'll miss you. I'll come and visit when I can, and you must write to me. I want to hear your news and about new friends you make. Let's get you downstairs, the bus will be arriving soon.'

With a soft sniffle, Nancy lifted her small bag and followed Kitty downstairs. The rest of the staff stood to say their goodbyes and both Kitty and Nancy stepped out onto the driveway where Jack stood beside his personal car.

'My old Ford needs a run out today. Fancy a ride instead of the bus?' he asked Nancy, giving Kitty a knowing wink.

Nancy turned and gave Kitty a questioning look, and Kitty gave an encouraging smile.

'Yes, please,' Nancy replied and gave a wide smile.

Jack settled them both into the car.

'I won't be a moment, I forgot something,' he said and walked to the side of the building.

He returned with a box and placed it onto Nancy's lap.

'You'll need to take this, bairn. He'll be lost without you.'

With caution, Nancy eased open the lid and peered inside to see Flop-Ear chewing on a dandelion leaf.

Her eyes widened with disbelief and joy.

'Really, I can take him?' she asked, stroking the ears of her beloved pet.

Kitty and Jack both replied with a yes and received a squeal of excitement in return.

The journey to Sunderland was uneventful, with Nancy chatting to Flop-Ear the whole time. When Kitty and Jack made their trip back to Fell Hall, they were confident Nancy's new life would bring her comfort.

As they drove along the driveway, Kitty noticed a military jeep parked at the front of the house. She swung a glance at Jack.

'Stanley's home. Something must be wrong with Jenny.'

Jack stopped the car and they both ran towards Stanley and Jenny's home. Halfway across the garden, Kitty heard her name called and she froze. The voice called out again and, without hesitation, she twirled around and saw Michael race across the grass towards her.

'Kitty. Kitty!' he called out with his arms wide open.

Without caring who was watching, they embraced with kisses so fierce Kitty's lips burned.

Eventually, they pulled back from each other, and she turned to speak with Jack, but with discretion he'd returned to his potting shed and left them to enjoy a private moment.

'Let me look at you.' Kitty stepped back from Michael.

He looked tired and hollow-eyed, but still handsome. His eyes sparkled and his lips twitched with a smile Kitty embedded into her heart.

'How long have you got here?' she whispered, hardly daring to hear his answer.

'Long enough. I'm staying at the castle for three days, then have to ship out with a new unit.' Michael kissed her before she could respond. Kitty clung to him, not wanting to let him go.

'I need to go to see to the staff and children. I'll clear my day and we can have some time together.' She linked her arm through his, pulling him close.

An hour later, they snuggled beneath a large tree in a small woodland area at the end of the garden. The staff were instructed to keep the children away for a few hours to give Kitty a bit of privacy with Michael.

'This is how it should be for us,' Kitty said as she leaned her head on his shoulder. Sunlight filtered through the canopy of trees above them and the only noise they could hear was a pair of pigeons cooing and a family of sparrows squabbling for food.

'One day, honey. One day we'll have our time together,' Michael replied, taking her hands in his and touching her ring. 'One day I'll add another to this finger. Just keep the faith and hope going. I love reading your letters. I'm sorry mine were fewer in number, but circumstances...'

Michael let his words filter away and she noticed his face pale.

'Was it bad where you were?' she asked.

He shook his head, but Kitty had no reason to believe him; his face told a different story.

'It's been hard, but others have had it worse than me.

I've got you in my thoughts, which keeps me going.' Michael kissed her again.

At the end of the day, Michael and Kitty had spent hours together alone or with the children. The chatted and played games until it was time for Michael to walk the short distance back to the army barracks set in Brancepeth Castle. At bedtime, Kitty settled down with a calm contentment, knowing her fiancé was nearby.

'...and that is how you tie off a sling.' Michael grinned down at the six small faces in front of him. Kitty stood up from her chair in the audience and addressed the children.

'What do we say for our first-aid lesson, children?'

The children called out in unison their thanks and rushed from the room armed with torn old sheets to practise, once dismissed.

'You made quite the impression,' Kitty said as Michael repacked his medical bag.

Michael laughed. ' I think a couple were hoping to see blood and guts.'

'God forbid,' Kitty muttered as she tidied away the chairs.

From outside, Kitty heard a car horn and the children cheering and shouting as they raced to greet it.

'Ah, Jo's here. The kids love her, and she brings treats to ensure they always will.' Kitty laughed.

'It will be great to see her again. She's a good friend to you and I want to thank her for taking care of you when you needed it most.' Michael leaned in and kissed the tip of her nose.

'Enough of that, young man,' Jo's voice rang out as she entered the room.

Michael laughed and gave her a hug.

'Hello again. Driving now, I hear. The British Army must be desperate,' he said and gave a belly laugh.

Jo gave him a friendly tap on the back and pulled away.

'Enough of your cheek. I'm glad you've put colour in our Kitty's cheeks. She needed to see you and I'm glad you made it to Brancepeth.' Jo gave a wink.

Kitty looked at them both and something puzzled her. Then it dawned on her that Jo had managed to get word to Michael somehow.

'You organised this, Jo?' she asked.

'She sure did. I received a note explaining you had been unwell; it appears someone asked if I could be tracked down and handed the letter. Sadly, I was unable to get leave when you needed me, but I came as soon as I could. I arranged transport to the castle and here I am.'

Kitty went to Jo and embraced her.

'So, you knew he was here?' she said.

Jo gave a flippant flick of her wrist. 'I have friends in high places,' she said and grinned.

'Thank you. *Thank you*,' Kitty said with feeling.

'My pleasure. Take your time here, the kiddies are going to help clean the car. Slave labour for their country. Duty calls.' Jo bowed and walked away laughing.

'Oh, I needed that, but we'd better slow down for dignity's sake,' Michael spoke softly into Kitty's hair as they pulled back from a deep kiss. Kitty's skin tingled with pleasure. The house was quiet, and they had the downstairs to themselves.

'I can't believe you have to leave tomorrow. When you are around, I forget the war. You bring happiness and excitement.' Kitty snuggled closer to him and Michael leaned in for another passionate embrace. Kitty wanted time to stand still as she melded her body into his as they lost themselves to showing as much loving as they dared. Michael caressed her neck and nuzzled her throat with tender kisses, which she returned. He stroked the top of her thigh, placing the palm of the other hand firmly at the back of her neck with his fingers stroking into her hair. They needed time to stand still, to take in newly formed memories of their love which would help them through the days when all seemed lost. For an hour they shared intimate moments without crossing the dignity line. It became their new perfect ending to another brief visit.

'Time to go,' Michael said as they stood together the following day. He stroked Kitty's cheek to stem the flow of tears.

Unable to speak, Kitty placed her forehead against his and inhaled, absorbing his fresh aroma. A pleasant shiver tingled through her body; once again, Michael, with a fresh haircut and shave, looked like the handsome doctor she'd first met in Birmingham. Their time together had refreshed him, and Kitty grabbed her camera for Jo to take a photograph of them together, not wanting to lose the moment when they both accepted their brief meetings filled with the deepest love for one another were all they needed to get them through the atrocities.

'Stay safe, darling. See you again soon.' Kitty gulped back her emotions and tried hard to not end their happy time together in more tears. She controlled her breathing to a steady pace to remain in control.

Michael saluted her. 'Yes, ma'am.'

She watched as he turned on his heel and, once again, walked away from her. Kitty guessed it was with a heart as heavy as her own, but she hoped he did not suffer the intense pain inside as she did; Michael did not deserve to have that kind of pain. [chapter ends]

Chapter Eight

Kitty heard the gravel spray against the garage wall and a car door slam before she saw it was Stanley rushing towards his home. She ran downstairs and raced after him in the garden, the warm May sunshine welcome on her skin, despite the goosebumps of fear forming on her bare arms.

'Stanley, is it Jenny? Nobody has said anything to me. Is she all right?'

'I'll be with you soon, Kitty. Jenny's fine, but I need to speak to her – I'll come and find you in a minute – don't go anywhere.'

Stanley's voice filtered across the garden as he moved at a speed which exacerbated his limp. Kitty stopped and caught her breath. Whatever had made Stanley rush home appeared to be important and she crossed her fingers he wasn't being moved away. Jenny was too weak not to have him return home every other day to check on her.

Trying not to overthink the problem – if there was one –

she went back inside the main house to reassure the staff about Jenny's welfare. The children, eager to draw Stanley into a game of cricket, whined their disappointment when she told them no; they were to sit quietly with their books and read.

She and the rest of the staff poured out milk for the children then mashed a pot of tea for themselves and took it into the main dining room, where they sat waiting for Stanley to put them out of their misery.

At last, they heard his stick tap against the flagstones and Kitty rose to meet him as he entered the room.

'We're in here, Stanley. We've made a pot if you want a cup,' she called out.

Stanley addressed the rest of the women in the room with a hello, before he turned to Kitty.

'Can we speak in private, please, Kitty?' he asked and looked to the doorway.

Kitty's heart sank to her stomach and as they headed for the old sitting room, now the quiet room for staff, her mind went over the worst-case scenarios as the look on Stanley's face suggested what he was about to tell her was bad news. Her aunt? Uncle? Michael!

He was here to tell her she had lost the love of her life. Her legs threated to give away at the thought, but she remained composed. Before she had the opportunity to sit down, Stanley spoke. His voice was calm and steady. The serious Stanley sat before her.

'This isn't easy, Kitty. I've only just heard the news from my commanding officer, and I felt it only right you heard it from me.' He shifted into a more comfortable standing position.

'It's Michael, isn't it? she said quietly, not really wanting to hear his reply.

'Wh-what? No, good gracious, no, Kitty, it's nothing like that. No one's died. Oh, dear girl, I'm sorry. I'm sorry I made you think it might be something horrific. It's bad news, but not as bad as the death of a loved one, goodness, no.'

Stanley's voice rushed through his speech and, as he spoke, Kitty relaxed a little.

'Bad news?' she asked.

Stanley gave an awkward smile. A reassuring, yet weak one. 'There's no painless way to say it, so here goes. Fell Hall has been requisitioned by the RAF for convalescing pilots.' He put his hand up to stop her interrupting. 'The children – the children are moving to a St Barnardo's home, where the staff are preparing families to take them in as we speak. They'll be safe and cared for. I'm sorry, Kitty, I have no say in the requisition, but I did have a say in the children's welfare. The MoD are in charge, and I cannot fight them on this.'

Unable to stand any longer, Stanley sat down, and Kitty followed; she was lost for words and sat with her hands in her lap, trying to come to terms with what Stanley had just announced.

'You will no doubt receive new orders from the Red Cross. I'm not sure what the set-up will be here with regards to medical support. Kitty?'

Kitty shook her head slowly side to side, biding her time

to compose herself and to understand what the result of his words might mean for the children and staff.

'When? How long have I got to prepare the children for this?' she asked and could hear the shake in her voice.

'They are arriving to prepare it all in three days.'

Kitty jumped to her feet. 'Three days? Oh, Stanley. How has Jenny taken the news?'

It was Stanley's turn to give a slow head shake. 'Not well, I'm afraid, and I have to get back to HQ. Go and see her later, Kitty? For me?'

'Of course. She must not be upset by all this. I'll be as upbeat as I can. She did a wonderful thing by setting up the home, but we all must accept changes have to be made. To have convalescing pilots is a good thing, too. You both can appreciate that from personal experience.'

Kitty walked over and touched his arm to reassure him.

'I'll always be grateful for what you did for the children of this area – and beyond. It's been an honour to live here and secure new homes for so many. But I will admit, your news has broken my heart.'

Stanley touched the back of her hand.

'Ours too, Kitty. This isn't the dream we'd planned,' he said, his tone soft and heavy with sadness.

Waving off the children on the battered bus sent to pick them up, Kitty hoped all involved would manage to come to terms with what happened. She had broken the news to the staff first, then they joined forces to explain to the children who were old enough to understand, and offer comfort where necessary. Eric was one of the luckier children; the adoptive parents of the Gaskin brothers offered him a home. Both Kitty and Stanley considered the parents gluttons for punishment, but happily organised his relocation. Kitty took comfort that Nancy was not one of the children she had to send away on the bus, but still found it tough to let them go. Now she understood a little of how mothers felt when they had to evacuate their children. It was a heart-wrench.

She had comforted Jenny as she promised and wrote letters of praise for the staff to give to their Red Cross recruitment officer. They spent the day packing away anything belonging to the Walker-Fells, and Jack – under Jenny's instruction – took them to the village hall where the ladies from the WI helped those in need of decent bedding, or anything relating to young children. They then spent the late afternoon waiting to hear whether they were to stay and work at Fell Hall, but, by the end of the day, they had heard nothing.

The following morning, the end of May slipped silently into June and the sun shone with a warmth not one member of staff felt appropriate for their unsettled mood. By 8 o'clock, they had finished all cleaning chores and were at a loss as to what to do. The sound of a car pulling up outside broke the silence around them and they all peered outside.

'Oh, it's only Jo. I expect she's come to comfort me. She knows me so well,' Kitty said with a sigh.

She pulled open the front door and greeted her friend with a half-hearted smile.

'Come to check up on me, Jo?' she asked, lifting her voice in an attempt at humour.

Jo slammed her car door closed and strode around to

face Kitty.

'No, I ruddy haven't. Have you had one of these?' she demanded, waving a piece of paper in Kitty's face. Her face was red with anger.

'Stop waving it around so I can read it, but no, I've not had any form of letter for several days. What is it?' she asked and made a grab for the letter.

Jo handed it to Kitty, who read it in silence as Jo impatiently tapped her foot.

'They are sending you away. Tomorrow. Where?' Kitty looked up from the letter in disbelief.

Jo kicked at the stones around her foot.

'They are. Apparently, I'm to travel on one of the trucks leaving with new recruits at dawn for a destination unknown. Another of their top-secret plans, no doubt. I thought I'd be here for longer. Anyway, what do you mean, check up on you? What's the matter? – oh, not Jenny. I thought it was rather quiet around here,' Jo said.

'Didn't you get my message? Jack left it at the guard house.' Kitty asked.

'Obviously not. I'm not a mind reader either, so what is going on?' Jo asked with deep sarcasm.

Kitty sighed. 'No need to bite my head off. The children have gone. Not noticed how they've not rushed out to see you? This place,' she waved her hand in no particular direction, 'is no longer a safe home for orphans. It's been requisitioned by the RAF. They move in tomorrow. I'm still waiting for instructions.'

'Cornwall? What is it with that place, and why on earth are they sending me there?'

Kitty took a deep breath before she raised her voice even louder and deafened the forever patient Maureen Deeks, on the other end of the telephone.

'Nurses are needed there and we have to send you where there are shortages.'

'At the expense of a roof over the heads of children,' Kitty retorted, not holding back her heavy sarcasm.

'Kitty, be careful not to become bitter. The children are in good hands, and you are needed to continue the nursing post you were originally contracted to carry out.'

Maureen Deeks' voice came across firm and in control. Kitty was fully aware she had received a verbal warning.

'Apologies, but I've moved around so much at short notice, this has come as a shock,' she replied, and followed through with a heavy sigh.

'As have the majority of those fighting in this war. Now, I've arranged transport and you will be collected first thing. Good luck, Kitty. I'll let your family know you are safe and will be in contact when you can.'

With a raising of her eyebrows, Kitty gave Maureen Deeks an 'I've no choice' face and, even though the woman could not see it, it made Kitty feel better.

'Thanks for offering, give them my love. No doubt I'll hear from you again in a few weeks,' Kitty said and heard the huff of disapproval down the telephone.

'Sarcasm is not becoming, Kitty. As I said, don't become bitter. Take care and stay safe,' Maureen Deeks said and ended the call before Kitty could say anything else.

'Oh, shut up,' Kitty muttered to the blackbird singing outside. He called in the dawn and Kitty was not ready to watch the sunrise spread its silver threads across the dewy lawn. She had no desire to watch the pale-yellow merge into gold of every shade and touch the top of the tree canopy. Beneath it, she and Michael last whispered their love to each other and forced themselves apart, breathing heavily with want and need for one another. She could not bear to listen to the happy bird perched in a leafy tree dappled with sun rays; it was not a happy day.

Her eyes still ached from crying after a tearful farewell with Jenny, Jack and Daphne. Stanley telephoned and wished her luck, and she could hardly speak with what felt like a large swelling in her throat where her emotions choked her.

Nor did she want to hand over another letter with a new address for Michael to eventually receive; she wanted life back to normal, as before the war, but with Michael a large part of it all. Kitty woke with a miserable cloud hanging over here and the parp of the horn outside did nothing to improve her mood. She dragged her kitbag off the bed and stomped downstairs. She gave a brief smile to Daphne and stepped outside.

'Ay, ay. We've a beauty travelling with us today, lads,' a cheerful voice rang out of a truck filled with soldiers, some several years younger than herself. Another voice told them to lock their lips and, to Kitty's surprise, Jo jumped down from the back.

'Hello, you, coming our way?' she asked Kitty.

Kitty handed her kitbag to the hovering soldier to one side of Jo and stared at her friend. The moment Jo grinned back at her, Kitty's mood brightened, and the sunshine warmed her shoulders when she realised they were to travel together.

'Are you going to Cornwall, too?' she whispered, hardly daring to say it out loud for fear of Jo's reply.

'You've got it, my lovely, we're not sure where though, you?' Kitty shook her head.

'No idea,' she said.

A sharp whistle from the driver caught their attention.

'Time to go, up you get,' Jo said. She guided Kitty over to the truck and helped her onto the rung leading into the back of the tarpaulin-covered transport.

A firm hand pulled her inside and a few cheeky remarks were thrown her way. Once seated, she watched as Jo leaped inside on her own; no one offered her a hand and Kitty knew Jo would have batted it away if they had. Sometimes Kitty wished she was as tough as her friend.

Sitting on the uncomfortable bench, trying hard to ignore the winks and leering stares, she felt as if she stood out. Despite the warmth of the air, she kept her cape around her shoulders and discreetly pulled it closed and over her knees.

Jo sat beside her and gave her a nudge with her elbow.

'They're a rough bunch but mean well. Don't be nervous,' she whispered.

Kitty made no reply. Her friendship with Jo meant there would be no point in explaining she wasn't nervous, simply not happy with the stares, which made her feel an object rather than a nurse heading off to another wartime challenge; Jo knew and would dash away anyone who took a step too far.

Chapter Nine

As they journeyed across country, the truck passengers dwindled as people were dropped off along the way. Kitty and Jo decided it was a vehicle filled with stragglers offloaded to fill gaps in various parts of England – the majority being Red Cross support.

Although Kitty enjoyed seeing parts of the country she had never visited, the eight-hour journey did nothing for frazzled nerves and bruised behinds. Both Kitty and Jo clambered down from the truck at the airbase they had arrived at, stretched and groaned, but all aches were forgotten when they took in the view of patchwork clifftops rolling downwards towards the clear blue sea beside the RAF station where they had parked, and both sighed with contentment.

'It's beautiful,' Kitty said and stretched her arms and legs, inhaling the sea air. 'Brought up by the sea, I always appreciate that smell, but the view! My goodness, the North

Sea is grey compared to this; it's incredible. Are we staying here? With the RAF?' Kitty said as she stretched again.

Jo shook her head and copied Kitty with a stretch. 'I'm not sure what's happening. I think two of the chaps travelling with us are transferring here. But—'

'Cooeee,' a female voice echoed across the field where they stood.

Both Kitty and Jo looked at each other in disbelief, then across to the woman striding towards them.

'It can't be. It ruddy well is. What the h—' Jo expressed with feeling, but stopped herself from saying anymore when Kitty nudged her in the ribs.

'Belle? What on earth is *she* doing here? I know she lives somewhere in Cornwall, but she's in uniform. Oh, no, please, she's not joining us again! Tell me she isn't...' Kitty exclaimed.

A huffing, plumper, but still glamorous, rosy-cheeked Belle joined them, carrying a large battered brown case.

'Hello, you two. Like old times, eh? I fought this, I can tell you.' Annabelle Farnsworth's appearance might have altered, but her plummy-toned voice had not, and Kitty was on the defensive. This was the woman who tried to destroy her relationship with Michael, and although she had tried to forgive, it was easier writing letters than seeing her face to face again.

'I came willingly, as did Jo. We got the call and were hustled away from our posts, but we didn't argue. It's for the best of others, not ourselves. I thought you'd given up on the RC,' she said and watched as the woman who'd once sneered at anything shabby or relating to the lower classes tucked in a stray hair from a very unkempt head.

'Yes, life changes when we least expect it. I didn't leave the Red Cross – my circumstances changed when Mummy became ill – but I've always helped where I can, which is why I've been dragged back onto the support list. I tried to avoid it,' she said as she bent to rub grass from a shoe, missing the *not surprised* look between Kitty and Jo, 'but they insisted I am duty bound and simply had no choice. I've worked long hours at the pub and am exhausted. They have no sympathy; I was rushed from my bed, hence the state I'm in. I had no time to make up and prepare myself.'

Belle droned on about her male companion sharing the bed with her, and how many fell at her feet begging her to marry them, whilst Jo and Kitty stood in stunned silence before they were beckoned over to join a small group of women outside the truck.

'Here goes, destination unknown,' Jo said and grabbed her bag. 'Come on, Kitty, let's bag the best seats.'

'Those trucks are dreadfully uncomfortable. I'd rather walk,' Belle called out after them.

Jo and Kitty giggled between them and upped their speed.

'You'd better hurry up or you will have to – they won't wait for a dillydally,' Jo shouted over her shoulder.

Upon giving their names they were told to wait before boarding the truck as they were to join one of three groups. Jo's name was called first and she was instructed to join a group of four waiting entry into the airbase. Kitty and Belle were directed to a group of six, four male Red Cross orderlies and two women – not in Red Cross uniform.

Jo's group were told they were staying at the RAF base, which they now knew to be Perranporth, and were marched through the entrance before she and Kitty could say goodbye. The other two groups were hurried onto the truck, and they drove away. Jo gave a wave and air-etched a message to write as they passed her by, and Kitty's heart sank. She did not want to write; she wanted to chat and enjoy Jo's company. She told herself to be grateful; she knew where her best friend was stationed, and they were at least in the same county.

The truck slowed down, and the other group were told they were allocated to a local hotel now converted into a first-aid centre and to walk the short distance to their posting. Half an hour later, Belle and the others were told to leave the truck, which was fine by Kitty as Belle had griped and moaned the whole journey.

Belle's mood did not improve once she found out her duties and Kitty could hear her voice getting louder.

'POW support? What is that, for goodness' sake?' she demanded from the allocating officer for the Red Cross.

'It is the new post you will carry out with dignity and care – and please do not shout. I will not tolerate the way you have just shown me disrespect, Miss Farnsworth.' The officer gave a deep, disapproving sigh. 'We all have a duty within the service to our country. Now kindly follow your other colleagues; show the residents we still have pride and decorum. You represent Great Britain and please do not forget such an important reminder.'

Belle puffed out her chest. 'Where am I? I live about half an hour away, but without signposts how am I supposed to know whereabouts in Cornwall you have dragged me!'

'You will be told everything you need to know when you go inside, Farnsworth. Now toddle off and do as you are told.'

Without waiting to see if Belle was going to do as instructed, the allocating officer turned heel and headed to the front of the truck.

Kitty leaned out just as Belle stamped a foot like a belligerent child. 'But I…'

Kitty shook her head at her.

'Belle, it's time to stop whining. See you around, maybe.'

With a sigh of relief, she leaned back onto the benched seating – her backside so numb she no longer registered discomfort. She was not lumbered with keeping Belle in check, a task harder than holding back the enemy, when she recalled their time at Birmingham.

'Here we are, this is your stop, Pattison. Good luck. Over there – register at the main building.'

Kitty looked across a large expanse of grass towards an array of huts.

Checking in and finding her quarters took less than five minutes. An interview with a senior nurse followed after Kitty dropped her bags onto her bed and joined her new colleagues.

'Welcome to RAF Trebelzue, Nurse Pattison. Your HQ report shows you have solid experience with returning airmen,' the ward sister said as she crossed Kitty's name from an attendee list.

'Yes, Sister, but I've not nursed for several months. The reason is—'

'Yes, yes, I see on your records,' the sister interrupted. 'You stepped away from nursing duties and had a couple of months playing with orphans. Well, it's back to the grind. Back on the horse.' The woman took a brief breath before launching into another speech at such a rapid pace, Kitty found it hard to keep up with her. 'I am also instructed you are no ordinary RC trainee nurse, but widely experienced in emergency search and rescue, which stands you in good stead here. We patch them up and move them on, but what we see and endure during their stay takes a strong stomach. Block H is your new home. I've taken the liberty of registering you with the local rescue team as valuable training and skill must not go to waste during wartime. You've travelled well; still neat and tidy, I see. Ensure it stays that way...'

The sharp bite of the woman's words was a temptation to fight back in her defence, but Kitty kept quiet. She resented the use of the words *playing with orphans* but accepted it would be futile and foolish to respond. Her main concern was offering the returning airmen her support without a repeat of her traumatic experience at Shotley Bridge.

'I will try my best, Sister. I am told my training programme has recommenced and I will have assessments as before. I do hope they won't coincide with any late-night recovery sessions if I'm called out. I tried to do too much at Shotley Bridge and ended up not able to give my best to my patients.'

The sister frowned at her. 'We all have sacrificed a lot – sleep included. It is war, Nurse Pattison – it's a tough situation. I will, however, ensure no assessments are carried out should you have to deal with an emergency. I'm not heartless after all.'

Kitty felt it best to say nothing. Her sarcastic 'you are all heart' would find her in deep water or worse.

For two weeks, Kitty worked the ward for limbless men. She wrote to Michael, Jenny, Trix and Jo, informing them where she was now living, and simply mentioned she was back nursing returning servicemen. The severity of the injuries meant rapid decisions to amputate were made, and Kitty's heart burned with sadness for so many when they woke from their anaesthetic and were told the news.

No one needed to hear the nightmares had returned. Her dreams of patients screaming with severe burns or severed limbs were still vivid; so much so, they evoked the gagging smell which, in turn, triggered more nightmares. It was a vicious circle of memories, but Kitty struggled through with the knowledge she had her best friend not far away and could make plans to meet with Jo and ensure she made good use of her day off. She bought a bicycle from a nurse who was leaving to marry and had no need of the bike due the fact she would be pushing a pram six months down the line.

A shout-out around the base meant the post had arrived and Kitty worked her way through endless bed baths and sheet changes wondering if there would be anything from Michael. His surprise visit at Fell Hall made her greedy for his touch and kisses – she definitely wanted more. The attention from other men on the base was flicked away like an annoying fly and earned her a cold shoulder at times. Each day she steeled herself against the fresh traumas which flowed through the doors, and if some people thought her an ice queen because she ignored their advances, it meant nothing to her. She no longer cared for flattery, since it seemed trivial in comparison to what went on around her, but even against the horrific wounds she dealt with, she no longer had the strength to release any pent-up emotions. The war, her sacrifices and losses had hardened her. Kitty no longer hid and cried when a patient died; she continued on to the next and the next, ensuring they received the best of care. So far, the search and rescue teams had not called for their backup crew, and she managed to get a few hours' unhindered sleep before a past terror – often the face of a burned patient gasping for air or screaming for a loved one when the morphine wore off – threatened to disturb her and the five other girls sleeping in the same hut.

Picking through the post pile, she picked out one letter and disappointment set in to find nothing from Michael. She recognised Jenny's handwriting on the envelope and instead of ripping it open for a quick read during her short tea break, she pushed it into her uniform pocket and chose to wait for a more leisurely moment to find out Jenny's news about Fell Hall.

Although she wasn't miserable or lonely, Kitty knew something was missing from her life – other than Michael's loving attention. As she walked back to her quarters, she heard a group of men laugh, followed by a giggle from a female, and she gave a sigh when she realised the laughter of children was one of the things that lifted her heart. Innocent, carefree laughter with no strings attached was a tonic for anyone having a difficult day. She touched the pocket where Jenny's letter sat waiting to be read. Was she ready to read about an empty house which held mixed memories? The answer was no, but the letter begged to be read.

Fell Hall,
Brancepeth
10ᵗʰ June 1942

Dear Kitty, I hope this letter finds you well and in good spirits (sorry, Jenny, no it doesn't.) *Personally, I wish I could say I am well, and my spirits are high, but sadly, Dr Andrews has told Stanley and I that my cancer has progressed, and my body can no longer cope with all I ask of it, meaning the war will outlast me should it continue through the summer months.* (Oh, Jenny, we knew it was coming, but not so soon – and I don't think the war will outrun you if that is the case. Now I'm sad.)

This letter is sent with love and thanks to you for sharing my dream in ensuring 'our' orphans had comfort and care. (The love and thanks are reciprocated, Jenny.)

Stanley has borne the news with his usual fortitude and strength, which helps me cope. With the knowledge that when I'm gone, he will survive. (With a broken heart, Jenny.)

Please, when time comes, write to him but do not expect a letter in return, he is not a letter writer.

My dear friend, it was a good day the day you walked onto his ward and took control of getting him back out into the world again. I wish you and Michael a lifetime of happiness and pray he returns to you whole and ready to embark on married life. (Me too!)

Don't read this with sadness. I have asked for Stanley to pass on a gift when you see each other again. A token of our friendship.

Be bold and brave, Kitty. (Oh, Jenny, I try, goodness knows, I try.)

Keep doing great things and be proud of your accomplishments.

I am grateful our paths crossed.

Your friend.

With love and affection,

Jenny x

The voice of response quietened inside Kitty's head as she laid down the letter. A letter she would never read again. She allowed the tears to flow free as she conjured up the image of Jenny reading to the children on the lawn of Fell Hall. A peaceful, graceful image. She focused hard and replaced the sad image of a waning friend with the one of her during her happiest hours when Kitty had known her, and soon the tears turned to a gentle smile – a comforting picture of peace and happiness. Confident the image was there to stay, Kitty tore the letter into pieces and placed it into her pocket ready to throw into the furnace at the back of the wards. Some letters were never meant to be placed in a box with pretty ribbons.

Chapter Ten

Although her legs were tired from a busy fortnight at work with minimal rest periods, Kitty chose to cycle rather than take the bus, and had arranged to meet Jo in a small village a short distance away. The scenery around her wound its beauty around her mind and body, and she released the pressures of work into its care.

She rode with determination through the narrow lanes and enjoyed the sense of freedom when freewheeling with the soft breeze in her hair. She needed today, despite flying along on her bicycle reminding her of Michael. She clung onto the hope they would be together again, but since his last visit and their deep intimacy, she chose to concentrate on each day rather than keep focusing on the future. A particularly dreadful day taught Kitty it was time to form a positive, protective barrier around herself to stop the ache of the many partings she had recently experienced in both her personal and her working life.

A brief note sent to her from Jo spurred Kitty to ask for

her day off to be swapped if possible. To her surprise there was no argument from the ward sister and a colleague stepped up to the request without a grumble.

'Hello, you,' Kitty called over to Jo, sitting on a wall opposite a large church. She looked a picture of health and her smile lifted Kitty; she stored it away for a day when she needed to draw on happier times.

Jo hopped down from the wall and put her arms around a surprised Kitty, who happily received the rare embrace. Jo usually flapped away any form of affection.

'What's going on? I'm happy to receive a hug and is that a hint of lipstick? Who are you and where is the real Jo Norfolk?' Kitty asked playfully and gave Jo a soft arm punch. 'How's things?

Jo grinned and stood with her feet astride and her hands in the pockets of a set of mechanic's dungarees. To Kitty, the lipstick seemed oddly out of place.

'Things are fine for me; I'm driving a vehicle around the camp whilst two or three others are distributing coffee and tea to the boys. It's quite a pleasant job. I'm responsible for the van and I never go hungry, but what about you? What duties did they allocate, is there even orphan care around here?'

Kitty shifted her feet into a more comfortable position and patted her hair away from her face. 'No orphans, sadly. I miss them so much. I'm more or less back on the same duties as Shotley Bridge: caring for limbless patients. I'm back on a search and rescue crew, too.'

With a harrumph of disapproval, Jo stood with her hands on her hips and stared at Kitty in disbelief.

'After all you've been through, they plonked you back into the middle of it all. Unbelievable! Be careful, Kitty. Don't burn yourself out like you did before, and if it gets too much, tell someone, get a transfer, call me, promise?' Jo's voice was loaded with concern and Kitty put her hand in Jo's.

'I promise. I'm fully aware of my limits now, and instead of volunteering to do extra duties on my day off, to take my mind off Michael becoming like my patients, I chose to spend it here with you.'

'So, want to tell me why we are meeting here – wherever here might be?'

Kitty pointed to an attractive stone building across the small square. 'Ah, here's the thing, now don't shout, but over there is Belle's place. I never realised my placement was so close. We bumped into each other, and she invited us over. It was one of those awkward moments when I couldn't say no. She caught me on a good day.' Kitty gave a giggle.

Jo scoffed and looked around her. 'Please don't tell me she's at home – *please!*'

'Don't be mad, Jo. I think it's best this way otherwise she'll just turn up at our places, and I couldn't cope with a Belle surprise. Listen, let's just go in, smile, and leave in an hour. Apparently, there's a lemonade and a pasty for us both today.'

Jo swung around and groaned as she gave Kitty a pleading look. 'She's in there? Do I really have to suffer her company on my precious day off? I never realised you were so cruel,' Jo said with a pretend whine to her voice, making Kitty giggle.

'Apparently she inherited this inn last year. I knew she inherited one in St Mawnan Smith, her main home, and now her father has given her this one. She wrote telling me about it all and asked me to visit on a day off. I was intrigued and agreed as it isn't far away and it's also her day off,' Kitty said and Jo gave a soft huff of exasperation.

'So you dragged me into the visit too. Kitty, you said you were my friend.'

Kitty lifted her eyebrows and cocked her head to one side, offering a theatrically innocent face.

'Think of the pasty. I'm rather fond of them since enjoying one my first week,' Kitty said, raising her voice to encourage some form of enthusiasm from Jo.

'Can't we have a look around the village first? Work up an appetite. I'm just not ready to walk into the spider's web yet.'

Kitty burst out laughing. 'I'm not climbing that hill until I go home!' she said and pointed to the steep hill in front of them, 'or that one,' and pointed to another leading into the village square. 'Besides, if I can forgive her for trying to take Michael away from me in Birmingham, you can cope with a meal and conversation with her.'

'You are a kind spirit, Kitty Pattison, and I'll do it for you, but you owe me one. I give in. Lead on and no more than an hour, right?' Jo gave Kitty a gentle push, only once again her strength unbalanced Kitty.

'Careful!' Kitty exclaimed as she stabilised herself by gripping onto the stone wall.

Jo gave a loud laugh. 'I remember the last time that happened; you fell onto Michael and the rest is history. I literally pushed you two together.'

'Hmm, true. Oh, no, she's seen us. No running away now,' Kitty said and waved at a well-groomed Belle striding across the square.

'You came. How wonderful.' Belle said and gave the smile of a gracious hostess. It was hard to imagine her being anything else in life.

'Belle,' Jo said and gave a weak smile.

'Isn't it a wonderful day for cycling? Come inside, you must be parched. It's early, but we can sit in the garden. I'm afraid it is all turned over to vegetables nowadays,' Belle said and walked towards her home.

Jo mimicked Belle under her breath. Kitty gave her a warning frown. This was their day off and Kitty wanted to relax, not referee Jo and Belle. Opposites to the core.

'I must say that was a delicious pasty. Did you make them?' Kitty asked Belle.

Belle dabbed at the corner of her mouth with a napkin. 'Gracious, no. I simply eat them. One of the ladies in the village follows a recipe my girl in Mawnan uses. She collects wild herbs and I'm convinced she uses a secret one in the pasties as I've tasted others and they are not the same. Oh, I am glad you came. It gets lonely here. I much prefer the other pub, there are more…'

'Soldiers,' Jo said and took a long drink of her lemonade.

Belle gave a laugh.

'Yes, that's very true. It's lovely here, but I did make the other one my home,' Belle said and gave a wistful sigh.

Kitty offered Belle a polite smile.

'It was nice of you to invite us here for lunch instead of going to see your man, Belle. Isn't it, Jo?'

Swallowing the last dregs of her drink, Jo nodded. 'Nice.'

Kitty heard the sarcasm, but Belle remained oblivious as she flicked her hair back from her face.

'What are you both doing with the RC reallocation? I'm packing boxes for British prisoners of war in a makeshift place I'm not allowed to mention. We've a few Italian ones in tents just recently and I've heard there are plans to build a more permanent one. I'm told I will remain attached to the group and my nurse training is no longer valid.'

Both Kitty and Jo listened intently to Belle, asked questions about the Italian men, and were given a vivid description of one dark-haired, handsome prisoner giving her the eye.

'Belle, don't get ideas. Put them right out of your head. Pack the boxes and return to your tent – alone,' Kitty said, deepening her voice into a warning tone, much like a headmistress.

Throwing back her head and giving a bright laugh, Belle looked at them both. 'Me, sleep in a tent? Bless you, no! I'm collected from the pub every day. I work from eight until two o'clock. It suits me for opening time.'

With her mouth wide open, Jo stared at Belle, and Kitty gave a wide-eyed stare of surprise.

'You get to sleep in your own bed?' Kitty asked.

Jo faked a cough. 'Now there's a novelty,' she said, her voice heavily laden with sarcasm.

Kitty saw Belle flinch.

'*Jo!*' Kitty glared at her friend.

'I'm sorry, but that is so unfair,' Jo exclaimed. 'Don't get me wrong, I love what I do, but the luxury of returning to my own home at the end of the day is – is a dream, a fantasy. You must have friends in high places, that's all I can say. Bed one of them, did you?'

Jo snapped out her final words so fiercely, Kitty thought she would pop a blood vessel. Her own thoughts were that Belle always came up smelling of roses, but she chose to keep her thoughts to herself for fear of the day ending on a sour note. There was enough conflict around them with the war, without sniping remarks ensuring it crept into her personal life again.

'It's a dream for many, Jo. Belle is just one of the luckier ones. How lovely you can enjoy some form of home life, Belle. Do you have a boyfriend to walk out with?' Kitty asked. She knew talking about walking out with men would soon turn Belle's mind away from Jo's remark.

Belle looked at her with a sadness in her eyes. 'I met someone – someone special. Daddy warned him off. He also had him moved to another unit. He is American and on a special something or other over here. Apparently, there will be more to follow if the war doesn't sort itself out,' Belle said and stroked the calf of her right leg. 'He kept me in stockings and chocolate. I miss him.'

With what Kitty considered a mocking laugh, Jo stood up. 'Miss *him* or the stockings? I think it would be the chocolate I'd be heartbroken about though. However, I bet there's a queue at your door ready to replace him,' she said, and Kitty knew it was time to get Jo out from Belle's company. Her friend had never pretended to like Belle, but Kitty felt there was no place for rudeness when they had enjoyed a generous meal at her table.

'I think we'd better leave you to it, Belle.'

Jo stood up and brushed crumbs from her clothes. 'Can't have your love life delayed, Belle. Bye.'

Before Kitty could step away from the table, Jo headed inside towards the front door.

Kitty gave Belle a friendly hug to stave off a haughty spat; she had noticed the flash of anger – and hurt – in her eyes. Belle and Jo were never ones to hold back their tempers when working together in Birmingham.

'Lunch was lovely, thank you,' she said.

They joined Jo in the square. Kitty felt bad her friend had not thanked Belle for lunch and wanted to make up for her rudeness.

'As I said inside, lunch was lovely. Wasn't it, Jo?' she called over to her friend, who was intent on kicking pebbles at a wall.

'Delicious,' Jo replied and, again, Kitty felt Jo had slighted Belle with a rude response. *Was a simple thank-you so hard to say?*

'Are you able to join us for a short walk before we head back?' she asked Belle and gave Jo a warning glare.

'I'm afraid I can't. I have to open up soon, but if you get the opportunity to visit St Mawnan Smith, I'll take you on a tour of the beautiful gardens nearby. Today, if you head for the pathway over there,' she pointed to the church, 'and follow it through Lanherne Woods, you will come out at

Mawgan Porth beach area. It's a pretty route if you have the time. Mind out for the Home Guard, they will be on patrol.'

'Nothing changed there then,' Jo muttered as they walked away, wheeling their bikes through the leafy lane.

'No, you both make me feel as if I'm in the middle of a tug-of-war game. Do you realise you sniped at her so much you forgot to say thank you for lunch, Jo? When did you lose your manners, for goodness' sake? I'm the one whose man she tried to steal, and I managed to forgive, and be gracious enough to accept her invitation. I don't know what's got into you. And how come you wear lipstick? Spill!'

Kitty stopped walking and waited for Jo to do the same, but she carried on.

'Jo. Wait.'

Ignoring Kitty's call, Jo continued, and Kitty could see by the set of her friend's shoulders she was annoyed.

'I'm sorry. I didn't mean to come across as schoolmarmish, but you were spoiling for a shout down. Be honest.'

Jo startled her by throwing her bike to one side and turning around with a face so red with anger Kitty felt her insides churn.

'Stop nagging, for crying out loud. I spent my time off doing what you wanted, isn't that enough for you? Why don't you turn around and go chat with your new best friend? I'm done here.'

Too shocked to say anything, Kitty watched Jo snatch up her bike.

'Jo! What's got into you? Stop. Slow down. *Jo!*'

Kitty watched Jo ride away, bewildered by the outcome of their day off together. On reflection she wondered if she had been wrong not to tell Jo of meeting Belle, but inside she knew, if-told, Jo would not have agreed to the visit and Kitty would have missed out on her company. Jo was a listener and made her laugh; she made days off fun.

Taking a moment to realise that Jo was heading back to Perranporth, she picked up her bicycle and took a slow walk, keeping to the path. After twenty minutes she saw the beach area and sat a while on a grassy bank, compiling a letter of apology in her head. Nearly losing Michael to Belle's antics in the past had taught her a hard lesson. She could not let Belle come between her and Jo.

Chapter Eleven

c/o Pinchinthorpe Surgery
6th June, 1942

Dear Kitty,

I am at my wits' end. The RC have called me back to ward nursing. I am extremely sad, but it is out of my hands. We have cancelled the wedding and regret the fact we did not marry sooner. I am to be ready in the morning – after receiving the telephone call four days ago! I will write to you as soon as I have a new address. Please, please write to Smithy. He's so sad and I know he will miss me terribly. I've never seen him cry before, but when we realised our wedding could not go ahead, he shed a few tears. I will do my bit for king and country – and Churchill, but as soon as we've caught our breath, we've decided to marry, and I will step down from the Red Cross. I will miss our lovely village. I do not think I'll cope living in a city again.

Take care, my dear friend,
Trixie

K itty folded the letter and tucked it away in her family and friends' box. Her heart went out to both Trix and Smithy; with their wedding three weeks away, this recall seemed cruel, but the Red Cross were not to know of their plans. They needed capable people to support others during war; whatever was happening outside of the prioritised needs of others was of no interest to any governing body.

She picked up her books and returned to her studies. As much as she wanted to write back to Trix, she would wait for her next letter. She would write to Smithy the following day.

'Nurse Pattison, are you with us?'

The ward sister's voice cut through the silence Kitty had created in her head. Her mind had become frantic with study, practical exams and thoughts on how to get to see Jo again. For two weeks her friend had ignored any form of communication from her, and Kitty had to accept she had tried to apologise and now it was up to Jo to decide how important their friendship was to her. She also fretted over the letter from Trix.

'Apologies, Sister. I was pondering the ward layout,' Kitty said and gave an apologetic smile.

The sister cocked her head to one side.

'Care to enlighten us?'

With a swift smile and grappling with a reply – *oh, I was just daydreaming,* would not get a favourable response – Kitty glanced around the room and pointed to one or two patients.

'When I worked in a unit like this one, we had patients unable to assist themselves due to locker placement on the wrong side of their amputation. I've noticed a few here and wondered if they would benefit from a swap around. We have been so busy I've only just had the opportunity to assess the situation.'

Kitty watched the face of the sister and waited for some form of disapproval, so she could continue listening to the sister's lecture. A muttering amongst the other staff members unnerved her as she reflected on her words. Secure in the knowledge she had not highlighted any failures in her remark, she relaxed a little, still watching the ward sister's face and waiting for their lesson to continue.

'An important observation, Nurse Pattison. Anyone else agree?' the sister said.

More mutterings amongst the staff resulted in a majority show of hands.

'We are due a new intake of patients. Let's use this unusually quiet spell to enable those patients to reach for something from their bedside cabinet. It's a time-saving project valuable project and will give us the opportunity to assess the patient's ability to a better degree.'

By the end of her shift, Kitty ached but her mind was no longer in a fretful state. It was far too exhausted to be in any other state than tired. The new patients arrived after the ward move-around and spring-clean – something that prompted Kitty to wonder if it was entirely necessary, but that was carried out with enthusiasm. All patients capable of helping themselves and others welcomed the move and the ward staff commented on their ability to concentrate on those who needed more intensive care. Her reward for thinking about the patients' needs was praise from the ward sister and encouragement to continue towards her final certificate. Little did they know she had been formulating ways of trying to get to Perranporth and hunting down Jo to speak face to face.

When she climbed into bed, Kitty felt settled and thought of Michael, remembering their last time together. Before she fell asleep, she concentrated her thoughts on him and melted into a dream state with him enfolding her in his arms.

The following afternoon, a large postal delivery arrived and Kitty stood back watching the eager young men awaiting the call to fly and protect, kiss envelopes or slope away, disappointed. She often had the same cold slap of feeling forgotten when her name was called. A letter from Michael was much needed. Not that she did not appreciate one from her aunt or Trix.

She envied Trix and disliked herself for her envy. In her latest letter her friend had written that her placement was compensation for leaving Smithy. Her request to train as a midwife was on her records and she now worked at Stockeld Park, a large mansion which was converted into a maternity home for mothers with children. Trix said she met women from all over Britain and she was happier at her placement than she thought she might be – she also added that Kitty would love it there with the children. It wasn't quite what Kitty had wanted to read, but she was certainly happy for Trix, especially when she read it was only an hour or so away from Smithy.

Cornwall
9th July 1942

Dear Aunt Lil and Uncle Frank,

Thank you for the painting. It captures the lighthouses and promenade in the most beautiful way. It is the perfect size to sit on my bedside cabinet and reminds me of you both, and of our times together at the beach. Your new tenant has a talent indeed. Billeted soldiers need a comfortable home and yours is a lucky young man as I know you will spoil him where you can. Goodness knows when I'll get the opportunity to come back to Parkeston to enjoy being spoilt myself, but I'll let you know as soon as I can get leave.

It is with great sadness I must tell you that Jenny Walker-Fells passed away yesterday. I have permission to return for the funeral, but I fear the twenty-four-hour turnaround from here to Brancepeth will be far too tight for me and there is no movement in my leave allowance, so I telephoned Stanley with my condolences and explained. He will be a lost soul for a while, but it sounds to me as if he accepted the loss with courage. It was no great surprise, just extremely sad for him. For us all.

It is weeks since I've heard from Jo. As I explained in my last letter, we had a falling out and she appears to have taken it hard. I've tried to get in touch, but she never returns my calls or acknowledges my letters. I'll leave her alone for a while and then try again.

Belle has contacted me several times and this time has invited me to her other inn along the opposite coastline. Imagine owning two inns before you are thirty! On my next day off I might cycle there just out of curiosity. I'll keep you updated.

I received a short letter from Michael. He is still declaring his love for me but, sadly, cannot tell me where he is working, though I get the impression he is on the move again. This top-secret business is not good for a relationship, so it is a good thing we've a strong one. Some days I feel our separation is so unfair – the war is slowly taking everything away from us. I say slowly, but in fact it's speeding up, going by the losses I see on a daily basis. I push myself to see positive things, but I will admit I'm struggling right now. Still, I work with good people and living near the sea again helps. Don't worry about me – I know that's easy to say, but I am fine here. I'm faring much better than when I was at Shotley Bridge. I'm a little wiser when it comes to looking after myself.

Trix is still struggling with being apart from Smithy and their wedding being on hold, but the maternity home she now works in is only an hour away from her home, so they are not so far apart, and she gets to do what she's always dreamed of. I will admit, it makes me miss the orphans when she writes about the children staying with their mothers.

I must go now as I've to attend a Home Guard meeting (or, as my colleague Vi calls it, the gathering of grandfathers). It's something to do with the search and rescue team I belong to, and, I must add, I really enjoy the friendship they have shown me.

It is beautiful here. The more I see of my small area, the more I fall in love with Cornwall, and one day, when the war is over, we will come as a family and enjoy the beauty of the bluest waters and most beautiful trees and flowers I have ever seen.

Take care of yourselves,

With much love, Kitty x

Chapter Twelve

Kitty lay on the grass shaded from the sun. She stretched out on her front, reading a well-worn magazine in an attempt to ignore physical exhaustion taking its toll on her body and the tormenting images in her mind. A raid in France in a place named Dieppe had brought about the most horrific injuries for hundreds of men, and she, along with many others, had been drafted in to help with the makeshift receiving stations. Over the weeks Kitty noticed the hardened wall of protection she'd put up around her emotions was slowly crumbling; she knew she had to rebuild the bricks of security or she'd fail her patients. Her own fears had to be placed to one side until she had completed their care. The sacrifices the men made on her behalf deserved only the best of her attention. She learned when a cheeky remark could bring a smile to a dying boy's lips, and that her ice queen persona was no longer needed. To become too hardened to the world around her meant she was shutting out the small things that mattered, and she realised they would not break her nerve, simply give her a fleeting moment of unrest, or a nightmare from which she would recover.

Kitty had thought hard about the change within her and put it down to a new maturity and confidence in her work. She'd always known her work was important, and that her self-doubt needed suppressing, but at last she felt relief she had achieved the fine balance she sought, which gave her a different approach to her self-care and preservation. She made a concerted effort to express her feelings in the form of a diary, and, when troubled, she walked to a quiet spot and vented to the sky her anger towards the enemy. Each time she shouted, she felt the release of tension, which enabled her to cope with whatever was thrown her way. A renewed courage to believe in herself pushed its way to the fore and Kitty embraced the person she'd become.

A week after her twenty-second birthday – one spent working a night shift and evacuating patients in the pouring rain – Kitty received notification of another move. When she questioned their reasoning, they gave none but promised her return to RAF Trebelzue would happen no later than the end of August. She tried to plead her case and asked to remain in the Newquay area as the constant moving around was not helping her with her studies and assessments. A quiet matron gave her an understanding smile and reassured her that once she heard the reason, she would understand; the matron was convinced Kitty was a credible member of the team to help in this particular case. She was encouraged to listen to the medical officer in charge of the transfer and then reconsider her request as decisions were never taken lightly when it came to wartime activities. Taking it as a gentle dismissal, Kitty joined the other bewildered Red Cross workers and rescue team who had also been called away from their duties.

Standing receiving their orders, they were told they were the all-important extra pair of hands needed for a top-secret venture which had resulted in a multitude of allied forces casualties. All thoughts of objecting to the move went from Kitty's mind. She had a duty to others and her own personal objection was pushed aside. She would do whatever was asked of her – those fighting for her freedom deserved nothing less.

The trucks they travelled in were shut off with tarpaulin, which hindered their view, but, as their destination drew closer, the passengers guessed they were still coastal from the odd seagull scream above the noise outside. The journey had taken just over an hour, and when they stepped down from the truck, the scene before them could only be described as chaos. They were offered a brief welcome to Plymouth and were swiftly taken to makeshift receiving tents and told to do their best. The organisation was not what Kitty was used to, but she was told everything had become a last-minute rescue ordeal for all involved as the powers that be had kept the raid a tight secret. No one had expected such a vast number of casualties, which had resulted in the frantic mobilisation of anyone free to aid the medical units.

Looking about her, Kitty saw the aftermath of men returning from a bloody battle and her adrenaline pumped renewed energy around her body. She helped those floundering for guidance on how to deal with some of the injuries, organised treatment areas and, within an hour, found herself heading up a small receiving tent of her own. As some around her died, Kitty came alive. Whenever she flagged with the awfulness of it all, she repeated her new mantra, *duty of care, it's my duty to care*, and it aided her focus on whatever new horror she faced.

A Canadian accent caught her attention at the doorway of the tent and her heart gave a little flip. She knew it wasn't Michael, but the voice made her feel close to him. She rushed over to the soldier in question and guided him to a chair. She removed the temporary bandage around his head and stemmed the flow of blood.

'This will sting, I'm sorry,' she said.

His clammy hand touched her arm and Kitty looked down at his face, twisted with pain.

'My friends, they – I, my friends…'

Kitty hushed him with a soft tone she often used on the children when they became distressed.

'They'll be taken care of in other places. Let's see to you first, and if I consider you fit enough, then maybe you can go look for them. You're Canadian – my fiancé is Canadian,' she said, distracting him from his distress.

Patient after patient received the tender care Kitty and her colleagues offered. The steady flow of Canadians was directed their way and Kitty was in awe of their strength and resilience when each one she tended relayed their story of attack and rescue. Each one carried guilt for surviving.

One nineteen-year-old sobbed for his mother and Kitty rushed to comfort him. She held him in her arms crooning words of comfort as his blood soaked through her dress. When his sobs subsided, she stroked his brow and tended his wounds. Medics and nurses moved around the tent in synchronised manoeuvres, guided by the needs of their patients. An air of control eventually settled and assessing and moving patients from the tent took precedence. There was no time for a break and adrenaline pumped through Kitty's body as she worked her way through fourteen hours of heartbreak. Eventually, she gave in to her tiredness and headed for a spare trestle bed in the corner of the rest tent. The noise surrounding her faded away as she slid into a deep sleep.

In what seemed like an hour but was in fact three, an orderly shook her gently by the shoulders and handed her a cup of tea and a bread roll with a precious slice of bacon nestling in the centre. Kitty gave him a grateful smile.

'I can't remember when I last ate something. Thank you,' she said.

He patted her shoulder in a fatherly fashion.

'I've watched you work. How do you do it? Where do you find the strength to carry on? It's carnage out there,' he said with a grim face, his voice cracking with emotion as he spoke.

Kitty swallowed her mouthful of roll and wiped her mouth before answering.

'I've been asked the same question several times. I think each patient gives me the strength. I cannot imagine what they've been through, but I know they deserve the best care I can offer them.'

The orderly raised an approving eyebrow and said, as he

walked away, 'If I ever need help, I'll pray you are by my side.'

'And I'll be there,' said Kitty and took a sip of her drink.

'Then you will be the luckiest man on the planet,' a voice called from inside the tent.

Kitty stopped sipping her tea and stared at the dishevelled medic coming towards her.

The orderly gave her an enormous grin. 'I'll leave you to it. I've a feeling this Canadian is not wounded, but a man definitely in need of some of that tender care you offer your patients.'

Kitty tried to move, but she froze with the shock of seeing Michael. 'Um, yes. My fiancé. Thank you for the tea,' she said just as Michael pulled her from the bed and into his arms.

The world around them continued with their activities, but Kitty and Michael took little notice. Eventually, he pulled away from their kisses and grabbed her hands. She looked down at the red, sore skin.

'The hands of Cinderella,' she said.

'My beautiful princess. Look at you. My shining light.'

Kitty spotted a colleague looking for somewhere to rest and waved them over.

'Let's leave them to it, Michael. Come outside for a walk. I need air.'

Hand in hand, they walked to the loading bay and pier where the wounded were still arriving. The evening was fading fast, and their rescuers worked at a frantic pace to get them into vehicles ready for transporting for care.

'Were you there?' Kitty asked Michael as he stared ahead.

He tweaked her hand.

'Dieppe? Sadly, yes. I tried to save so many, but it was a helpless situation. I should imagine Hell sums up what I saw. Fellow Canadians were amongst the allies and hundreds fell, their blood soaking the sand. The Germans pushed through, and we lost command of a vital area. I left with the last boat and am due rest, but I need to go back, I…'

Kitty gripped his hand and tried to control the screaming inside.

'Stay here and help the men here. We need the help,' she said, not liking the sound of pleading in her voice, but Michael was hers to worry about and seeing the state of him, her worry levels had increased tenfold. Her body shook with the fear of him returning, and he must have sensed her trembling and draped his arm around her shoulder. She leaned her head into his body, not wanting to see any more of the scene in front of them. Still, they had to see the atrocities in order to tell their stories and ensure another generation never suffered this kind of fight for freedom again.

'Please don't go, Michael. Get involved here, make yourself valuable here and stay. I don't think I can bear it anymore without you around. I was so happy at Fell Hall when life seemed slower paced, and even though short, our times together were less frantic. Just as I thought we had that opportunity to embrace our love with physical contact once more, I lose you to this damned war again.' Kitty drew breath and held back a threatening sob. 'Why can't we have a life of peace where we can talk of a future not just in letters but hand in hand? I know I sound as if I'm whining like a child, but seeing you leave is the hardest part of loving you. Letting go of your hand means another splinter of fear in my heart.'

Michael manoeuvred in front of her and peered into her face. She saw the grime etched into his skin, but, most of all, she saw the pain of all he had seen. And, once again, she knew she had to let him go. His duty, and hers, was not to dream and walk hand in hand, it was to dig deep inside their souls and find renewed strength to offer hope and support to others. She saw his love for her and knew it was not the fading kind; she just had to trust fate would give her the happiness they looked for when it was all over. Life had dealt them many blows, and she had to trust her instinct that they would survive and move forward into a better world filled with freedom and peace.

'I'm sorry. I let my emotions get the better of me. It was the surprise of seeing you here. Of course you must go, the same as I have to head back to work now. We are the hands of hope and although they are tired and sore, they are much needed by those brave men. Go and help them, Michael, but as soon as you can, come and find me,' Kitty said, her words barely whispered as he stroked her face. His eyes, red with dust and sadness, filled with tears. One tipped the brim and Kitty stroked it away.

'I love you, Kitty. I adore your bravery. You are what keeps me going when we're in the thick of it all. I don't want to leave you, Cinderella, but this prince has ogres to fight. I'm better out there in the mud and dirt, giving my support to my brothers. I'll be in touch as soon as I can. When I saw your name on the duty board, I can't tell you how my heart swelled with pride. It was so full it nearly burst. I love all that you are, loving, kind, caring and selfless. I cannot wait until you are my wife. I'll be the proudest man, the proudest husband. I wake every day wondering what good thing I did to be given such a gift as your love.'

Michael placed his hands on her cheeks and a soft kiss on her lips. Kitty accepted the kiss with the same tenderness before allowing her tongue to seek out his and their kiss to reach a heady height of passion born out of fear and intense love. Her chest ached inside with grief when he dropped another soft kiss on her brow, whispered his love and walked away. His silhouette wound its way towards the gridlock of vehicles marked with large red crosses, and Kitty knelt on the ground and opened her heart to let the sadness pour from her. Once she released her tears, she composed herself and, loosening her filthy apron, walked to the washrooms and readied herself for another shift.

After a particularly hard shift, Kitty stood looking out to sea, as she inhaled the fresh air she mentally sent her love to Michael across water. Sea tainted with the blood of the courageous.

Chapter Thirteen

K itty eased off her shoes and wriggled her toes. She looked at the calendar: 3rd September, 1942. Three years of war dragged them down and there seemed to be no let up. Every day was a battle to find something to uplift the mood. Newspapers were filled with desperate news of defeat or small victories, and the local church bulletin board slowly filled with names of those who'd died protecting them, or a family asking for prayers for a missing relative.

Kitty stared at the pile of letters sitting on her bedside cabinet and resisted the temptation to dive right in and read them before she undressed and washed. The horrors of August were tucked to the back of her mind for the majority of the time when she moved back to Trebelzue. She thought of Michael and men like him and used her calming technique of shouting to the sky whenever she felt the need. She had brushed off the praise given her and denied she had gone above and beyond for many a patient. Her discussions with Matron and her ward sister were about Kitty's future and not the past. It was the only way she could cope and keep her mind intact. If she allowed any form of insanity to creep her way, Kitty would have failed Michael. She'd once promised him she would remain strong and support his brothers-in-arms. Her duty of care was carried out to its fullest and she returned to the airbase knowing she had fulfilled her promise.

Once she was settled in bed, she laid out her recent post and tore open a letter with Nancy's neat yet still childlike scrawl.

Dear Kitty,

I miss you. Flop-Ear said hello. My cousin is teaching me to knit. I have a kind teacher twice a week and she makes me happy. We read and I can do my sums without using my fingers now. She said my spelling and writing is advanced for my age and the war disruption. I had to look that word up and I agree with her, my schoolwork is disrupted. I miss our lessons at Fell Hall.

My auntie sent material for two new dresses for my birthday, and I helped make them. They have big hems and are a bit loose for me to grow into them, but I am still skinny so I laughed and said I think it will be when I am grown up before I grow out of them. One of the dresses is blue and reminded me of Jenny's pretty dress she wore the day I arrived after the bombing. I wrote to Eric, David and Peter, but only Eric wrote back.

How is your friend, Jo? She made us laugh.

I have to peel the vegetables for tea, so must finish writing.

Love from Nancy and Flop-Ear x

Smiling at the mention of the blue dress and the memory of a little girl, Kitty placed the letter to one side and tore open one in Jo's handwriting. She scanned for the address at the top of the page and saw the space was blank. The letter was the first she had received since Jo's refusal to take her last telephone call at the end of July.

Kitty,

Just a note to say I'm on the move. Wishing you well for the future.

Jo

Kitty stared in disbelief at the scant words across the page. They looked lost. Although she did not expect Jo to apologise for her original outburst or lack of communication, she had expected more from the contents of the envelope in her hand. A tremor of anger rose inside her as she wondered if, by leaving off her new address, Jo expected her to try and track her down. Then she thought it through and decided Jo might not have one to send yet. However, the wishing her well for the future read as a final message. Kitty also knew it would have taken Jo a lot of hand-writhing to write a letter in the first place as the stubborn side of Jo rarely relented over anything.

Putting the letter with Nancy's, she moved on to one from her aunt informing her they were still looking after billeted men, and the apple tree was fruitful again this year.

Stanley's news in his letter was of an upbeat nature, and, reading between the lines, Kitty guessed he rarely returned to Fell Hall cottage. She could imagine him thriving on the challenges thrown his way and figuring out the course for the British air force pilots to follow and do their worst.

Pulling the covers to her chin, having saved the best until last, she prepared herself to read Michael's letter. She smiled at the memories of his kisses. Stroking the official envelope, then slipping the grubby paper from inside it, Kitty sighed at the amount of black pen marks crossing out what the censors considered vital information, not to be passed along to those who do not need to know. The lines broke the flow of his words and Kitty spent time trying her best to assess what he might have tried to tell her. Michael shared his sadness for the loss of his fellow man, and his happiness when she and he were together, but nothing told her of his whereabouts in the world.

Darling Kitty,

Life here in— means the men are— and we can no longer— but somehow we manage to keep our spirits up and enjoy the local life, albeit—

Our next move in a couple of weeks, is to— is on— a date with the enemy once again and we won't be dancing!

I miss you and can't wait until we can share a pasty once again. Remember the pasty?

There are days I want to forget— a place of darkness and then there are memories of pasty eating with you, and I know we'll enjoy one together again one day. I do hope you remember the pasty.

Take care, my sweetheart.

Forever yours,
Michael x

Kitty pondered his words about them sharing a pasty together again in a couple of weeks and how it was a treasured memory of his. His words puzzled her as it was not a memory they shared and it worried her; had he written the wrong memory to the wrong girl? Kitty reprimanded herself: the idea was ridiculous; Michael was a faithful man. Slowly, she reread his letter to try and work out his meaning, and then it occurred to her he had deliberately put in sentences to be crossed out in the hope the pasty message was missed. Which it was. Michael was to be posted to Cornwall!

She held the letter to her chest and closed her eyes.

'Someone's had good news, going by the smile on her face,' said one of her roommates, squeezing her foot as they walked by her bed.

Kitty opened her eyes and grinned. 'I think Michael might be coming to Cornwall with his unit soon,' she said.

Another voice cut in from across the room. 'Let's hope you're not posted elsewhere then.'

The girl's words hit hard. Kitty's nomadic life with the Red Cross was bound to interfere with Michael's new posting. Suddenly, the smile receded and a small frown replaced it and she listened as the other girls in the room berated their colleague for ruining Kitty's moment. Without speaking, Kitty rose from her bed and left the room. She needed to find the moon, to look at it and reconnect with

Michael in positive thoughts. She wondered if they'd stand together, staring at it, hand in hand once again.

The better September weather gave in to a damp start for October and it suited Kitty's mood. She waited for Michael to contact her, but she had no response to her letters. She received letters from Trix and Smithy sharing their joy about their work and ability to meet each other once a week. Again, although she was thrilled for them both, it did nothing to lift the darkness she allowed to drift over her. Jo made no attempt to get in touch, and Belle's letter of invitation to visit looked a tempting offer. Having passed more assessments and entering her final year of training, Kitty travelled back to Harwich for a four-day visit with her aunt and uncle, who panicked upon her arrival, concerned about where she would sleep. After a word with a neighbour, Kitty insisted it was her and not the billeted soldier who slept in the woman's home. Kitty knew only too well what it was like to be moved from pillar to post and the young man needed stability for the short while he was based in Essex. News of fighting abroad and the stories brought back by the wounded men would mean once he left British soil, a comfortable bed and a home-cooked meal would be a distant dream. She was not going to be the one to deprive him.

Kitty did her best to enjoy the visit, but by the third day she no longer felt part of the splintered families surrounding her. From her bedroom window she spotted the back of a telegram boy who was knocking on the door of the house opposite. A cool blast of reality hit her. Death had touched their street yet again – and her personally. She lost a schoolfriend and playmate in the soldier son of her neighbour. Working through the horrid outcomes of war had altered a large part of her life. Losing her cousin who'd taken his role as big brother was hard, but she moved away with the comfort of Hamilton Street tucked in her mind, and now the war encroached yet again on the place she had always thought of as a safe haven. In her innocence, when she left home, she never dreamed the war would distort the image she carried with her of the tearful farewell with her aunt and uncle, the little ones cheering her on to the end of the road, and neighbours calling out their good wishes. Her once happy, contented village was now filled with fraught parents, grieving residents and the lost sound of children chattering on their way home from school – most of them now living hundreds of miles away for their safety. Barricades stood where open ground once allowed residents the freedom to roam, and vegetables replaced the colourful flowers in every garden. The ornate metal fencing and gates had been uprooted when the call from the government came for ammunition support, and the gaps which marked their boundaries stood out like the scars of battle, jagged and unsightly.

Even her walk along the promenade did nothing to make Kitty want to stay longer. After a heart-to-heart with her aunt about her unsettled feelings, they decided it was due to the thought that Michael was based somewhere in Cornwall and when she was there working, he did not seem so far away. Her aunt understood her dilemma and was not offended by Kitty's confession of wanting to return to Cornwall.

'Kitty, I might be a lot older than you, but I can still remember what it was like to be in love – yes, you might grin, but I love your uncle despite his faults and ways.' Lil tapped Kitty's arm in jest. 'Promise me you will come home when you can; we understand it won't be every time you get leave. Just don't forget us, but know we do not expect to be the centre of your world. You have a life to live despite this war.'

Kitty embraced her aunt.

'Thank you for understanding. I have a lot on my mind, and it tends to make me a little selfish,' she said and placed a kiss on her aunt's cheek.

'Kitty, you are the least selfish person I know. Find a little happiness and get a rest for a few days. You will be with your Michael before you know it and grab those moments,' Lil replied, giving Kitty's cheek a little tweak.

On the day she was due to return to Newquay, Kitty had a change of heart and chose to make her way to Mawnan Smith instead. There was an acceptance by her adoptive parents that their niece had grown up and ready to fully fly the nest. They purchased her ticket with their blessing, and both expressed their concern that she was overworking to hide her worries. It was a tearful farewell, and Kitty left carrying sadness but no guilt, thanks to their encouragement and support.

Once on the train, she slid into a state of composed calm and knew their concerns about her health and welfare were valid. She had promised she would walk and clear her mind, chat and relax with Belle as best she could, and she knew she would try and do as she promised. Belle might not be her favourite person, but the girl obviously thought enough of Kitty to reach out on more than one occasion inviting her to stay. She was no replacement for Jo, but with Trix not around, Kitty needed someone who leaned towards a more carefree attitude, to remind her life wasn't all about work.

Chapter Fourteen

The journey was long-drawn-out because of the disrupted train service, but eventually Kitty arrived in the village in the hope Belle would not be put out by her unannounced arrival. Kitty knew if she was to return to the airbase, she would throw herself into work for the rest of her leave instead of relaxing.

Stepping onto the platform, Kitty wound her way through the vast throng of servicemen and women towards the exit. Geography had never been her strongpoint at school, and she had no clue how big Cornwall was, but she imagined it to be overspilling with visitors in uniform. She had never seen so many people on one station.

The bus journey into Belle's village was a pleasant one, with several local passengers offering smiles and words of encouragement to those defending them. By the time she reached the edge of the village, it occurred to Kitty she had no idea where The Stargazy Inn was. From out of nowhere, a noise overhead disturbed the peace and she was reminded of war once again. A low and fierce dogfight above had people rushing in different directions to avoid bullets, although there was no siren sound to send people to safety. It was a situation which needed a shelter of some kind, but Kitty had no idea where to go. She turned in confusion when someone grabbed her arm and pulled her into a garden across the narrow lane.

'Quickly, with me! I'm Conwenna Veryan, but to put you out of your misery, you can call me Wenna,' a woman said as they ran. Her laugh had a softness to it and Kitty warmed to her straightaway.

As they reached an Anderson shelter at the bottom of the garden, Wenna hustled Kitty inside, bent low to catch her breath, then stood up and grinned at her. 'And you are?' she asked with a loud laugh.

Kitty had no choice but to laugh with her; the woman had a wonderful, friendly aura about her.

'I'm Kathryn Pattison, but you can call me Kitty – seeing as how we are friends,' she said and added a belly laugh of her own.

A sea of faces stared at her as she sat down next to Wenna; each one gave her a beaming smile.

'Irene, my eldest, Jimmy, my youngest, and Ruth, my ma,' Wenna said as she introduced her family to Kitty.

'Sit down, my lovely. And you must be parched. Wenna, a cup of tea – nettle for me will do. Please, call me Ruth.'

The tiny woman sat on a chair which threatened to swallow her up; her feet dangled a foot from the floor. Kitty loved the soft burr in her voice, a strong Cornish tone.

'Herb tea?' Irene asked. Kitty smiled her thanks, still confused by what had just happened.

'Welcome to our rainy day den. Dad made it before he went away. It's to keep us safe,' Jimmy said.

'Your den? Oh, you lucky things,' Kitty said, and her heart went out to the man who'd created the space where children played in safety. Irene sat on a heap of cushions, and Kitty noticed seats which would make comfortable beds. There was an array of blankets, and books heaped on shelves. Tinned food and other items for cooking were stacked against the other side of the room. Rugs lined the floor and hung from the walls. It had a cosy feel, and Kitty felt sure the oil lamps added to the feeling when lit against the darkness. It was the best shelter she had ever seen.

'This is incredible,' she said.

Wenna handed her the tin mug filled with steaming herb tea and Kitty mused at how relaxed everyone was.

A rumble overhead told them the planes were still on the chase.

'My Jeffra did his best before he left, and when the news arrived that he was killed in action, we found ourselves using this as a place of comfort. Ironic really, but the war altered our way of thinking about what is important, and the place where my man put his last energy into helping his family is here – so why not use it as a den and not a place to sit and be terrified?' Wenna said.

Ruth and Kitty both offered their agreement, but Irene tossed her book aside and huffed before Kitty could offer her condolences.

'Here she goes, Miss Moody,' Jimmy teased and was rewarded with a clip around the ear from his grandmother.

'The war interrupted everything. A cosy shelter won't change that – or bring Dad home,' Irene muttered and made no effort to hide the resentment or sadness in her voice.

'I'm sorry, Irene. It must be hard for you all,' Kitty said, feeling for the girl, who was aged around thirteen. A tender age to have life turned upside down.

'You've got a funny accent,' Jimmy said, interrupting the adult talk, and Kitty wondered if this was to deflect from his own sadness.

'I'm not from Cornwall,' Kitty replied.

'What is your story, Kitty? How come you've ended up in our Anderson shelter – aside from me dragging you here?' Wenna asked.

'The short story is that I was sent here! The longer story is that I think my fiancé is somewhere in Cornwall, but I have no clue where he is based. My family are in East Anglia, and I've been shipped to Birmingham, pulled up in Leeds for minutes, only to be sent onto Scotland. I then transferred to Shotley Bridge, near Durham, and am now based at RAF Trebelzue, but a short while ago I was sent for three weeks to Plymouth. I've nursed, cared for orphans in a private home, and am now back nursing.'

Ruth shifted in her seat and groaned, rubbing her back. 'Gracious, I'm surprised you aren't hiding somewhere to catch your breath with all that travellin'. Are you here for a mission? We've got a couple of American visitors in the village turning heads. Something's afoot, I swear,' she said.

Kitty shook her head. 'No, I'm on leave. If there's

something secret going on, I doubt the Americans would be out in the open. I suspect they've brought machinery over or are learning about the coastline and how we work over here now they're part of the war. I've travelled from Essex where I had four days with family and now I'm visiting a friend. She owns an inn, but I wasn't sure where it was from the bus stop,' she said.

Wenna stood up and stretched her legs. 'Listen to her, simply travelled from Essex. I struggle travellin' to Truro some days. Right, it's much quieter out there now, not sure we needed to have stayed here so long, there was no siren, but best be safe. I know where your friend lives – I'm surprised you— I'll walk with you,' she said, and Kitty guessed what she didn't say aloud.

'Thank you. We're Red Cross colleagues more than close friends, but I need a rest so thought I'd take advantage of her offer to stay,' Kitty said and also stood up.

Ruth struggled out of her chair and Jimmy moved to her side. He helped collect her knitting together and, with tenderness, he held her hand, guiding her outside into the evening air.

'Don't you be letting that girl run you ragged while you're here. She uses people, especially men and that poor deaf mute of a girl; treats her like a skivvy,' she said to Kitty with a motherly tone to her voice.

'Ma,' Wenna cut in with a warning tone to hers, and Kitty guessed Belle had created enough gossip to keep the villagers entertained for months.

'Belle is one of a kind, but she knows better than to try and boss me around. We've had our spats and overcome them, but I appreciate you thinking of me, Ruth,' Kitty said and gave a friendly smile. For a moment, she felt a profound when she thought of Jo and Belle; there was no comparison in the depth of their friendship with her, and she hoped the time apart would heal the argument between her and Jo.

'You come back and visit, my lovely. Don't be shy,' Ruth said.

'Bye, and thank you all for making me so welcome,' Kitty said as she and Wenna walked towards the lane. It had amazed her how quickly a friendship circle was formed in the shelter.

'Here we are, The Stargazy Inn. I'll leave you here, my lovely. The deaf girl my ma spoke about is Meryn Tremayne. She's had a hard life; she had a devastating accident just beyond Blackberry Lane as girl of eight or nine. Lost her parents and brought up by a drunken uncle – an oddball I would never trust. He had crooked eyes, sly too. Then another family took her in when he died. Your friend has taken on the girl and, yes, she overworks her, but at least she's safe in someone's care. She's not long turned fourteen, but the pub is her home, not just a place of work, so it's best she stays there. See you again, don't be a stranger.' Wenna spoke hardly taking a breath, and gave Kitty a wave goodbye.

Chapter Fifteen

Outside the inn was a large group of soldiers who offered Kitty all kinds of compliments; she guessed they were off-duty men from the beach patrol. She gave a polite grin and walked inside the whitewashed building. She stood by the door looking across at the bar where Belle courted several more soldiers at one end, her tinkling laugh filling the whole room. A scene which did not surprise Kitty in the slightest.

An elderly man served beer from a pump and a young girl, who Kitty assumed was Meryn Tremayne, wiped tables and collected glasses. She lifted her face to Kitty. Dark circles framed deep pools of black, surrounded by thick lashes. She gave a flick of her head towards Belle as if to show who to speak with, and, as quickly as she had looked up, she dropped her head and concentrated on her glass collecting.

Kitty pushed her way through the men and called over

to Belle. The men gathered around her parted and Kitty had no choice but to approach the bar between them.

'Kitty! What a wonderful surprise,' Belle said above the noise. 'Come around this way and through the back.' She pointed to a small opening at the end of the bar and lifted the top to allow Kitty through into her living quarters.

Kitty smiled to herself as Belle made apologies to her attentive audience, much like an actress taking a bow. She looked equally glamorous.

'Did you send word you were coming? I'm sorry I'm not prepared for you; I must have missed a message. Meryn can't be trusted to hand them over sometimes,' Belle said.

With an apologetic smile, Kitty gave a slightly embarrassed shake of her head. Maybe she had been wrong in just turning up and putting Belle in an awkward position. 'I'm so sorry to drop in just like this, it's a spur of the moment thing. I was back in Essex, but had a desperate need to escape from war horrors on the wards. I'll happily find somewhere to stay, but just wanted to say hello.'

The curls on Belle's head flowed gracefully as she grabbed Kitty's bag and nudged her towards a large, comfortable chair. She mesmerised Kitty with her sleek movements. Belle always maintained an air of fashionable perfection even during dire shortages of cosmetics and clothing.

'You will sit and relax. I've a spare room for you, and Meryn will take your ration book tomorrow to get your allowances. We'll have fun. She's deaf, so just ignore her. She works hard and that's all I want from her.'

Taken aback by Belle's remarks, Kitty removed her jacket and sat down.

'Be kind, Belle. I'm sure you don't mean that – you can't just ignore another human being. Anyway, I noticed you look busy, you must be rushed off your feet,' she said, changing the subject.

Adjusting her curls and pouting into a mirror, then pouring two large brandies, Belle gave a giggle. 'Darling, I am in Heaven. They are so attentive and enjoy the company of women. Some need training on how to treat a lady, but we get there in the end. They've helped me get over my man.'

Kitty gave a teasing laugh as she accepted her drink. 'Ha, so have they found one – a lady?'

Belle flounced over to the chair opposite.

'Ooh, listen to you relaxing already. Anyway, how's your man? Do you hear much from Trix? Such a timid little thing,' she said.

Kitty did not appreciate the dismissive comment. 'Michael is well; he was when I last heard from him. Trix is not as timid as you think, she is a strong woman and knee-deep in delivering babies close to her home. Her wedding is on hold, but she and Smithy are still happy to see each other each week. Not heard from Jo lately as we've both been busy and I ended up in a medical unit after the Dieppe rescue,' Kitty said. Not wanting to get into a discussion about Jo, she tagged her comment to the end of her statement in the hope Belle would move on to something else. It was a foolish hope.

'Jo's a funny one. Sometimes she's so masculine in her

ways; a true tomboy. I struggle with her sense of humour, too. You two are so different I am surprised you are such tight friends.' Belle drank the last dregs of her brandy.

'Jo's a good friend and they are hard to come by in this fast-moving life of ours. She's worth getting to know, but, I agree, we're like chalk and cheese. Much like you and me really if you think about it. Still, here we are, enjoying five minutes together,' Kitty said in a calm voice. Belle's outspoken ways were hard to understand at times and Kitty wasn't sure she wanted to keep ignoring the snipes and unkind remarks. On the other hand, she also wanted to enjoy the uplifting, fun side of Belle. To experience the company of someone a little more light-hearted on tough days. She would never be able to form a friendship with her like she had with Jo and Trix, but when Belle wasn't flitting around and flirting, she had a side of her – a confidence as a woman – Kitty secretly admired.

Belle gave a brief nod. Kitty wasn't sure if it was one of agreement or not, but watched as Belle fluffed out her hair and puckered her lips in front of the mirror before she smoothed down her dress and spoke. 'Anyway, I must call last orders and get the lads off the front garden before I'm told off for lighting up the sky with their cigarettes. Honestly, the Fire Watch and Home Guard have taken to flexing their muscles since the khaki boys arrived. Like cats marking their territory. Give me fifteen minutes and I'll show you to your room.'

Kitty smiled her thanks and watched Belle walk from the room, before stretching out and allowing the last of the brandy to warm her into a comfortable state of calm. The day had been a long one, but the tiredness she felt was not brought on by stress, merely from many hours of travel. She listened to Belle's laugh outside the window and soon silence washed over the building, bringing with it a calm atmosphere. Now she was no longer interested in Michael, Belle no longer felt like a threat to their relationship, and Kitty relaxed.

The following morning, Kitty was woken by a tapping at her door; a quick glance at the clock on the dresser across the room told her it was 7 o'clock.

'Come in, Belle,' she called out.

Nothing happened. Then it occurred to her that Meryn might be on the other side, and she slipped out of bed.

Meryn was standing on the other side of the door, beaming, and she held out a tray of tea and toast.

'Thank you, Meryn. This is very kind of you,' she said, slow and clear. Meryn was the first deaf person she had met and was unsure how to communicate with her without embarrassing her or herself.

Meryn handed her the tray and rummaged around in her apron pocket. She pulled out a small scrap of paper with *ration book please* written across the top and *welcome to Mawnan Smith* below.

'Thank you, I'll fetch my book,' Kitty said, but Meryn's expression did not change from the smile.

After enjoying a leisurely breakfast and changing into a fresh blue dress with white plimsolls, Kitty felt refreshed and ready for a day of relaxation. She went downstairs in search of Belle, and somewhere to leave her tray. The place was quiet, and Kitty guessed Belle might be on duty, although Kitty could not recall hearing a truck pull up early.

A clattering sound came from a room beyond the main living area. Kitty guessed it was the kitchen and walked towards the noise. She pushed open the heavy door and entered a large, beamed room. Meryn was rolling out pastry with her back to Kitty, and Kitty could see large batches of pasties waiting to be put into the oven. Mounds of chopped vegetables were in several bowls, and what she assumed were herbs were in heaps on a chopping board, their fragrance suggesting they had not long been prepared. Knowing there was no point announcing her arrival with a verbal greeting, but not wanting to startle Meryn by touching her, she placed the tray by the sink and walked around the large pine table where Meryn worked and waved her hand to capture her attention. Meryn looked up from her task. Kitty was rewarded with a beaming smile.

Pointing to the pasties, Kitty rubbed her stomach and licked her lips. Meryn gave a wide grin and pointed to the clock. She shook her head and then raised one finger, telling Kitty they would be ready at one o'clock. Kitty asked after Belle, but again, Meryn stood without expression. Kitty noticed a slate and chalk on one side of the table and scribbled down Belle's name with a question mark. Meryn shrugged her shoulders and returned to her pastry-making. Kitty, in no doubt she had been dismissed, left the room and went into the public area of the inn. Behind the bar she saw a middle-aged man moving bottles and barrels. He looked up as the door creaked, announcing someone entering.

'Morning,' Kitty said brightly and gave him a beaming smile.

'Morning,' the man muttered. He lowered a crate, then stood upright rubbing his back.

'Anything I can help with?' Kitty asked, hoping the answer would be in the negative as she had no idea about the inside of an inn and its workings.

'No, my lover, you are here to rest. Miss Belle told me you are to feel free to enjoy a drink on the house and to wander our fine village.' The man gave her a toothless smile and she watched as the ash from his cigarette dropped to the floor, 'I take it it's a bit early for a tipple of brandy for 'e?'

Kitty gave a laugh. 'You take it right, Mr...'

The man stepped towards her, spat on his right hand and wiped it clean down his unclean trousers. Kitty cringed, but knew she had to shake it or be seen as a snob.

'Pots. They call me Pots on account I'm the pot-man 'ere.' He thrust his hand in hers and gave a hearty shake.

'Nice to meet you, Pots. I'm Kitty.'

'Aye, Miss Belle told me. Now, the weather's fine, but the tide is brewing up a breeze. Take a right out of here and walk Blackberry Lane. The view is a bit different due to the boys building whatever it is they build, but it is a view worth starin' at. Get back 'ere for one and Meryn will have them pasties out and ready,' Pots said and gave another toothless grin. 'A glass will have your name on it, too. God rest 'er soul, my sister was a Red Cross girl during the Great War, and she deserved more 'an a brandy for what she had to do. Always got time for girls like you and the boss.'

Kitty had no time to respond as Pots disappeared through a small hatch in the floor as nimbly as a child.

She heaved open the heavy door and looked around the courtyard. It was pretty and well kept. With not a soldier in sight, Kitty was able to stand still and take in her environment. She took Pots' advice and walked towards a hedged lane she took to be the one both he and Wenna referred to as Blackberry Lane. The weather was in her favour and as she reached a bend, the view left her breathless. Turquoise water shimmied alongside golden sands, with jagged rock formations in varied shades of beiges and browns. Looking down and to her left, there was a lot of activity as Pots had mentioned, but to her right she noticed a large rock area which hinted at having an opening. She walked a few more feet and saw a well-worn pathway going down to the beach. It appeared not to have the same restrictive barriers as the active areas. She took a few steps down and followed the curved manmade walkway until she reached the sand. The darkness and damp sand told her the tide came right to the edge of the shore and had not long turned back, leaving a small pool of water to shine in the sunlight. Pre-war, Kitty would have had no hesitation in splashing away her worries or frustrations, but now the beaches were forbidden places. After watching the small ripples shine and calling out to her to paddle, she took a tentative step onto the beach, waiting to be shouted at or for a warning shot of some description to be fired her way, but nothing happened. She quickly slipped off her shoes, dipped her toes and allowed the lukewarm sea to trickle over them. Hidden from the soldiers by the large rocky cove, she took another step until her feet were fully immersed in the water. She closed her eyes with bliss, the sensation transporting her back to happier times. She stood for a few minutes, absorbing the healing powers of standing on a beach barefoot once again, when she got the shock of a lifetime as someone touched her arm. She had not heard anyone approach and had to suppress a scream. To her left, Meryn stared at her with her finger to her lips. She pointed to Kitty's feet in the water and then to herself.

A calmer Kitty gave a sigh of relief. 'Of course, come on in,' she said.

After about ten minutes, Meryn touched Kitty's arm again. She pointed to the working end of the beach and made signs of a boat on water. It took a few seconds, and then her actions registered with Kitty. A patrol boat was due. They climbed back up the hill, and, at the top, Kitty spotted a wicker basket filled with greenery.

'Is it yours?' she asked and pointed at the basket, then at Meryn. The pointing action felt rude, but it was the only way she was able to communicate with the girl.

Meryn walked to the basket, lifted nettles and other vegetation to reveal large blackberries and waved her hand towards the bushes across the pathway. During the walk home, Kitty helped pick the fruit and watched with fascination as Meryn gathered what she could only assume were edible plants. The more time she spent in her company, the more she wanted to learn about her past and what she had to share in the present.

Chapter Sixteen

Belle came and went. Sometimes to work and other times to enjoy the company of a new male friend. She appeared oblivious to the fact she had not spent time with Kitty during the four days she was there. Their one brief afternoon together was spent sitting on a bench in the most beautiful gardens Kitty had seen. Belle told her all she knew about the place and how an American friend romanced her on many an evening under the trees.

Trebah Gardens did not deserve the cheapness Belle tarnished it with in the way she told her stories, but Kitty could imagine herself in Michael's arms on a starlit night, enjoying the privacy of the shadows cast by the beautiful trees. Suddenly, the ache for Michael became too strong and from out of nowhere tears threatened and Kitty gave a sigh she had no control over.

'I recognise that sigh – the loss and waiting sigh,' Belle said. 'Move on, find a man you can be with in the moment –

stop wasting your life on one you never see. Look at me, I found a way.'

A flash of resentment passed through Kitty as she listened to Belle's thoughtless advice. She thought about her time off spent with other people and the tears took over her willpower and fell endlessly down her cheeks and dripped from her chin. She made no effort to stem the flow.

Belle got up from the seat. 'If you are going to sit and wallow in self-pity all day, then I'm heading back to the inn to enjoy the company of fun people. When you've finished crying, come and join me. I'm not callous, Kitty. I know you think I am, but I am a survivor of lost love.'

Kitty listened to Belle walk away. She admired the resilience she had found to bounce back after declaring a loving relationship. Deep inside, Kitty felt it wasn't a true love, not like the one she shared with Michael. If Belle had experienced true love, she would be as broken as Kitty felt sitting on the bench looking out across the vast waters, wondering whether to return when the moon appeared so at least she would know Michael would be looking at it too.

After a while of what Belle referred to as wallowing, Kitty took a slow walk along a path filling with shadows as the sunshine flickered between the trees. Her emotions mixed into a mash of happiness and sadness. Then she thought of Meryn and Wenna, two people who also had a lot to deal with in life. Although they had never had a conversation, she felt a kinship with Meryn, and wondered if orphans did connect on a deeper level when they first met, sharing a silent understanding of not having parents to nurture them through the troubles met during life, or of building happy memories together. She shuddered at the thought of the pain Wenna must suffer each time she thought of her husband lying somewhere in foreign soil.

Brushing aside the miserable mood, which had obliterated the contentment she had felt paddling on the beach with Meryn, she strode with purpose to the inn. The courtyard was empty, but voices drifted from inside through the open door. She stood and watched Belle play her part as landlady, Pots chatting with two men at the end of the bar and Meryn moving gracefully between tables. She was a beautiful young woman and Kitty wondered if she was happy inside her silent world or if she yearned to hold a conversation. Her smile was her words and her pencil her voice, and Kitty wanted to get to know her better. She calmed Kitty. There was an aura about her which slowed Kitty's heartrate and levelled out her emotions. Before she acknowledged Belle, Kitty walked over and placed her hand over Meryn's. She looked into her face and gave her a wide smile, one she hoped conveyed the hope that Meryn would trust her as a new friend. Tomorrow, she would ask her to guide her back to Wenna and ask Belle if she could buy a few pasties to take as a gift. She would write to Jo, Trix, her aunt and uncle, and Michael with upbeat letters. Always looking on the dark side of life was bringing her mood back into a place she had no intention of entering if possible.

'Belle, thanks for giving me a moment out there,' she said.

With a tap-tap on the counter, Belle beckoned her to join her behind the bar.

'I've poured you a brandy and want you to start enjoying your stay. Flirt a little, have fun.'

Kitty laughed. 'I'm not good at flirting, I think you are the expert at that – not being rude. I watch how you make men relax, but stay a safe distance from their wandering hands,' she said.

With a shake of her head, Belle jutted her chin towards the group of four soldiers. 'This lot know where they stand with me. Each one has made a pass and experienced rejection, haven't you, lads?' Belle said, the latter sentence – directed at the men – said in a louder voice.

'Haven't we what, Miss Belle?' one asked.

'Lost out on love with me!'

A roar of laughter from all four men made Kitty laugh, too. Belle had the magic touch of being the perfect hostess.

'Don't think me rude, Belle, but this brandy is so good, it must be expensive. Let me pay for my drinks. You'll never make a living giving me free food and drink every day,' Kitty said in a lowered tone to prevent the men from overhearing.

Belle gave a tut, dismissing Kitty's remark, and moved her to one side as she went to serve a returning customer.

'I need no payment. You deserve a treat.'

Kitty watched as she leaned across the counter, sharing just enough cleavage to keep the man wanting, and whispered to him. He was not in uniform, older but not elderly – certainly not the type of man Kitty would expect Belle to flirt with. His face had a slyness to it; his eyes shifted from Belle to Kitty and then to the soldiers. He had a nervousness about him. On spotting Kitty looking their way, he gave a nod and raised his glass to her, and she felt an embarrassed blush cross her cheeks. She raised hers back out of politeness. The man downed his pint of beer, wiped his hand across his mouth in appreciation and walked away. From the corner of her eye, she saw Meryn watching him leave and, pulling a small notebook from her pocket, scribble something down. She did the same when another male, slightly younger but not in uniform, came an hour later and went through the same scenario with Belle as the older one had. He had a cockiness about him; he joked with the soldiers, but they limited their laughter to a polite round of ha-has and then ignored him. As he walked out of the inn, Kitty noticed him wink at Meryn, who appeared to be caught off-guard and dipped her head so her hair fell over her face. The man gave a laugh and Kitty made a mental note to mention it to Belle. Meryn was a vulnerable young woman and Belle had a duty to watch over her.

Kitty wondered if Meryn suspected black market movement between the inn and the men. It was, after all, the first thing which popped into Kitty's head when she saw the second man's visit.

Belle never showed signs of tiredness and Kitty wondered how much work she had to do with the prisoners of war. Her work at the inn appeared limited, and after working with her in Birmingham, Kitty's impression was that Belle did just enough to make others think she was busy, but actually saved her energy for whatever she considered the more pleasurable side of the war. As she stood looking at Belle, Kitty wondered if she could ever turn her life around to limiting the amount of energy she spent on caring for and about others. Somehow she could not see herself playing the part of an actress, which is what Belle's role in life appeared to be, the more Kitty watched her.

Last orders were called, and the bar emptied. Kitty joined Meryn in collecting the remaining glasses. She handed her the note she had prepared at the bar, asking Meryn for help the following day, and Meryn wrote she would be free after two o'clock and would be happy to join Kitty.

Belle agreed to the extra pasties and for Kitty to pay for them. By the time Kitty settled down to sleep, her mind was back into holiday mode.

The following morning was spent writing letters. The hardest one was to Jo via the Red Cross rather than direct, but she was determined to not allow Jo to ignore her over and over. She made up her mind to keep on trying to repair their friendship.

Newquay
August 1942

Dear Jo,

I hope this letter finds you well, and you will see your way to replying. Our friendship must find a way through our last disagreement. You are my best friend, please remember that and forgive me if I said things to hurt you and make you feel Belle has all my attention, for that simply is not true!

Anyway, here is my news. After a spell at an emergency callout base, I took myself home to see Lil and Frank but could not settle, so took up Belle's offer of visiting her at Mawnan Smith. It was a long journey from Parkeston to Cornwall, but worth it as where she is living is the prettiest of places. The inn is a whitewashed building set in its own ground, it's not huge but comfortable and quaint. The beach is cordoned off, but there is one part which is secluded although still manned by patrol boats, and I managed to sneak in a paddle with the deaf girl Belle employs. She's a pretty girl who cannot hear or speak, she only smiles. We communicate through writing. Belle moves around her as if she doesn't really exist, simply writing down long lists and thrusting them at her. I like Meryn. In fact, we will be spending a few hours together today when she plans to show me around the village. One family took me into their shelter the moment I stepped off the bus; the planes were extremely low and the bullets could be heard pinging from rooftops as ours fought the enemy back across the waters. I'm going to visit them today, too. I do hope driving still makes you happy. I miss our chats. Let's make up and move forward. I know our friendship isn't years old, but I consider you my best friend.

When I was in Plymouth, I heard the Red Cross girls from America would be joining us soo., I wonder if we'll get to work with any of them. With the number of patients arriving back in Britain, extra support is valuable.

Stanley wrote to say he has earned promotion and is moving to RAF bases around the country. I'm not sure what rank or what he is doing, but it is wonderful he isn't hiding in sadness after Jenny's death. I had a note from the Gaskin brothers, along with a photograph of them on the farm during harvest. They are so tall now. I bet they are still a pair of devils. They will always have my heart as they were so kind to the other orphans.

Anyway, I must not dwell on the past. Belle is trying to teach me to flirt to forget Michael, but she will not win that battle! I still have no idea where he is or which unit he is with. I send my letters to the original base address he gave me and sometimes I get a reply, so I know at least one or two of my hundred plus letters arrive. I have visions of a plane load dropping and all addressed to him; imagine!

Take care, my friend,

Kitty x

Chapter Seventeen

The rest of her time off was spent with Meryn in the afternoon and Belle in the evening. Everything was calm and peaceful during the day and lively with laughter during the evening.

Belle's description when they were in private, of the Italian prisoners building a new camp and of how she and the others prepared boxes to send abroad, sounded the ideal posting for Belle. The more she heard, the more Kitty realised that although her final year of training and the extra emergency callouts were arduous work, they were all she wanted to focus on. Her body and mind were reenergised with the comfortable walks and friendly note exchanges with Meryn, and they agreed to write to each other once a week. Wenna and her family also asked for her address and said they wanted to keep in touch, so Kitty left on the bus with a full heart and new friends, ready to face new challenges back at her temporary home. Belle was the perfect hostess, and although Kitty would never place her in her best friend zone, she decided she could now consider her a friend rather than an irritation trying to steal Kitty's man from under her nose.

'We have news filtering in from various quarters that Britain has attacked the German army in Egypt. It is the kind of news our patients could do with hearing, so you have permission to mention it if you think your patient will benefit,' Matron announced at a hastily put together meeting for all nursing staff. Kitty's heart skipped a beat at the news. The teams parted, and Kitty noticed shoulders back and upbeat chatter. The attack had brought hope, the October sky bloomed with blue, and cotton clouds scudded their way across in a leisurely fashion. Although tired from her duties, Kitty was happy in her work – she'd agree, if asked, she had been happier helping orphan children, but for the present the men learning to live with life-changing injuries were her priority.

She claimed her post from a grinning male who bounced around like an overgrown puppy, and she returned the smile. His broad shoulders and wide chest told her he was a man who enjoyed the physical side of the army life. His tanned skin suggested he'd not long returned from a stint abroad.

'Someone's happy,' she said.

'It's a boy. I've got a son,' he replied, waving his own letter in front of her.

'Oh, that's wonderful news. Congratulations! I hope you get to see him soon,' she said.

'Tomorrow. I've been granted leave as the wife is staying

with her mother in Yeovil, a couple of hours away,' he replied.

Kitty walked away thinking about how happy news spread contentment faster than a wildfire. Everywhere she looked, she saw happy faces, and, looking down at her post, she knew she added to the smiles. Both Michael and Jo had written to her, along with Meryn, Wenna and Trix. Although she was due back on duty within the hour, Kitty knew she would not sleep, and headed for the canteen for food and to beg several cups of tea in a flask to take back to her room, so she could read her post in peace.

M McCarthy
Medic, Eighth Army
Sept 42

My darling Kitty,

Thank you for your letters and news. It frustrates me as this must be brief as I am heading out to pastures new, and we are due to land soon. We've not sailed the North Sea thank goodness, as I've heard that is rough this time of year. There is a lot of sunshine ahead so my uniform will dry out, but I suspect the sand will fill my boots. I am joining a new unit (the Eighth Army) and I'm told they come from all over the British Empire. I wonder if I'll be the only Canadian medic fighting in the British Army amongst them. As I understand it, it is a large force and the medical supplies on the plane also suggest it might be true. (Ah, Michael, you beat the black pen brigade once again with your clever words.)

Stay safe, my darling, and try not to worry about me, but I know you will as I do you. I have confirmed you as my next of kin – I cannot remember if I told you. Anyway, I will be home and celebrating the end of the war before we know it; we're a determined bunch.

Take care, sweetheart.

My love always, no matter what, Michael xx

Kitty pondered his letter and read it again. Sun and sand suggested a hot country and with Matron talking about Egypt, Kitty's gut feeling was that Michael was heading over there. Although the thought was scary, she had a rough idea of where he was in the world. As much as she loved receiving his letters, she found them heart-breaking, too. Sometimes her mind created images she had to push to its darkest corners. Michael *would* come home; the war *will* end – these were the positive thoughts she repeated over and over.

She opened Trix's letter and absorbed the stories of new lives entering the world and of the antics some of the children got up to at the maternity hospital. Again, a twinge of envy sneaked into Kitty's core. Wenna wrote of the weather and of how the children were missing their father and the sad news that her mother Ruth had fallen during a recent rush down the garden path to the shelter. She was badly bruised and frailer than when Kitty first met her.

Sitting looking at Jo's letter, she chose to read Meryn's first; her letters were usually filled with little snippets of gossip from the village which meant nothing to Kitty but amused her all the same. Jo's she'd read later, because although letters were usually a good distraction, Kitty feared the rejection of her friendship.

Stargazy Inn,
Mawnan Smith
October 1942

Dear Kitty,

Where do I begin? I am trusting you with my thoughts in this letter, so please be respectful of what you will read. I must share this with someone, but am not sure who I can trust anymore. I made up a secret and shared it with someone who told Belle. It was a silly one, but I wanted to sound out the woman, although it cost me a day's pay. I pretended to confess to eating extra bacon from the ration store. Belle's temper wasn't good that day, but at least I knew the woman wasn't who I thought she might be – a friend.

As you know, I cannot hear or speak. What you don't know is that I can lipread. I taught myself to keep my face from giving away what I'd read and have learned a lot of things over the years. It protects me, but gives me a sense of belonging. Only once did I let down my guard. I was nine and the man punished me for laughing at what he said when he tried to take me into a back alley, but my uncle came out to offload an empty barrel and sent him on his way with a black eye. From that day, I trained myself to look without being noticed.

I'm worried that Belle is going to get into a lot of trouble with two men. I've written down the conversations. If you can come and visit us again soon, I will show you. I am deeply worried by it all.

Please help.
Meryn

Kitty glanced at her clock; time to leave for duty, but not before she read through Meryn's letter for a second time and popped Jo's on the dresser for reading after her shift. Meryn's words were more than enough to take in before work. What sort of trouble was Belle about to get into now? In two days Kitty was on a day off and she had intended to study and get her hair cut, but instead – weather allowing – she would ride down to Mawnan Smith and pay Meryn a visit. She had possibly misread the conversations, but was worried enough to reach out to Kitty; a quick visit would put both their minds at rest.

Although letters were usually a good distraction, she feared the rejection of friendship in Jo's.

Autumn shades gradually crept into the area and added to the beauty of her surroundings, so Kitty slipped back to her room to collect Jo's letter and took herself outdoors to rid herself of the ward smells. Her days were a cycle of work: grab a few hours' sleep, grab a plate of food and work. An exhausting shift had its good moments that day, when patients on the mend broke out into song and filled the ward with an uplifting atmosphere. There were giggles when one patient proposed to a nurse and she handed him a letter from his wife, and even the ward sister broke out into a smile at the joke. Kitty hoped Jo wouldn't ruin the semi-relaxed state she was in with harsh words, and pulled the letter from the envelope. She hesitated before unfolding it, then holding her breath, Kitty started to read.

England
Joanne Norfolk

Kitty,
    Your letters are annoying the postie, so stop sending them.
Let's meet instead.
    J

Those few words meant more than an essay of apologies. Jo had placed her 'sorry' between the lines and hidden it with humour. Kitty let out a huge sigh. Joanne Norfolk, your humour needs work!

She allowed the autumn sunshine to warm her face. It was time to go to her room to rest and to allow her mind to release the tension. Her concern for Michael would never change, Meryn's worries would be offloaded another day and Trix was content enough. At last, it was time to sleep for longer and study when refreshed, but it all depended upon Hitler. Kitty hoped he had no missions up his sleeve; the next few days might pave the way for a calmer November.

Chapter Eighteen

K itty's good luck came in the form of a guard at the gates. He asked where she was headed so early in the morning, and she explained a friend needed help. He told her to wait out ten minutes and a supply truck would be driving into Truro, making her journey on her bike a much shorter one than the three-hour ride she had planned. Forty minutes after leaving the camp, they pulled into Truro, and Kitty was told by the truck driver if she could make her way back to Truro for five o'clock, he promised he would wait and take her back with him.

The mild, dull weather held out for most of her ride to Mawnan Smith, but it felt like summer when Kitty arrived hot and thirsty at eight-thirty. The inn was closed at the front door, but Kitty knew she would find Meryn round the back, working in the kitchen. She wheeled her bike to the back garden and propped it against the wall.

She could see Meryn working in the kitchen. Then she noticed Belle walk in wearing her Red Cross uniform. Kitty went to step forward to knock on the window, then she saw Meryn turn to face Belle and stare in her usual blank manner. Kitty now knew Meryn understood every word Belle was shouting at her by reading her lips. She held her position, poised to walk in if things became more heated than they already were. Belle's voice carried through the window, calling Meryn a sneak, lazy and unreliable. To Kitty's dismay she was not swift enough to prevent Belle's raised arm from slapping Meryn across the face. With no hesitation or announcement, Kitty rushed through the door. Belle stared at her, but Kitty ignored her and rushed to Meryn's side. She turned the girl's face to hers and saw the expected flash of red across her cheek. She swung around and confronted Belle. 'What on earth is going on, Belle? Whatever has that poor girl done that you need to hit her so hard?' she said, still shocked she had witnessed such a horrible act.

'What are you doing here, is more to the point? Another unannounced visit from Goody-Two-Shoes,' Belle said, her voice nasty with sarcasm.

Meryn moved from away from Kitty and stepped outside. Kitty placed herself in the doorway to stop Belle rushing after her.

'I came to visit Wenna, but thought I'd try and catch you before you went to work. I'd hate for you to hear I'd visited and not said hello. Now that would be rude, don't you think? I also came to share a bit of news,' Kitty said, her voice level and calm, despite the anger. 'What I did not expect was to see you strike that poor girl.'

Belle gave a snort of a laugh, a sneering sound.

'Poor girl? She's a lazy good-for-nothing. I sent her on an errand, and she failed to carry it out. It was extremely important, and I do not have the time to do it myself. The blessed Red Cross insist I keep packing boxes like some skivvy,' Belle said.

Kitty ignored the childish rant. It was no secret Belle only enjoyed whatever she wanted to do, not what was asked of her. If anyone was lazy in the room, it was Annabelle Farnsworth. Any further thought of visiting her as a friend flew from Kitty's mind when she saw only angry rage pour from Belle.

'If it is that important, send Pots but don't hit Meryn. I'm sure there's a perfectly good reason she couldn't help you. She came across as a willing worker when I was here,' Kitty said and moved to the back door. 'She's not the enemy, Belle. She's a deaf and dumb girl trying to make her way through this war. She felt safe here, she told me.'

'Have many *chats*, did you?' Belle asked. Again, her voice was snarky, and Kitty was no longer prepared to stand by and listen.

'Go to work, Belle. I'll help Meryn, and I'll make arrangements to meet her at Wenna's from now on and that way I won't put extra pressure on you. Oh, and by the way – my news. I passed the test to take the last set of exams. Can you believe I actually made it through to the final year?'

'I have no doubt you will go all the way, Miss Goody-Two-Shoes. Bully for you,' Belle bit back.

Kitty's mind raced with what was so important that Belle had slumped to the depths of hitting out at Meryn.

Was she in trouble because the delivery hadn't been made? Or was it to do with the hints made in Meryn's letter?

She rushed out to find Meryn and saw her running along Blackberry Lane. She was about to call out to her, then realised it was fruitless; Meryn would not hear her. She dashed back to the inn, grabbed her bicycle and bounced her way down the uneven path, eventually catching up with Meryn. She dropped her bike to the ground and grabbed Meryn's arm; the girl turned around in a defensive attempt to hit out, but calmed when she saw it was Kitty. Her face was streaked with tears and where she had torn off her hair covering, her hair was tussled and a mess. Kitty's heart went out to her; she could see the distress in Meryn's eyes and the frustration due to the lack of voice.

'I'll help,' Kitty said and rounded her mouth around her words to ensure Meryn could read her lips.

Meryn buried her head in Kitty's chest and Kitty comforted her until she felt Meryn had calmed down enough to work out what to do next.

'Let's go somewhere and you can tell me what happened,' she said, getting used to the fact she could speak, and Meryn understood.

Kitty guided Meryn to the end of the lane and back to the inn. She left her outside and went to check if Belle had left for work. Pots sat drinking from a cup; Kitty had learned from her previous visit it would not be tea, no matter the time of day.

'Hello, Pots. I dropped by to say hello to Belle and am off to see Wenna. Meryn will be with me for a few hours, so I doubt there'll be a pasty for lunch,' she said with a smile.

'Heard there was bother. No mind, my lover, I'll keep house. Belle wasn't in the best of moods when she left. She's got something on her mind, I can tell,' Pots said.

Not wanting to get into a lengthy conversation with a man who was fishing for gossip, Kitty glanced around for Meryn's coat and the bag she always carried. Outside, she encouraged Meryn to put on the coat and to join her in her visit to Wenna.

As they approached Wenna's home, she heard singing and the sound comforted her; it also saddened her to think Meryn could not hear the beautiful voice singing about mermaids and lovers.

She gestured for Meryn to stand a while and when she heard the silence at the end of the song, gave a tap on the door.

'Kitty!' Wenna said and embraced Kitty with a lung-crushing hug. She glanced over at Meryn, who gave her a shy smile.

'What a beautiful voice you have – sorry, but I couldn't help but hear. The song was wonderful. Anyway, I haven't got many hours before I must return, but I need a quiet place to communicate with Meryn. Belle slapped her when I arrived, and I'm certain it is not the first time. Meryn's a dear and she works hard for a roof over her head; she doesn't deserve Belle's treatment, no matter what the problem was,' she said as Wenna ushered them into the kitchen.

Wenna looked at Meryn and gave her a motherly smile, one which touched Kitty's heart too.

'Use the den. There's no one here; the children are with

Mother in her place across the road for an hour,' she said to Kitty.

Once settled in seats in the cosy shelter, Kitty pulled out a notepad and pen from her bag and handed it to Meryn.

'You said you thought Belle could be in trouble of sorts – what kind of trouble? What happened to make her attack you like that? I received your letter – am I right in assuming it is connected to your problem today?' she asked.

Meryn sat back in the chair and processed what Kitty asked her. Kitty could see the uncertainty in her mind.

'It's safe to talk to me, Meryn. I promise. Let's start with building more trust. You trusted me enough to write to me. It wasn't a mistake, I promise. Let's talk about what we have in common. I'll start.'

Kitty sat and relayed her past, including losing her parents, and then shared her fears of the future. She spoke to Meryn more as a close friend rather than a new acquaintance. Slowly, the tension eased in Meryn's shoulders and Kitty watched her body take a more relaxed position in the chair. She took a while writing down her words and Kitty sat patiently as if she was listening. Once she had finished, Meryn handed her the pad to read.

I wasn't born deaf, and I used to speak before I was nine. My mother and I had a dreadful accident when an old mineshaft broke open as we walked a field. She fell first and onto the rocks below the hole. We'd fallen into a seam which ran above an old cove just before hightide. I hit my head so badly going down and as I landed, my eardrums were badly damaged, and the old gases and dust damaged my throat and voice box. Sadly, Ma never recovered. My father drank himself into a stupor. She was pregnant and only a few weeks off delivery, according to my uncle. Dad walked into the sea and never returned. His body was found along the coast a few days later. When my uncle died, a woman took me in and then left me standing outside the house which belonged to Pots and his wife, promising to return. She left me with a note for Pots. His wife was a horrid woman and when he walked out on her, he took me with him and begged Belle's family to let me work and live at the inn. I pretended not to read lips to learn more about the world I live in and what was going on in the village. When Belle came, she just used me as a skivvy – still does. I'm not lucky like you, having loving family to take you under their wing. I just exist.

Meryn's words choked Kitty. She worried Belle would continue to mistreat Meryn and worried for her safety.

'I could help get you away from her if that's what you need,' Kitty said.

With a shake of her head, Meryn snatched up the pencil.

I want to stay. Someone needs to keep a watch on Belle because I think she is a spy! She has a lot of whispering talks with men who are not soldiers, and has started walking a dog belonging to an old man in the village.

Kitty read the words with amazement, and she supressed a small giggle threatening to ruin the trust between them. 'What on earth makes you think Belle is a spy, Meryn?'

Meryn handed Kitty an unposted letter and sat back, giving Kitty time to read.

Belle is in business with two men, and they bring brandy – a lot of brandy and other things, to the inn through the secret passages, but she doesn't pay them any money from what I can see. I can see them walk from the beach through the hidden lane off Blackberry, from my room. Belle hates dogs! I became fascinated and now I keep a close eye on the men, and I think they are bringing it over from France through the old smugglers' cave where we paddled. She's received a large batch of sugar and butter recently, which she told me I must take to a man in the next village in basketloads every morning. He gave me a letter for Belle, but I don't think it is always money. Sometimes the envelopes are thick or firmer. Fake ID or ration books?

Last night, another two men came into the inn, with a local fisherman. They talked about meeting a boat. She said something about new papers and a special package being delivered. I do think it is something serious.

One of the men said there would be a man waiting at the main cove mouth from eleven to eleven-thirty, and he was to be taken to Plymouth before dawn. They said they were to get English money, cigarettes, and clothes for him. I thought I saw them bring him into the back of the inn. Belle also spoke to Pots about going to Paris sometime soon. Is the Red Cross sending her over there, do you know?

Kitty put her hand over her mouth in deep thought after she had finished reading. Once she had digested what she'd read, she faced Meryn again.

'What else was said?' she asked. Meryn licked the end of the pencil before turning the paper over and scribbling down her reply.

Belle was going to take him halfway, and his companion was due the day after, further along the coast. She joked about getting the army to do the job for them.

'Take him in what? Car, boat?'

She persuaded a group of soldiers to go to a dance in Truro on the evening off. The man went with them as her injured cousin. When I saw them leave, he had a bandage around his throat and his arm in a sling.

Kitty let out a frustrated huff and gathered up the scraps of paper.

'We must burn these. Let me think about what to do with this information,' she said.

Meryn scribbled another message and handed it to her.

Believe me? Do you think the men are spies?

Kitty scanned the note, then looked at Meryn.

'I believe you, and I've a horrid feeling Belle has got herself into something dangerous. I don't think she knows what it is she is doing.'

Meryn spread out her hands face upwards, shrugged and frowned.

'Do *you* think she knows?' Kitty asked her.

With a sharp nod of her head, Meryn wrote down her reply.

Yes. I don't trust her.

Chapter Nineteen

Meryn told her Belle had a day off in two days and they left a message with Pots that Wenna would give Meryn a roof over her head for two days whilst Kitty organised another day off and would return to speak with Belle. She swapped shifts with a colleague and got the all-clear from the ward sister after she explained she had a deaf relative in need of urgent rehousing.

Kitty wasted no time in getting a lift to the inn and confronting a disgruntled Belle wiping down tables.

'If you've come to beg for that lazy, good-for-nothing girl, you can forget it. I'll get someone else – someone with gratitude for a decent roof over their head,' Belle snapped at her as she walked into the bar.

Kitty ignored the huff of dismissal.

'She should come back here, Belle. This is her home. Goodness knows, the poor girl has been through enough. You're not heartless. At least let her stay until she gets somewhere else to live and work.'

Belle slapped down her cloth onto a table and sat in a seat. 'I'm worn out and in no mood to argue,' she said with an exaggerated sigh.

Kitty saw her opportunity and gave a loud tut. 'Worn out? Then don't you need the help of someone who can just pick up where she left off? Don't be so stubborn. What on earth did she do to make you so angry with her?' she asked.

Belle traced a fingernail across the table. 'I found her sneaking around down in the cellar, in the long room off the main one. She can't be trusted. I think she took a bottle of brandy from my store down there,' she said and continued trailing her finger into a figure of eight.

Kitty gave a slight laugh. 'Oh, come on, Belle. Meryn *stealing* from you. Really? And although I've only known her a short while, I've never seen her break the law drinking alcohol, despite living in a pub. Have you thought that she might be looking for escape routes or hiding places in case of invasion? She's deaf and it might help if you understood her world during wartime. She can't hear the siren; she must run for shelter after seeing others run and guess that's where they are headed.' Kitty drew breath; she found it incredible that someone she knew couldn't take the time to consider what changes the war had made to Meryn's life, but then she reminded herself: had Belle ever given thought to anyone but herself? Her selfish attitude was no surprise to Kitty.

Belle huffed with impatience. 'Is this lecture going to take long?' she asked.

As annoyed as she was at Belle's rudeness, Kitty was not going to let Belle off the hook.

'You know she's a good worker and has been loyal. Let her come back home. It's more than a place of work for her, you know that, Belle,' Kitty said.

With another dramatic huff, Belle stood up and looked around the room. It was obvious Meryn or someone else was needed; Belle was not a cleaner.

'I suppose I *could* give her another chance. The last one, mind you. If she sneaks around here again, I will ask her to leave,' Belle said and threw down the cloth.

Not wanting to suggest Belle had something to hide, Kitty gave her a smile.

'Thank you, it makes sense. You work during the day and can't keep on top of everything here. I'll fetch her and bring her home. I've got to get back, but will visit you all again soon. I'll send a message beforehand. Don't worry, no more unannounced visits.'

Back at Wenna's home, Kitty gave Meryn the good news and they planned to write as usual. If there was anything Meryn was concerned about, she would write the code words: *let's go paddling again* and Kitty would try her best to get to Meryn as soon as she could.

September gave way to October, but no sooner than the beauty of that autumn month came in, it lost its hold against the chilly grip of November winds and Kitty was left wondering what she had managed to do during October apart from work. The war dragged on, but the months flew by – none of it made sense. Some days she and her colleagues reflected on their lives before the war and the conversations would eventually dwindle into private silences as each person realised there would be something they would never do again, or someone they would never see. Those moments were painful reminders, but made them more determined to focus on the job and try in some small way to move the war effort in the right direction. Shrugging off the thoughts of the past month, Kitty strode with purpose along paths edged with tan and emerald-green foliage giving over to the reds, browns and blacks of winter.

As she walked, she watched the vapours from her exhalation drift towards the west, meaning the east wind was not ready to release its cruel and unwanted grip on Great Britain. She had left the south and lived in mid- to north counties for well over two years, and there was a definite difference between temperatures which defined the borders. In his letters Michael wrote of discomfort and Kitty read between the lines that things were worse than he put into words, and it made her accept the temperature changes without moaning.

Her latest visit to Trix meant she had to sacrifice the warmer climes of Cornwall, but Kitty did so with no regrets. Her days on shift were long and hard and it was time to have fun with friends.

Smith and Trix had reached the conclusion that their love was too strong to flail beneath Hitler's threats, and that Trix could still do her duty and commit to Great Britain's fight against the world's most hideous tyrant. They wanted a family and to bring it up in their village, and Kitty envied their ability to walk the pathway towards their desires. Her friends deserved her support, and she gave promises she prayed she could keep, just to be by their side.

The fresh smell of newly ironed clothes greeted Kitty as she stepped through the back door of her friend's home. A pot of prepared vegetables sat on the unlit stove.

Shrugging off her coat, she accepted the steaming cup of weak tea and grinned at her smiling friend.

'Church flowers done. The ladies are lovely, and you would think it was their own daughter getting married. You've made a huge impression here, Trix. Nervous?'

'A little. But I'm more excited, I think. The ladies needed something to bring joy into their lives and we adore them as much as they appear to enjoy our appearance in their village,' Trix replied, she hugged her cup close and drew her feet up on the chair. Kitty did the same.

'I just think it is wonderful the way they've taken over the organisation of your wedding and your wedding dress. Oh, what a pretty gift! It's incredible to think this time tomorrow you will be Mrs Gordon Smith. I wonder what he'll do when he sees you walking down the aisle in such a beautiful outfit.'

Kitty tilted her head towards the petite white gown hanging across the room on a cupboard door. A fur shoulder cape hanging next to it would ensure the bride did not freeze. It was a gift from a widower treated by Smithy. He'd offered the cape, which had been worn by his wife at their wedding. Trix explained to her how three local women, upon hearing Trix was going to wear her Sunday-best brown tweed suit to get married in, decided she deserved to have a lace dress to make up for the disappointment of not having family at her side, and pooled their own dresses, creating one for Trix. All three women had lost their only sons and had no daughters to pass along their own gowns to, and their affection for their GP and his fiancée was shown in every stitch they sewed. Each offered their husband or father to walk her down the aisle, but Trix declined. Without her father at her side, she chose to walk alone.

'What time is Jo due to arrive?' Trix asked Kitty.

'Seven. She's going straight to Smithy, so we won't see her until the wedding. I'm pleased she accepted your invitation,' Kitty replied.

'There was no hesitation on her part, she replied within days of me sending it. I do hope you both will get along again. You are both stubborn and life is too short to lose such a strong friendship.'

'We will be fine once we've seen each other again. Don't worry yourself,' Kitty said, hoping her words would come true. A wedding was the perfect place to renew a friendship. 'I wonder how the locals will take it when they see a best woman instead of a best man,' Kitty said with a giggle.

'They will be shocked, but amused, I'm sure. It is so sad Michael isn't in the country, Gordon would have loved him to be here today, but his oldest friend will keep him calm – so long as she doesn't offer him too many drinks to settle his nerves,' Trix said with genuine concern. 'Oh my goodness. I don't think I could cope if I found Smithy drunk at the altar.'

Kitty laughed. 'Relax, everything will be fine. Jo will take her role seriously; she knows how important it is to you both. After supper I will put rollers in your hair. Do you want to keep your usual style, or do you want to do something different? It's grown enough to have a few curls around your face; it will look so pretty. And your veil is beautiful,' Kitty said, taking her mind off Michael not able to attend and the thought of Jo getting Smithy drunk on his wedding day; she truly hoped her role of Trix's only bridesmaid did not become a tough one.

The early morning mists sat on the hillside and Kitty's eyes turned skyward. Dawn managed to break through the soft clouds, and the few small grey ones eased their way towards the south. It promised to be a pleasant autumnal day and a welcome surprise considering the days leading up to the wedding. The ceremony was due to take place at St Nicholas Church, in neighbouring Guisborough, and, thanks to the devoted village residents, everything was organised. If rain held off, Trix was travelling with Kate in a horse and trap used by the greengrocer for out-of-village deliveries. If not, the local taxi booked to take Smithy would return to take the bride and her attendant. Everything was in order; now all they had to do was witness the couple deliver their vows.

A stray tear rolled down Kitty's cheek as she stared out of the window. She whispered loving thoughts to Michael and begged for him to stay safe so they could enjoy a wedding day together in the future. Her eyes wandered to the navy-blue dress hanging on the wardrobe door and she wondered how many years it would be before she got the opportunity to turn around and see a lace wedding dress waiting for *her* to wear. She heard Trix finish in the bathroom and made her way across the small landing. She and Trix had moved from Trix's cottage into the surgery house after their supper the previous evening, and Smithy's landlady had prepared a room for Jo. Trix was seated at the kitchen table when Kitty went downstairs. An array of fresh-picked flowers and greenery from the garden lay across the table and a mass of pink and white satin ribbons, saved over the years, were laid out in assorted lengths.

'There's porridge on the stove,' Trix said, greeting Kitty with a beaming smile. 'I hope the weather holds out, it's fresh and uplifting out there. Smell this.'

Trix held out a delicate rose for Kitty to appreciate. A calmness settled around them and they ate breakfast in silence before creating a posy and bouquet of roses and greenery, bound with the satin ribbons. Trix insisted on making several buttonholes and asked Kitty to walk them round to Smithy for him to offer to those supporting him during the day.

Voices chatting in jovial tones told Kitty Smithy was relaxed, and Jo was in a good mood. The landlady let her into the house; they both beamed at her.

'How's my wife-to-be?' Smithy asked before the door had clicked shut.

'Hello, Smithy, Jo, Mrs Wetherby,' Kitty said with a relaxed laugh. 'She's fine, more than fine, she's blooming and incredibly relaxed. I'm the nervous one. I've strict instructions to make sure Smithy doesn't pin his buttonhole upside down. That said, it is your job today, Jo. So, I'll rush back and help Trix steam her suit.'

As she turned, Kitty gave Jo a wink. 'Have you got a minute, Jo? It's about the transport. The clouds are gathering, look,' she said and was grateful Jo took the hint and headed for the door. They stepped outside.

'Make sure Smithy turns around as Trix comes down the aisle. He's in for one heck of a surprise,' Kitty said and put her finger to her lips, 'I'll say no more. See you at the church and good luck. It's a good day, Jo. A good day.'

'I'll do as you ask and, yes, it's a good day for once. We'll catch up later, and, before you say it, I'll not get him drunk,' Jo said and patted Kitty's shoulder.

As she walked back to Trix, Kitty noticed how unburdened she felt after talking with Jo. It was as if nothing had altered their friendship, and with all the other issues she faced in life, she was grateful they could move forward.

As she and Trix stepped outside in their wedding outfits, a loud cheer rang out from those staying behind to organise the wedding buffet in the small village hall. Kitty was saddened by the lack of children calling out their good wishes. In the past, in her own street, the youngsters would chant and dance; now she wondered if there were any left at home to carry on the tradition. This village cried out for young voices on a day like today.

The weather held over enough for the horse to trot through the lanes to the church. Grateful for blankets and Trix's cape, they waved and smiled at anyone calling out their good wishes. Kitty crossed her fingers the war would not interfere with such a special day. Only two days before, there was news of another bombing attack on Canterbury city, and not a day went by when unwelcome news failed to filter its way around the barracks. But a romantic wedding between two friends deserved a war-free atmosphere.

'Now I'm nervous,' Trix whispered as they stood in the church porch waiting to make a grand entrance and Kitty fussed around Trix's veil. 'What if he's not inside?'

'Who, Father Christmas?' Kitty joked. 'Of course Smithy will be there, he idolises you and wants this marriage as much as you do, so stop putting yourself through something which will not happen.'

Trix checked her flowers for the umpteenth time and Kitty placed a calming hand over her friend's. The first notes of the organ filtered through the gaps in the doors and the vicar pulled them open, greeting Trix and Kitty. He reassured Trix her groom was in his place and waiting impatiently for her arrival. Just before they stepped inside, Jo appeared in her freshly cleaned navy-blue uniform coat and hat. Kitty was impressed by the rolled curls and smudge of lipstick Jo wore to complete the smart look. Something or someone had changed her friend, and Kitty was determined to find out more after the service. Right now, she was puzzled as to what Jo wanted with them when she was supposed to be at Smithy's side.

'Trix, Smithy cannot bear you walking down the aisle without support. Kitty is behind you, and he asked if I could escort you to his side. A little unorthodox, I'll grant you, but it is his wish and not my place to argue,' Jo said and held out the crook of her arm for Trix to take hold.

Leaving no time for Kitty to question Jo, she moved Trix into a formal position in readiness for their slow walk down the long aisle.

Kitty buried her nose in her posy, inhaled the sweet rose perfume and took her first step around the corner into the main aisle of the church. Even from behind, Trix looked perfect. Her veil was yards long and Kitty concentrated on keeping her steps short. Jo had her left arm behind her back and her shoulders were straight and as proud as any father's might be on such an occasion. Kitty could not wait to see Smithy's face and his reaction to Trix in her gown and she took a small, barely noticeable side-step to see around Trix.

Smithy beamed back at them, and his hand went to his eyes as he dabbed away tears. The perfect image. The head of the man in front of him remained facing forward, a pair of crutches leaning on the pew beside him; an elderly man and woman sat further along; then Kitty took a stealthy glance along the row behind and saw what she assumed were family members, and three of the doctors from Birmingham, there to support the groom. She turned her head towards the other side of the room and saw the local women and a smattering of husbands filling the gaps in Trix's family seats. They slowed to a halt as Jo handed over Trix to a grinning Smithy, and, as Kitty took the bouquet from Trix, Jo joined her in the front row.

'You need to be on the other side – best woman duties,' Kitty whispered urgently to Jo.

Jo turned and just gave her a smile. 'All covered. I've done my bit,' she said and moved to get a better view of the commencing ceremony. When the vicar requested the wedding rings, the man with crutches struggled to his feet and shuffled to Smithy's side. As Kitty moved into a better position, she realised she was staring at her fiancé. His skin was heavily tanned, his face much thinner and his hair cropped short, but his smiling eyes had not changed, and they expressed their love in one glance across to her. It took all of Kitty's control not to run to him, and she checked her mouth wasn't wide open with shock when Trix turned to give her a knowing smile. Kitty's willpower showed respect for the couple expressing their vows. She watched as they exchanged rings and returned her stare to Michael. She did not want to seem uninterested in the wedding ceremony, but from the moment she saw him again, Michael was the only person she wanted to look at. She noticed he had lost a little weight, but her main concern was the crutches and large white cast on his right leg. He had obviously experienced a broken bone, and the service could not finish quick enough so she could find out what happened.

Outside they threw rose petals and cheered. Kitty concentrated on completing her role without letting Trix down, but the moment she could move to Michael's side, she could not hold back.

'Darling, what are you doing here? What happened to your leg? What a wonderful surprise,' she said in a gush of whispered joy.

'Surprised? I was shot, I'll explain later. Oh, they want a photograph, off you go,' Michael said with a light laugh.

'Stay where you are!' Kitty instructed and knew the smile on her face would be a permanent fixture for the rest of the day.

Chapter Twenty

'And you knew! I cannot believe any of you didn't let the cat out of the bag. Your wedding day is a good day and not just for you! A wonderful surprise!' Kitty exclaimed to the laughing group of friends.

'As much as I was honoured to be asked to stand in for Michael, I can't tell you how thrilled I was when I heard he was injured and coming home,' Jo said.

Smithy coughed from laughing so much. 'Jo, you have a way with words, but I'm sure Michael understands you weren't thrilled he was injured.'

The banter carried on and the only thing Kitty found overwhelming about the day was the happiness she felt. Trix said much the same. They all stood together admiring the rare sight of a real three-tiered wedding cake, instead of a single with cardboard enhancements due to rationing, set on the table amongst other delicious treats – some of which Michael had managed to bring home from Egypt.

'As soon as word got through to Smithy that I'd been

shot, he used his status as my GP to enquire after my health and it was all go. It was agreed I could continue my sick leave in England and I was shipped out on a medical supply plane from Egypt. Smithy's plan to get me as best man worked, and then the plan to surprise Kitty was hatched. I couldn't come empty-handed,' Michael explained to his small audience.

Outside under the clouds, Kitty and Michael listened to the fading music before enjoying yet another lingering kiss.

'What an incredible day,' Kitty said as they agreed to return inside and continue their roles helping the married couple. All speeches had been made and toasts drunk, and the relaxed satisfaction of a job well done settled on many shoulders. Dancing on crutches was not something either Kitty nor Michael relished, so they chose to sit and watch the graceful, the naturally ungraceful and the inebriated move around the floor.

'I hope we have a wedding day like this, and you look just as beautiful as you do today. I've missed your beautiful smile. It was just as well I was on crutches; I wanted to run and scoop you up. I've missed you so much, Kitty. More than you'll ever know,' Michael said, taking Kitty by surprise with the tone of his voice. It was soft and earnest.

She squeezed his hand. 'If the war moves in the right direction, it could be this time next year,' she said, her own voice filled with hope.

Michael gave a returning wave to Smithy and said nothing. He struggled to his feet, then turned to Kitty.

'I announce the departure of Mr and Mrs Gordon Smith.

I cannot believe how she's tamed him, and the job is ideal for him. He's so happy'

'And so is their bridesmaid,' Kitty said and walked towards Trix and Smithy beside him. Jo joined them.

'Have fun in Bournemouth, Mrs Smith,' Kitty said to Trix as they hugged farewell.

'Thank you for making my day such a happy one and making me feel special. Enjoy Michael while you've got him and make our home yours for as long as you want,' Trix replied.

Back at the surgery, Kitty and Michael changed into less formal wear. Michael's pain caught him out now and then, and Kitty instructed him to stop walking on the leg. A bullet had shattered a bone and she wondered how much of an infection risk the leg might be under. Michael reassured her Smithy had everything under control and organised whilst he was away on his honeymoon for the week. Michael had offered to man the surgery for emergencies should they arise, and Kitty was unsure he should remain alone. Her leave was over in twenty-four hours. She relaxed more when he said his old landlady had offered her support for the week.

'There are two beds in the guest room; you need sleep by the looks of you, sleepyhead,' Michael said when Kitty yawned for the umpteenth time.

'I know, I think Jo and I should take that room and you take Smithy's, or we can make you a bed up in the back room when Jo gets back from her clearing-up duties. I can't believe she offered; something's changed in Jo, and I'm determined to find out what it is. In the meantime, we must sort out where you will stay after the honeymooners' return,' Kitty said and leaned back in her chair.

'I'll make do on the couch. You and Jo take the room,' Michael said and raised his hand to stop Kitty objecting. 'Believe me, if you saw my accommodation in Egypt, you would realise the couch is nothing but luxury.'

A tap at the door made them both jump. Kitty rose to answer it and peered into the darkness from the hallway, then frowned at seeing Jo on the other side.

'What are you knocking for? Get inside, don't let the heat out, come into the sitting room, it's nice and warm,' Kitty said, ushering Jo into the room.

'I wasn't sure what I'd be walking into,' Jo said with a cheeky grin. 'Evening, Michael, enjoy the day?'

Michael grinned back and shook his head. 'You haven't changed a bit, Jo Norfolk. Surprising Kitty is a habit of mine and it always reminds me we deserve a little happiness now and then. What's making you happy, Jo? I can see it in your eyes,' he said.

Pleased Michael asked Jo the burning question in her own mind, because he made it sound less nosy, Kitty noticed a slight flush across Jo's cheeks and jumped into the conversation with a teasing response, ready to show Jo their friendship was still important to her.

'I think you hit a nerve, Michael. Jo's blushing.'

Jo shrugged off her jacket, kicked off her shoes and slumped into a chair. She ran her fingers through her hair, flicking out her rolled curls and patting it into a smoother style.

'Give over, you two. I'm not blushing and there is no

nerve to hit. I've been instructed to *pretty up* and smile more. I've practised – I hate it, but, as explained to me, it cheers up the likes of him,' she said, jutting a thumb towards Michael. 'I'd rather have oil on my hands over lipstick on my lips, but who am I to deny a soldier a cuppa and my beauty before facing the enemy? That's downright cruel,' Jo said, pouting.

All three burst out laughing.

'Oh, Jo, you've let me down. I thought you had a secret lover!' Kitty exclaimed.

With an amused shake of her head, Jo looked over at Michael. 'All romance and roses is our Kitty.' She turned her attention to Kitty. 'You should know by now I'll never have a lover – a close mechanic friend, yes, but a lover is not for me. Too many tears and tantrums come with a romance.'

Kitty gave a soft smile with raised eyebrows. 'Michael, do you think a close mechanic friend is the true cause of the lipstick and curls in our Jo?' she said, teasing her friend further.

Michael sat back with an amused look on his face.

'I think she's caught you out, Jo. Confess or it will be torture until daylight, and I need some rest,' he said, stretching his arms above his head.

Jo wagged a finger at him. 'Stop it, you. I've nothing to confess, so stop stirring the pot of troublemaking. Now, I've an early ride back to camp in the morning, so I'll head upstairs. What's the room arrangements, Kitty?'

'Michael wants the couch, so you and I will share the guest room. That way it will leave the marriage bed freshly made up for their return. No point in creating washing where we don't need to. We've got tomorrow and then I have to head back to work, so let's have breakfast together and make plans to meet up again soon,' Kitty replied.

After Jo went upstairs and Kitty prepared Michael a bed with some of her covers, they sat holding hands in the dark of the room. Moonlight filtered through a small gap Kitty made in the curtains and the room regained a cosy feel, despite the fire embers dying in the grate.

'How long do you think you have before you get signed fit for duty?' Kitty asked Michael, wishing it wasn't a question needing an answer.

She heard his intake of breath and gentle exhalation. 'I don't know, sweetheart. The leg heals daily, and I know Smithy wants to ensure I stay for your sake by taking over my care, but I have a duty to the country and, as a medic, I know it won't be too long. As soon as the leg can bear my weight and I've built up the strength, I'll be flown back.'

Kitty accepted his answer in silence. Words could not express how she felt about him fighting abroad. It was as if she was already mourning a loss. Michael lay sideways on the large couch and patted for her to lie beside him, and Kitty did not hesitate to snuggle against him when he pulled the blanket to their shoulders. Their kisses were passionate and filled with desire, but eventually sleep and sensibility took hold and they slept in each other's arms until the rattle of the milkman's crate woke them.

'So you've been to visit Belle? Oh, my word, you *were* desperate for friends,' Jo said in a light-hearted tease to Kitty.

'Yes, but I'm stuck with you because Belle is still full of

herself, unlike you, who are all heart and loving,' Kitty retaliated with a friendly retort. Everything had fallen back into place with her and Jo, and, with Michael to wake up beside, the day promised to be a good one. A breakfast of boiled eggs and fresh bread was enjoyed around the large pine table and all three were refreshed from a good night's sleep. The weather outside was autumnal and when Kitty put the ashes onto the vegetable plot first thing that morning, the air was crisp and fresh with a minimal breeze. The temperature had a southern rather than a northern bite.

'What are you two lovebirds up to when I leave?' Jo asked as she and Kitty washed and dried the breakfast dishes, and Michael washed in the bathroom at the back of the building.

'Depending on Michael's leg, I'm going to suggest a walk to the stream at the end of the village and then we must work out where he goes from here. I can't get more leave, so the thought of him staying with Trix and Smithy does upset me a little,' Kitty replied.

Folding the tea towel, Jo gave a short *ha-ha*. 'Listen, I'll organise something when I'm back at the barracks. I'll get him a room somewhere and with the medical team to hand, he can get his leg checked out when needed. If he's only got a brief time here, then at least you will be able to see him after work. I'll try and get somewhere no more than a decent cycle ride there and back, and on a bus route for Michael.'

Kitty sighed. 'I would not know where to start,' she said.

'I've got quite a few contacts around the different areas nowadays, so trust me, it will be done. Just get yourselves back to Cornwall and I'll do the rest,' Jo said and Kitty pulled her in for a hug.

'Oh, Jo, I've missed your organisation of my life. I'd be grateful if you can help Michael and me. Smithy and Trix won't want a wounded soldier to worry about when they are just starting married life, and Michael won't want to be a burden.'

'Me a burden?' Michael's voice interrupted the moment. Kitty explained Jo's plan and Michael agreed for Jo to go ahead.

'There's no point in me hanging around here missing you, Kitty. I might as well fly back to the unit if that's the case. No offence meant to Smithy, who got me home in the first place, but he'll understand my need to be around you more than him and Trix,' he said.

'I'll let you know later tonight once I've sorted something out. So, listen out for the surgery telephone,' Jo said.

The rest of the day was made up of farewells. First to Jo and then to the village friends of Trix and Smithy. In the afternoon they sat reading by the log fire, untouched by the outside world. The tranquillity was broken when Kitty spent time preparing a vegetable stew with chunks of ham left over from the wedding feast. It was six hours of domestic bliss; a peek into the future. Michael's leg ached and she fussed over him, ensuring he was comfortable and as pain-free as possible. Just after nine in the evening, the telephone rang and she rushed to answer it, praying Jo had managed to work her magic.

'Kitty?' Jo's voice echoed down the line.

'I'm here,' Kitty replied.

'Listen, the plan is…'

Jo reeled off all instructions for the following day and Kitty was left in amazement at what her friend had achieved in what little time she had spent back home.

Chapter Twenty-One

'The food's better without the sun turning it rancid and the sand adding extra crunch each mouthful,' Michael said after Kitty asked how he was faring at the home of a couple willing to give him a room. It turned out that Jo had helped rescue the man and his wife after their car swerved into a ditch down a dark lane with no white guiding lines.

It was pure chance Jo chose to return home cross country and spotted their shielded torch flickering low to the ground in the hope they could gain someone's attention. She towed them free, and took them for a medical check over, before making arrangements for their vehicle to be returned to them the following day. Their gratitude was to invite Jo for a homecooked meal, and they formed a friendship which meant when she asked Tom and Maud if they might know anyone who could help Michael, and explained about Kitty, they were more than willing to offer him a place in their own home. They prepared him a downstairs room in their cottage, which was the ideal set-up for Michael.

Even better was the fact they lived on the outskirts of Newquay, which meant Kitty's visits after a day shift only took three-quarters of an hour on her bicycle. One afternoon it rained heavily and Maude loaned her the use of a large dressing gown as she fussed around drying out Kitty's clothing. Kitty protested, but Maude insisted. She wanted Michael to enjoy his time before he had to fly back and put his life on the line once again. Kitty knew it was a fruitless argument and spent the precious two hours she had with him listening to small snippets of his war away from British shores.

One day, one of Kitty's colleagues called for help when her boyfriend called to say he was home on leave. Although it was only a week since Trix's wedding, and Kitty's official leave was over, by swapping shifts to help her out Kitty gained a free day, and insisted she and Michael made the most of it together. Plans were made to spend time with Meryn. Kitty wanted to introduce her to Michael and Jo, with the view to letting them in on Meryn's concerns of Belle was supplying information to the enemy.

Jo drove them to Mawnan Smith in Tom's car, using valuable petrol coupons gathered from grateful people whose cars and vans she fixed in the surrounding villages. Most garages were closed due to fuel shortages, and able-bodied mechanics had joined the army to fix tanks rather than the baker's delivery van. Along the way they sang songs and ignored the mizzle threatening to dampen their day. Jo parked the car at the inn, and Kitty slipped inside to see if Belle was around.

'Well, there's a sight for tired eyes,' Pots said as he rolled a barrel across the floor.

'Hello, Pots, is the lady of the house around?' Kitty asked.

Standing straight from his stoop and stretching his back, Pots shook his head. 'As far as I'm aware, she's still enjoying a visit with friends in Bodmin,' he said and peered around her to look outside the open door. 'Have you got company with you this time? The girl is in the kitchen baking, I'll get her to fetch you breakfast.'

'It's my fiancé and best friend. I'll slip through and see Meryn; we've eaten and are heading to Wenna's for a quick visit. We'll be back for pasties and a drink later,' Kitty replied and made her way through to the kitchen.

Meryn was in her usual place rolling out the pastry. Kitty walked to the front of the table so Meryn could see her.

'Hello, Meryn. How are you?' she said, ensuring Meryn could read her lips.

Meryn wiped her hands down her apron and raced around the table to hug Kitty, her face alight with happiness.

'Well, that was a warm greeting if ever there was one,' Kitty said and gave Meryn a genuine smile of gratitude, then indicated Meryn should remove her pinafore and follow her. Meryn pointed to the clock and raised ten fingers, then pointed to the pastry and prepared pasties.

'We'll come back – I'll take my friends for a walk down Blackberry Lane,' Kitty said.

'I should imagine that paddle you enjoyed was the last one of the season,' Jo said when Kitty pointed out the rockpool below and told them how Meryn had taken her down the hidden pathway to enjoy the clear water.

'It was still warm then, but I'm not going to try today. Besides, look, there's the patrol boat working with the tide,' Kitty said as the boat slipped into view. 'They are closer this time, and I reckon they've heard about the smugglers' coves along the coastline. Meryn told me a lot about the history of this area. We must go to the gardens and take a stroll when she has finished in the kitchen. We'll need to work up an appetite to eat one of her pasties. You might have eaten a few in Cornwall, but never one like Meryn's,' Kitty said and realised she sounded like a proud mother singing her child's praises.

Michael rubbed his stomach. 'I can't wait.'

Back at the inn, Meryn was waiting by the car. She pointed to Michael's crutches and creased her face as if in pain.

Kitty shook her head. She was not prepared to let the others know Meryn could lip read yet and wanted her to know she had kept her word.

'Meryn will write down any questions or answers, so if you have any, do the same,' she said to Michael and Jo. 'It annoys me when Belle ignores her. I've said many times, just because she is deaf doesn't mean she cannot be involved in our conversations.'

She knew Meryn had read her lips and admired how

straight-faced she remained; no one would have a clue she understood what was said. Kitty wasn't sure she would ever be able to do the same.

'The view was exhilarating, but I'm exhausted. My leg aches so I'll not be walking anywhere else today,' Michael said.

Jo pushed her empty plate away from her. 'I agree about the view and about aching legs, and, thanks to that incredible pasty, I'll not be able to move for a while yet. You are right, Kitty, they are the best in Cornwall so far!'

They sat for a while chatting about what they had seen around the village that day and Meryn went back to work. A few customers came and went, keeping Pots occupied.

About an hour before they were due to leave, Belle made an appearance and, on seeing Kitty, Michael and Jo, turned on her actress personality.

'Darlings, what a wonderful surprise! I wish I'd known you were visiting today. Naughty Kitty, I'd love to have spent time with Michael. Poor thing, you're injured,' she said and gushed around him with false sympathy and loaded flirtation. It irritated Kitty and she could see Jo was put out at Belle's attempt to ignore her.

'Thanks to Jo, we were able to take a last-minute drive out somewhere and I suggested we come to visit you but did warn them you are extremely busy with Red Cross business and running this place. I also told them it was worth the drive to enjoy one of Meryn's pasties. She's such an asset and The Stargazy has a reputation for them.'

Belle gave a slight puff of indignation. 'It's me they come to visit, not some old pasty rolled out by a deaf mute. I bring *class* to this place. Once I've removed that ragged cloth of a uniform, I show them what they are missing.'

'I bet,' Jo said with a sarcastic laugh and Michael laughed with her until Kitty shot them a stare.

'I'm sure you are right. Delicious food and good company are ideal companions for an inn by the sea. Ah, here's a few of the chaps working nearby, we'll say our goodbyes. If it is all right with you, I'll go and say 'bye to Meryn?' Kitty asked as she pointed to several soldiers walking through the door. Belle walked away, waggling her fingers in a dismissive manner. 'Yes, but don't keep her too long, she has tables to clear,' she called out.

Michael gathered up his crutches and Jo stood aside to let him join Kitty.

'Can that woman get any ruder?' he asked.

Jo joined them. 'She's not changed one bit, has she?'

Kitty did not reply to either question, simply choosing to leave them hanging as statements. She went through the back to speak with Meryn.

A hasty exchange of written notes showed Belle had not given Meryn any cause for alarm, but she did mention Belle was still meeting the fisherman and friends once a week. The discussion always seemed to be about black-market items, and no more mention of moving strangers across Britain. However, she did notice food disappearing from the pantry and Pots would always ask if there were spare items if he was short of something for a meal. Belle never cooked and was rarely in the kitchen. Meryn said she was going to move the items later that day and when Belle wasn't around, she was going to sleep on a truckle bed in the corner as it was warmer in the kitchen, so if anyone was sneaking around, she would know. Meryn promised to keep a safe distance and to contact Kitty without hesitation via Wenna, should she need help.

'At last, something positive and, dare I say it, there is light at the end of the tunnel. What wonderful news. Maybe it will all be over next month; *this* Christmas!' Kitty said, referring to the predictions of the war ending by Christmas each year since it started. She and Michael sat listening to the news on the radio and it was announced Britain and her allies had defeated Hitler's army at a second battle in El Alamein.

Michael shifted in his seat and said nothing. He put his head in his hands and Kitty remained standing in front of him. This was not the reaction she had expected from him. Watching the tears drip from his fingers onto the stone floor, she slipped into the small kitchen to fetch water. Maude stood looking outside at Tom smoking his cigarette in a dark corner of the garden, hidden from the evening sky.

'How is Michael?' Maude asked.

Kitty thought for a moment before answering. 'Sad. I wasn't expecting him to be sad,' she said.

Maude turned away from the window, her own face damp with happy tears.

'We all have different emotions, I suppose. Tom is angry because he is too old to fight for king and country, you and I are happy because there is hope, and I suspect Michael is remembering those who died to bring about this victory. He will also feel very guilty about not being there to tend them, so go easy on him. Just give him space to let out his emotions. Bottled up, they will fester. Take him a drop of Tom's rhubarb wine, it will help him sleep.'

Kitty returned to Michael's sitting room area where he was now sitting dry-faced and handed him the drink.

'Something to help you sleep, according to Maude,' she said.

Michael took a sip and his face twisted with the sourness of the mixture.

'I'm sorry,' he said.

'What for?' Kitty asked.

'I need to go back. I'm ready. I've no pain and I've walked without crutches with no problems for a while now, and the wound has healed. I *must* return, there will be casualties. They fought and fell whilst I had a holiday away from it all,' he said, his voice deep and cracked with emotion.

Kitty laid down her glass and knelt in front of him.

'If you must, then go, but only for the right reasons, not because you feel guilty about spending time with me – or being injured. We deserved this time. It will see us through our darkest days. Everything happens for a reason. We are a ceremony away from being family; I'll be your only family member if we marry, and as orphans we've been through our own kind of Hell, so a little happiness during a dreadful, evil time in our lives is earned – well earned and not given. Lose the guilt, soldier, and take the love with you,' she said, putting her hands on his cheeks and kissing his lips. It broke her heart to know she had no choice in letting him go again, but she also understood his reasoning. Her loyalty to her nursing career was why they were not married, and it was not her place to prevent him from doing his duty.

'I'm sorry, Kitty, I don't want to leave you, but it is time.'

The tenderness in his kiss transported Kitty away from what lay ahead and led her down a path of breathless passion so fierce both had to pull back. It wasn't until she turned the corner of the street that Kitty allowed her own tears to flow. Then came the anger and she shouted to the empty sky and shadowed lane as she pedalled furiously towards home.

'He's mine! You can't take him from me, he's mine!'

Chapter Twenty-Two

A few days later, Kitty stood on the edge of the cliff after shift and let the wind blow her hair from her face. She released loving thoughts of – and to – Michael on the wind and let peace wrap itself around her tired body and mind. Their farewell sat like a heavy stone inside her chest, and she mourned his leaving as much as if Michael had died.

Loud church bells rang out for the first time since 1940 and were celebrated by everyone except herself. Prime Minister Churchill announced the ringing of the bells for that day only, as an announcement of victory, but Kitty heard them as a personal win for the enemy. With the news of the Eighth Army, nicknamed The Desert Rats, forging forward in its fight, Michael's main aim became rejoining his unit. Before she had time to absorb the information, he was confirmed medically fit and had secured his flight for that morning, leaving her to stand on British soil, alone, and, yet again, waiting for news. Although a breakthrough had been made against Hitler's defences, the war abroad was far from over and Kitty felt abandoned. She knew it was selfish, but the joy of others did nothing to help her feel uplifted, and she could not bring herself to join Jo and others in their celebrations. She volunteered to cover another nurse's shift. Her fight was against pain and death, and her victory celebrations were recorded as survival against the odds when she wrote on patient notes.

As the weeks drifted closer to Christmas, in some ways, Kitty wished Michael had never come home without it being permanent; their parting had come at a price – her mind tormented her not only when she slept, but during the daytime. Each man brought into the ward with devastating injuries wore Michael's face. She nursed them as if they were him, then mourned their leaving, either as a living patient or a man in a box, in the same way. Kitty's torment sat inside her body like a stone, but she shared her feelings with no one, not even Jo. She joined in with parties and dances, always volunteering for anything connected with children, and wrote letters to Trix, her family, Meryn and Wenna each week, and sent Michael her love every day without fail. Her laughter was fake; nothing in life made her smiles true ones.

Kitty made her life circular and protected by not allowing the outside world to pull her true feelings from her body and offer her nothing but false hope. Her aim was to see out 1942 tending to those who were alone and afraid, not dance until her feet ached; they would ache with the burden of serving her country during its time of need. Kitty focused her mind on everything but what might be happening to Michael and on her own desire to be strong for when he did return home. Whenever the word *if* came into her thoughts, she pushed against it hard until *when* had the stronger hold.

However, when midnight struck and 1943 slid into play, despite trying to suppress memories, she found herself reminiscing over the year Belle lied, and tried to destroy the relationship between her and Michael. Kitty, in survival mode, reminded herself of how the plan failed.

Her memories drifted back to a snowy night, a painful ankle and the strong arms of the man who rescued her in her hour of need. To their reconciliation, and the night she fell in love. The time she vowed nothing and no one would come between them again.

When Kitty climbed into her bed, January 1943 ticked into its eighth hour and the power of happier memories settled the turmoil in her mind. At last she understood the new year brought with it the opportunity to make way for fresh beginnings and leave behind the darker days. Memories were all she needed to hold her up and give her the strength to believe the war would end in their favour.

Cornwall slowly emerged from the winter months and, as always, the frosts and occasional snow flurry had not destroyed its beauty. The March weather was mild and spring flowers pushed their way through thawed-out ground. Much like the seasons, Kitty had dark days and bright ones. With winter well and truly gone, she felt a little brighter.

Kitty woke from a night shift to find she had received a batch of letters. They brought mixed news, but Kitty no longer felt sadness or regret when she read them. Instead, she looked to the positives. The letter from her aunt and uncle reassured her all was well back home, and Stanley wrote to tell her he no longer owned Fell Hall. He had signed it over to the Gaskin brothers and Eric, for when the army no longer had use of it, and they were to do whatever suited them when they turned twenty-one. The three boys were like the sons he never had, despite them being adopted by his farmer friend. Jenny had suggested it before she died. He also wrote that his temporary home, aside from the air base, was a one-roomed cottage on the farm. Kitty wrote back and said she fully understood why he'd made the decision and knew he would never marry again. She promised to visit him and the boys at the farm one day.

The best letter she received was from Michael. He sent her a photograph of himself beside a camel, with a brief note to say he was not ready to ride one yet, but it was something he intended to do before the month was out. Something about the wording of that sentence made Kitty's heart flip and she wondered if he was heading elsewhere in April. Michael had a clever way of writing coded messages which slipped past the censor's eagle eye. Before the month was out – not next month, or in a few weeks. Suddenly, it occurred to Kitty she was assuming the end of March, but the letter was dated the first week of January. If it was a code for moving on, it had already taken place and Michael might have taken his first camel ride. All she could do now was ride the wheel of waiting to find out where in the world he was and what new horrors he faced.

Only Meryn's letter gave her cause for concern when she

spoke of weather and of how she had enjoyed paddling in the rock pool now it was warmer. It was their code. Meryn suspected Belle's activities again, and, as soon as she was able, Kitty begged a lift into Truro with her bicycle and went to Mawnan Smith to give Meryn her support and reassure her she was a friend to be trusted.

Chapter Twenty-Three

K itty wasted no time in drawing Meryn away from the kitchen and they walked to a bench overlooking the bay from Trebah Gardens. Below them the army activity had increased, and Kitty noticed the presence of American soldiers around the gardens and through the village. Large trucks loaded with equipment to aid the British fight were unloaded at the end of Blackberry Lane and transported with care and a lot of noise down the narrow, winding lanes to the beach below. She was pleased to see Blackberry Lane itself was untouched.

'What's the news, Meryn?' Kitty asked.

Meryn handed her a prepared note. Records of her findings.

Belle and the men discussed the arrival of the American forces, and she was instructed to learn as much about their reasons for being in Cornwall as she could.

In mid-March, another piece of cargo will arrive, and she was to escort it to Falmouth the following day.

Belle left the village with a man on the bus to Falmouth – 25th March.

It happened two more times during the month.

In April, she was to travel to London to meet a friend and bring them back to stay overnight at the inn. She made two more trips.

Every month is the same; a new friend is tucked away in the secret rooms off the kitchen.

End of April. I became suspicious. She told me she is going to London again soon.

I think they are back to smuggling people. If they were British, it would not be so secretive, would it? I also think she is up to something at the POW centre. She said they are building extensions for the new accommodation, and she must be there for longer hours. We both know Belle does not work extra hours – something is going on there, too.

Kitty folded the paper and put it into her coat pocket.

'We'll keep this as a record and, if you can, keep watching her and see what happens after her London trip. I'm going to speak with someone, as I do think she's mixed up in something illegal. I'll try and find out more about the POW situation, too. Don't worry,' Kitty said quietly, ensuring she mouthed her words for Meryn to follow.

Meryn understood and reached out for Kitty's hand.

'You are doing a good thing, Meryn. I'm with you all the way, don't be afraid.'

'Another visit, Kitty? I take it you've come on a pity visit to see my kitchen help,' Belle said with a sniping tone as Kitty walked into the bar, pushing her way through the groups of soldiers filling the room.

'I've come to see you both,' Kitty said. 'I needed a break and always feel relaxed here. Mind you, there are a lot more customers than when I came in last.'

Belle looked around the room and smiled. 'Yes, more Yanks arrived. They drifted in a few at a time, but they are thirsty and in need of female company. I can offer both. They are generous and know how to treat a woman, so, the more the merrier, I say,' she said.

'You certainly can, Belle. How's work?' Kitty asked.

Belle moved to serve a customer, but Kitty got the distinct impression she was avoiding answering Kitty's question. She watched Belle use her charm on the soldier and encouraged him to join her at the end of the bar.

'Meet my friend, Eli Bevis,' Belle said to Kitty.

'Howdy, ma'am. It's a pleasure to meet you.'

The man held out his hand and Kitty feared his grip might crush hers. He was tall, strong, and stood with broad shoulders. His smile was wide and friendly, and his accent had a singing lilt to it, and Kitty could see why Belle warmed to him.

'Welcome to Great Britain, Eli. I'm Kitty, a friend of Belle's. We met through our Red Cross work,' Kitty said and eased her hand from his firm grip.

A loud banging of bottles from the far end of the bar made Kitty jump. Belle shook her head at Pots and excused herself from Kitty and Eli's company.

'I'd best be leavin', Kitty. Belle doesn't need this kinda

trouble,' Eli said and went to step away. Kitty put her hand on his arm.

'Belle can deal with them, she has a certain charm,' she said.

'No, ma'am. It's me they are banging for – I must go.'

Kitty stepped in his way to prevent him leaving. She swung a glance behind her to see Belle in full chiding mode with three soldiers and noticed the tension rising.

'Eli, what have you done wrong? Whatever it is, I'm sure we can sort it out,' Kitty said, trying to reassure the man, who no longer looked tall and confident. His smile became lost in his frown and he looked worried.

'I was born with the wrong colour skin, ma'am. I apologise for disturbing your time with Belle.'

His answer confused Kitty; she did not grasp what he meant, but she could see the three soldiers heading their way would be classified as white soldiers if skin tone was recorded on their files.

'Is this dog troublin' you, ma'am?' one soldier asked.

Kitty made a pretence of looking around. She did see soldiers spilling outside at great speed and guessed there was trouble brewing.

'I'm sorry. I haven't seen a dog around here, so no, he gave me no bother,' she said with an emphasised innocence and added Britishness to her voice.

The men crowded around Eli and leaned into him.

'Get your sorry carcass out of here,' one threatened. His voice was gravelly, as if he meant the man serious harm, and was loud enough to be heard by those nearby. There were some muttered words Kitty had never come across, and their attitudes confused her even more.

'I'm sorry. I truly don't understand what he has done wrong,' she said, but the men ignored her as they narrowed their eyes and glared at Eli. Kitty shuddered at the goading the soldiers heaped on Eli, and he put up his hands and edged backwards.

'I'm leaving. Nice to meet you. Ladies, goodnight,' Eli said and moved away from the bar, keeping his distance from the men.

Kitty stepped to one side, squeezing past one of the three men.

'Stay where you are, Eli. Belle, do you think this man should leave?' she called over to the bar.

Belle moved into the middle of the room with her arms crossed in front of her chest. Kitty saw temper in her face.

'He is my guest. He stays,' she said.

A soldier stepped forward. 'I am sorry, ma'am, but we have rules. He cannot stay. Leave it to the men – you ladies need not worry your pretty heads about this, we'll sort it out with your pa over there.' He pointed to Pots at the bar.

Belle rose to her full height, overshadowing the soldier. For a second, Kitty felt the soldiers should fear Belle over Hitler.

'Firstly, I do not worry my pretty head over anything, and Pots is not my father. Second, *I* own this place. Yes, me. Not Pots. So, as I said, *I* decide who gets to drink here. Everyone is welcome unless they misbehave. Understood. Now, I don't know what your grievance with this man is, but he is welcome here anytime and I will not tolerate violence amongst my customers. If you think you cannot stay in the same room and be civil, then please take your custom elsewhere.' Belle's voice boomed out and no one could doubt her authority.

One of the three men walked towards her.

'We obviously have different ways of thinking. Things are different back home,' he said to Belle.

Belle's hands moved to her hips, and she stood with purpose.

'Well, that's as maybe, but you are not back home, you are in my country, and in my pub,' Belle said and lowered her arms. She pointed outside, then to the bar. 'If you'd like to finish your drinks, please do, and I'd appreciate you bringing manners with you the next time. And yes, there will be a next time if you all respect each other. Kitty, how's Jo?' Belle cut her conversation with them so they could not respond and moved towards Kitty, leaving the men standing awkward, unsure whether to stay or leave. It wasn't until Kitty turned back to the bar that she noticed Eli had slipped away through the living quarters during Belle's speech.

'Belle, I'm going to say goodbye to Meryn, and will leave you to keep the peace inside – and good luck. Eli has gone, so fingers crossed these chaps will sober up and forget this by tomorrow,' Kitty said as Belle moved back behind the bar.

Belle screwed up her mouth and threw a disapproving glance towards the men, now slapping each other on the back and laughing.

'Sadly, those three are the worst of a great bunch of men

and, for some reason, they always manage to upset everyone enough to walk out and leave. I'll speak with Eli when I see him again; he'll be the third man they've driven out, and all because of their skin colour. Segregation is what they call it. I was surprised to find it amongst their forces, though. I suppose we must try and understand why, but it's hard,' Belle said. 'One thing you must agree with though, when you drop by; there's never a dull moment around here. Yes, my lovely – another?' Belle walked away to serve her customer before Kitty could respond.

Meryn wasn't in the kitchen or in her room. Kitty felt guilty for just walking in, but knocking would never bring Meryn to the door.

Outside, the customers had left and Pots cleared away the tables.

'Have you seen Meryn?' Kitty asked him.

'I sent her down the lane,' he said, pointing towards Blackberry Lane. 'She's showing the boy places to run and hide if things get out of hand in there again.' He glanced back at the inn. 'Not that I think he'll be back. Belle winds them in then out again, she loves the drama. Those three were bad apples amongst a barrel of good ones.'

Kitty walked over to her bicycle. 'I'll come back on my next day off, Pots.' She touched Meryn's note in her pocket. 'Let's hope drama doesn't raise its head again anytime soon. Take care,' Kitty said, and headed to Wenna's house to say hello before riding back to Truro to catch her lift home.

Kitty received another note from Meryn during Easter and when the girl arrived with a bunch of daffodils and a request they meet when Kitty finished her morning shift,

Kitty sensed something serious had happened back at Mawnan Smith.

She changed her uniform and rushed to the bus stop where Meryn had asked to be met.

Meryn sat on the grass beside a large woven bag and Kitty noticed dark rings under her eyes when Meryn looked up at her. April had not been kind to Meryn, Kitty could see it in her face. With her young friend arriving in such a state, Kitty guessed it had something to do with Belle. If it was something else, Meryn would have turned to Wenna – her new mother hen.

Both agreed it was time to hand Belle over to the authorities, but Kitty had no clue where to start, so Meryn suggested she return to the pub and continue her recorded notes until Kitty had worked it out. She confessed to originally feeling scared and alone and had hoped she could stay with Kitty for a while, but now they'd talked she was ready to continue what she'd started. Kitty promised to join her again as soon as she could, but for now, she had to think about the next step in confirming their fears about Belle and the men she met.

A fortnight later, another message from Meryn told Kitty there had been no more meetings in the pub and Belle was there more often than not. They met for a picnic to talk more, and both agreed they'd overreacted and should push it to the back of their minds. The months ticked into summer with no further news of extraordinary meetings and Kitty heaved a sigh of relief. She had enough to worry about with her final studies.

Chapter Twenty-Four

K itty pushed open the door to the examination room door and took several deep breaths. This was it, the day she had dreaded. Just over an hour later, she took her final assessment, and it was all over until results day in September. What a way to spend her twenty-third birthday! At least she had a more relaxed evening planned with friends.

Tom and Maude often welcomed both Jo and Kitty for an overnight stay, always grateful to Jo for rescuing them. Kitty was always made welcome and comfortable in their home, and especially enjoyed the visits when all four enjoyed an evening playing cards or sitting quietly listening to the radio followed by a discussion or debate over current affairs. Japanese attacks on supply ships and the battle in Tunisia brought conflicting emotions into the home: fear and hope. Tom had a calm manner and always succeeded in restoring their belief an invasion would never take place.

Jo and Kitty's friendship repaired itself as if their spat

had never happened. They spent their time off together and Jo helped Kitty smile again. Their visits created a strong bond with Tom and Maude, and it often felt like returning to a loving home. Sometimes Kitty felt guilty for not visiting her aunt and uncle, and she made plans to visit on her next official leave. Tonight, the radio presenter spoke about Japanese attacking supply ships, and another successful advance for Great Britain and her allies in Tunisia. A discussion about spies causing chaos came about and, when they went to bed, Kitty chose to share Meryn's findings with Jo.

'And she thought Belle is a spy? Why haven't you said anything before? The authorities need to know!' Jo's reaction was just as Kitty expected and she sat low in her chair whilst Jo twitched her way around the room in a thinking frenzy. The warmth of the sherry Jo had poured earlier – a birthday gift from Kitty herself – rolled through her veins, giving the same sensation as cuddling a favourite toy.

'Because I was not convinced the word of a fifteen-year-old lip-reading deaf girl and the occasional visitor to the pub would be listened to without proper evidence. You have to admit, it sounds crazy. Belle loves drama and excitement in her life. One flattering remark and she'll run around a man until she's drained him dry. If the well stays full, she'll cling on until the next exciting adventure turns her head, but spying against England for flattery? I'm not so sure. The more I thought about it, the more I realised it would be hard work, and we both know she avoids that like the plague,' Kitty said and allowed the vapours of another sip of her drink to warm her throat, 'Meryn never ventures far, so to turn up here and unburden herself made me nervous. She recorded every detail from the start of the year and it reads believably enough, but when it all stopped just after Easter, neither of us were really certain we'd read the situation properly. *But* the reason I am confiding in you now is that it appears the meetings and city visits have started up again. I've reassured Meryn I will act on it now, so I have to speak with someone who will decide whether it is worth investigating and let them decide how far to let it run, or whether to shut Belle down – or lock her up, immediately.'

Kitty took a long sip of her drink and Jo sat staring at her in disbelief.

'It sounds ridiculous, doesn't it?' Kitty said, 'but I have everything Meryn has seen written down; don't take my word for it, read them. In that box, on the table, there's quite a story. Read them and we'll talk more in the morning. I need your sensible head right now, Jo.'

Kitty walked into the room where Jo sat reading one of the notes written by Meryn. Sunshine flooded the room and Kitty shielded her eyes from its bright glare.

'Have you read them all?' she asked Jo.

'This is the last one,' Joe said, waving the letter at her.

'What did you make of it all?' Kitty asked.

'Buying from the black market for business is one thing, but possible people smuggling?' Jo replied.

Kitty joined her at the table and tapped the box. 'If I take these to the police, Meryn will be the one to suffer if Belle was found to be innocent. It's a difficult decision to make, which is why I need your advice, your input. I can't do this alone,' she said.

Jo folded away the last letter and put the lid on the box. 'I think it's best if we keep quiet for the moment. I agree with your sentiment; the observations of a deaf lip-reader and an occasional visitor, a young woman, are possibly going to be put at the back of the queue – brushed aside as hysterics. They say, report every little thing, but it doesn't mean they are taken seriously when folk do just that – I'm in on this but I think we need more facts, find out more about who the people are, and if Belle is still transporting. They might be our own people for all we know, or members of her family. It's been a few months now and I would have thought someone else might have noticed by now and reported something. Are you certain Meryn isn't an attention seeker? Harsh, I know, but, well...' Jo said, shrugging her shoulders. She stopped pacing and stood by the window, lifting her face to enjoy the warmth of the sun. 'What about this friend of yours, the woman with the children, can she be trusted?'

'I'm sure she could, but I don't want to bring her into all of this; she's widowed, and Belle could create problems in the village for her. And I'm not sure about Pots, the pot man – he could be tied up in it all as well for all I know,' Kitty replied.

'Or there might be nothing going on at all and Meryn has a fertile imagination,' said Jo.

Kitty wiped and put away her breakfast dish as Jo expressed something Kitty had thought about the second time she met with Meryn.

'Let's hope there's nothing to worry about, but I trust Meryn is telling the truth and believes Belle is assisting the enemy. Meryn has a lot to lose – I'm not sure she would risk losing her home. If it is true, Meryn would have to be moved to somewhere safe and we would have to really trust the person we tell.'

Chapter Twenty-Five

'Remind me why I am sitting on damp rocks?' Jo demanded with fake indignity as she and Kitty made a pretence of gathering seaweed for Meryn. They had arrived in Mawnan Smith and gone to the cove in the hope of finding evidence to back up Meryn's latest report of a small boat entering and leaving the previous evening. She had seen two men walk down Blackberry Lane shortly afterwards.

'Can you think of any other way of spending your day off?' Kitty asked.

Jo swung her a look. 'Um, yes. I can think of several,' she replied. 'When's the tide on the turn?'

'Around ten minutes' time, but I think we've seen enough. There are definitely signs of a boat being dragged onto the sand and more than one set of footprints,' Kitty said. 'Let's go back and go tell the police.'

'The local ones? How do you know they aren't in on this, too? Something tells me any small boat moving across these waters has support from up there.' Jo pointed to the area where the army were building defences. 'Or up there.' She pointed towards the village. 'What if the boat belongs to an innocent fisherman? We have to be sure about this, Kitty.'

'In Meryn's note she mentions seeing a brief flash of light on the water just after the patrol returned, each time she's watched from the shadows in the lane. I think the fisherman gave an all-clear signal; it makes sense. You've read the other things she's recorded. It's time we spoke with someone. Let's head back,' Kitty said and pulled another clump of seaweed from the cove.

As they walked along Blackberry Lane towards the inn, Jo nudged Kitty. 'Is that the three men with Belle?'

Kitty looked to where Jo pointed, and they both stepped out of sight.

'Blast, I thought she was at work. We'll sneak round the back, give this to Meryn and leave. I'll tell Meryn what we saw, and we can plan to come back another time and then report it. We can't leave it much longer or we'll be breaking the law ourselves. You know she said there's another traveller arriving, and Belle mentioned she is leaving to visit her parents tomorrow. I think tonight is when the traveller will arrive. It's all too much of a coincidence. I'll speak with Meryn. Stay here,' Kitty said.

Meryn was standing by the sink when Kitty rushed into the yard. She ran outside to take the basket and Kitty beckoned her to a hidden corner at the end of the courtyard.

'There's something going on. We are heading to another police station to tell them just in case the local ones can't be trusted. Pack a bag and go to Wenna when you finish work and I'll explain it all to her, but we've got to get back. Wenna will keep me informed. We will make sure you are safe. Belle doesn't know we are here. She's with the three men and we've just seen her go inside, so go about your business as usual. Understand?'

Meryn nodded.

'Sorry it's rushed,' Kitty said.

Meryn grabbed Kitty's hands and pulled her towards the kitchen. She snatched up a pencil and paper.

We must stop the enemy, she scribbled, and then put the paper into her pinafore pocket.

Kitty gave a nod of agreement and left Meryn working as if nothing had happened.

After telling Wenna Meryn might need a place to stay at short notice, and all would be explained later, Kitty and Jo decided to approach the Home Guard as they could not find the local policeman, and time for them to return home was running out. They chose to speak to the captain of the Truro branch on the way home, once they tracked him down to the village hall and explained the situation. He was sensitive to their concerns about Meryn, and accepted Kitty's garbled apology and reason for not speaking out earlier. He appreciated her concern that the original findings were not substantial enough, but after skimming through the more recent notes, he confirmed their fears. He took their own details and promised they were not wasting his time.

For two weeks Wenna updated them with no-news-to-tell telephone calls. Once told there was a matter of security issues, she agreed to watch over Meryn – who continued to work as usual. She reported back that Belle hadn't returned from visiting her parents as expected, and that when Pots asked Wenna to help behind the bar until Belle's return, she agreed without hesitation.

A telephone call from the Red Cross office led to a request for a meeting with Kitty one morning, and her stomach sank when she received the news from her ward sister. Another move was no doubt on the cards; right on top of Christmas was not a great time to choose to land her in the company of strangers. She approached the sister's office with a nervous tension. Kitty had made up her mind to fight the move; her final exam results were due, and she could not cope with adding to her nerves with another upheaval within the Red Cross.

They tapped on the door and received permission to enter.

'Nurse Pattison, good morning.' A woman in a Red Cross uniform stood alongside a police officer. Kitty was taken aback at the sight of them both.

'Good morning,' she replied in a cautious tone.

'Please, sit. And don't look so nervous. We need to ask you about Annabelle Farnsworth,' the woman said.

'Belle? Is this to do with—'

'Do you know of her whereabouts?' the policeman asked in a deep and firm voice. Hostile was a word which sprang to Kitty's mind and her thoughts froze. She composed herself before answering. 'If she's not at her home in Mawnan Smith, then no, I do not know where she is. I do know she was to visit her parents a couple of weeks ago. May I ask why you've both come here to ask me?'

The policeman remained standing when the woman sat down and encouraged Kitty to do the same.

'We know you and Joanne Norfolk are friends of hers and visit her regularly. Her parents say they haven't seen her for months, and the young girl who works for her said she's not been at home since you last visited. We wondered if you knew where she was – it is important, Nurse Pattison,' the woman said.

Kitty took a moment to digest what was being said. Belle was missing and the Red Cross and police were together asking after her whereabouts, and she concluded it must relate to the Home Guard situation. They had believed them and followed through.

'Is she not at the camp – at work?' she asked, directing her attention to the woman rather than the fierce face of the policeman.

The woman looked to the policeman and Kitty gave an inward sigh. He was in charge, that much was obvious. She just wished his face wasn't so stern. She gave him a soft smile, but gained nothing back.

'No, she is not. I have here notification of your visit to the Home Guard at Truro with regard to national security and giving the name Annabelle Farnsworth as a person of interest – along with notes recording unusual activities on her part. We need to track down this young woman as a matter of urgency,' the policeman said and, to Kitty's relief, his voice softened slightly. 'We really do, Miss Pattison.'

Kitty looked to the Red Cross woman and then back at him.

'You believe us. I didn't want to waste anyone's time.'

The woman stood up. 'You did the right thing. If you do hear from her, you must inform the police straight away, understood? This has to remain quiet, Nurse Pattison, so please – well, you understand.

'We'll be in touch again. We have Joanne Norfolk to speak to next. Your young friend at the inn was most helpful and her mother certainly ensured she had her support.' The policeman held out his hand, his face stern once more.

Kitty smiled. Wenna the mother hen had protected Meryn from the nerve-wracking ordeal. The sooner they found Belle, the better. It would be dealt with, and another worry could be released to the past.

When Kitty returned to the ward, she found beds being moved in to accommodate the many extra patients arriving that afternoon. Her colleagues were exhausted, and she relieved a few for a well-earned rest. The ward sister gave Kitty the task of overseeing the new patients, and, when they arrived, she clerked them in and worked tirelessly tending to their medical needs. A new courage surged through her body and Kitty knew she was in control and would cope with whatever came her way. Jo's support and input in her life had helped her through the terrible days. By the end of the shift the ward sister made Kitty realise she *could* take control as a registered nurse, and Kitty promised herself she would fulfil her drive towards helping the war effort and wounded, but she also aimed towards another dream for the future. Orphan care. The war orphans and Meryn played heavy on her mind.

'So, both of us have given statements now?' Kitty asked Jo that evening, after Jo made a telephone call suggesting they meet.

'About Belle, yes. Did you know three Italian POWs are on the run too, and they suspect Belle helped them escape?'

Kitty stared at Jo in disbelief. Her friend brought fresh news.

'You're joking? Do you think she's with *them*?'

Jo picked up the keys to the truck she had borrowed and went to the door. 'Who knows? Anyway, I can't stay any longer, I dropped off a couple off in town, but I'm on a half day tomorrow, shall we meet up around two?' she said.

Kitty shook her head, 'I'm not free for three days – only in the evenings. Listen, if either one of us hears from Belle, we must hand her over to the authorities.'

'Agreed, this is beyond black market stuff, although that's bad enough. I'll see you at the end of the week. Cinema?' Jo asked.

'Sounds ideal. It's been a busy time lately, but all is good, and worrying about Meryn isn't so bad now Wenna is watching over her. I'll see you Friday.'

Chapter Twenty-Six

September brought with it more drama surrounding Annabelle Farnsworth. Jo's post now took her to several remote training camps supplying food and drink to the armed forces, so they were not able to meet so often. On her last visit to Kitty, she told her they had taken supplies to the Italian POW camp near to where Belle worked, and the place was a hotbed of gossip. In true Jo style, she gleaned as many snippets as possible to share with Kitty.

The authorities had recaptured one of the Italian POWs hiding out at Falmouth. He told them Belle smuggled vital information abroad in parcels addressed to enemy informants with British names. She also helped him and his friends to try and get out of the country.

On the back of this information, The Stargazy Inn became a source of interest, and it was discovered a sergeant in the British Army, a member of the local constabulary and the three men Belle held regular meetings with were all involved in transporting infiltrators into Great

Britain, along with black market items. They named Belle as the head of the smuggling unit and suggested her father had dealings with the group, too. A countrywide search for Belle and her parents was ordered.

There wasn't a day went by when Jo did not send Kitty news about Belle, who was now the main topic of conversation amongst the Red Cross staff. Guilt crept in for Kitty, and she held back what she learned from Meryn and Wenna. The last thing she wanted to do was to make Meryn feel as she did – wrong for not speaking out earlier. The delay had given Belle the opportunity to run and carry out more crimes against the country. Every day Kitty chided herself for doubting what Meryn had shared. She was angry at Belle and her family for betraying England, and shocked to think it was real and not something out of a novel from the camp library. The further the investigation went, the more angry and guilty she became – it was no longer a secret within the Red Cross or the hospital, and each person who began their training with Belle in Birmingham was questioned on more than one occasion.

Jo and Kitty were the first, followed by Trix and Smithy. They were asked to name people they might know Belle had contact with, and Kitty gave Michael's name as a colleague, but it wasn't until after her meeting and she was talking with Jo and Trix that Kitty recalled someone who had the character to draw Belle into something so sinister and dangerous.

She requested another meeting with the investigator and handed them Eddie Dobson's name. He was the soldier she met on the train the day she left home, who stirred up trouble in Birmingham. He and Belle were extremely close in those days, and Kitty never found him trustworthy. She recalled he abused the army petrol, and was always wheeling and dealing, or creating trouble. His last posting was abroad, on the front line, and Kitty suspected he and Belle had never lost touch.

In mid-September, Jo visited and told her the group she worked alongside were moving out and she had orders to go with them. New entertainment vans were arriving, and she was to drive one around with three American women from the United States Red Cross. Kitty tried to be happy for her friend, but it saddened her to think she would be alone again. The Stargazy Inn was closed for investigation and Meryn now lived with Wenna. She had permission to collect her personal items from the inn, and after Pots spoke to the authorities, Meryn was allowed to continue using the oven and baking her pasties until the inn's supplies ran out. The Home Guard sent two middle-aged men to protect the property and keep Meryn safe whilst at work. Meryn wrote to Kitty with any news which came her way, but with regards to the inn, until Belle and her family were brought in for questioning, there was not a lot to report.

The more Kitty reflected on Belle and Eddie's situation, the more she realised he might well have had a hold on Belle. She still found it hard to believe Belle was the instigator of the national attacks on behalf of Hitler. Eddie, on the other hand, often gave her a reason to be irritated and she thought back to when they first met on the train to Birmingham in 1940; never in her wildest dreams did she think of him as a man betraying Great Britain – he was a brash, cocky soldier seeking out a naive girl. When he hooked up with Belle, Kitty could only imagine he fell for her and she found a way to recruit him into her ring of spies. Kitty still found it incredible to think of them both locked up in prison on several accounts of treason. Their capture came about when word filtered through that Belle's mother could not cope with the interrogation and within forty-eight hours gave up her husband, her daughter and her daughter's friend, offering the past and present plans of the enemy crossings from France to Cornwall.

As she sat trying to block out the sounds of construction of the last of the buildings on the RAF base, Kitty noticed a lot more activity than usual. The name of the base had changed from RAF Trebelzue to RAF St Mawgan, and the American air force Air Transport Command had moved in alongside the RAF's overseas unit, since when the number of people stationed there had risen rapidly. She looked out of the small library window, and it soon became obvious a major part of a fresh batch of America's air force were moving in that day. It was announced that a large rescue mission was landing with casualties, and all wards were to increase their bed capacity by six. Just what she wanted on her first day in charge of a full ward!

She gave up reading papers on new techniques, as all thoughts filtered back to Belle and her crimes, plus the noise became a distraction. She packed up her books and walked across the grounds to the calls and whistles of the new arrivals. She was joined by her colleagues, who chattered like excited schoolgirls. Kitty simply smiled politely and tried to keep her pre-duty nerves in check.

During the night she chatted with new members of staff from the American medical team and learned of new techniques and where some of them lived. Their arrival brought the distraction she so desperately needed. She explained what she could about the British way of life to those who asked questions, and enjoyed hearing about the cultural differences. The American team brought with them an air of excitement after the nightmares of the bombings. They listened to her stories about her rescues in her earlier postings and reassured her Britain was no longer alone. Someone hinted that Germany would be facing much the same sooner rather than later. A sense of relief overwhelmed her by the time she'd finished work, and she retired to her room to rest. Their support and protection of Great Britain were most welcome.

Two days later, the words of her colleagues became facts and the skies filled with American planes during the daytime and, at night, the British took over. They dropped their bombs over Germany and returned tired but triumphant. Kitty listened to their exchanges and comparisons in the canteen and felt guilty when her heart went out the German people, the innocent victims of the raids. Somewhere amongst the rubble would be a nurse much like herself, pulling out the dying and injured, reassuring those who were alive she had done her best to find their relatives. Kitty understood the nightmare the German nurse in her own rescue team would be suffering.

She questioned herself over her mixed feelings about becoming a nurse, but realised it was part of growing up and finding her strengths. The war was not ending any day soon; it was about to explode into other countries and extend its tentacles of death. It was the war to end all wars, but did not know when to end its own life.

Kitty placed herself back into the circle of work and rest, but fully aware of the need to protect her own well-being.

Her refusal to accept the attentions of eager airmen eventually earned her the name Ice Queen. At first it hurt, but Kitty dealt with it by not focusing on it too much; she knew she had brought it on herself but refused to punish herself for her reasons. Her love and loyalty to Michael would never alter and no American, Canadian or Brit would change that fact. Whilst he was fighting in Tunisia, she was not going to let down her guard and flirt with other soldiers, no matter how many sticks of gum or nylons they wanted to throw her way.

After one tiring shift, she took time to sit with a cup of tea and read a letter waiting for her from Meryn.

She looked forward to reading who had done what in the village, but the contents were upsetting as Meryn expressed feelings of unhappiness.

Dear Kitty,

Forgive me for writing this letter, but I need to get something off my chest. I am so miserable. My life is difficult in Wenna's home. I appreciate her taking me in, but it is cramped and no matter how hard I try to help her mother, it is not good enough for her. I've witnessed words between them and Wenna is under enough pressure with Irene running to flirt with soldiers with her friends, and looking after her mother, that I think I should look for a new home. I get frowned at by people angry about Belle and I'm sure they think I was involved, too. I miss you when you are not around, too.

I will try and find somewhere else. It will take a lot to reassure Wenna I don't not feel welcome; you know how she'll fret over me. I'll let you know where I am soon.

Take care.

With affection,

Meryn

After reading the letter and knowing Meryn enough to know it had taken a while to confess her feelings, Kitty had no hesitation in approaching Tom and Maude and asking if they would consider taking Meryn in for a week, so the three of them could help her through a challenging time in her life.

The days spent together were a success; so much so, Tom and Maude invited Meryn to live with them on a permanent basis. She expressed her joy at the room by clapping her hands. Tom wasted no time taking his car to fetch her belongings and Maude took her under her wing. Kitty walked away knowing she'd made the right decision by contacting them.

Chapter Twenty-Seven

K itty closed the door behind her, walked down the corridor and stepped outside, her body still shaking. She bent over, took large gulps of the sea air and allowed her body to release tension from her neck to her toes.

She had done it. Thanks to the Red Cross, she was now a fully qualified nurse! The proof was in the letter she held in her hand. As she looked out at the many bodies going about their business amongst the planes with no clue, there was no one she could call out to and share the news. The staff on the ward would pat her back and offer their congratulations, then move on with their day. She knew that for a fact as she had done it herself in the past.

She felt deflated and her thoughts went to Michael. How she wished she could telephone him – even better, run to him and shout her joy. Instead, she turned around and walked to her room to pack her bag. She was granted leave, which meant a four-day break with her aunt and uncle, then joining Trix and Smithy at their home, followed by a nostalgic two days in Durham at the bed and breakfast she and Michael referred to as their place. She needed to feel close to him. The travel was not going to be easy, but she made arrangements, and, provided the enemy kept to their side of the world, she might make all her connections and enjoy a well-earned rest. Kitty needed a change in scenery in the hope she could draw some sense of where or what she should do next with her life.

Jo had already used her leave and left Kitty in tears when she announced she was moving on and driving her food truck with the American team to feed the forces around the blitzed towns and cities. Apparently, coffee, doughnuts and music were their speciality. Jo was so fired up about it all and Kitty could see it brought out the best in her. The subtle changes were more than just a dash of lipstick. Jo related to the Americans far more than to her British colleagues. Their relaxed style suited her, and Kitty wished her well and meant it. She was lonely without her best friend, but rejoiced in the fact their friendship was stronger than ever. She also missed Trix, but found solace in Tom, Maude and Meryn.

'Telegram for K. Pattison.'

Kitty froze when she heard her surname. Her hand gripped the handle of her new suitcase – a gift from Maude – and she took a moment before turning around. Several of the girls from her room looked her way, and she saw relief flash across their faces, then a swift glance of pity.

'I'm Kitty Pattison – is it, is it for me?' she asked, not sure if she wanted to know the answer.

'It has Pattison K., residing at this section, so I will

assume it is, yes,' said the young messenger boy. He looked so young and troubled, and she wondered how many families were tormented by the telegrams he delivered with dignity. He stood in his navy and red uniform, and she wanted to reach out and straighten his pillbox hat and reassure him no matter what her telegram said, he was not responsible for its contents, but she could not speak. Time stood still.

Kitty did not envy him his job as he handed her the envelope. She noticed the sweat across his top lip and wondered if it was due to nerves or riding his bike uphill. Shaking herself from unnecessary thoughts, she rummaged in her bag and pulled out her coin purse.

'Don't wait for a reply. I can't open it just yet,' she said and pressed a penny into his palm. 'It's all I have, but thanks for all you do,' she said, keeping her voice soft.

'Not many people say that. Thank you. I hope it is good news,' the boy said and walked away.

Kitty felt the stares of the people surrounding her, all waiting to offer her pity. She placed the telegram in her handbag. If it was grave news, it could wait. She had a long journey ahead and unwelcome news would not be the ideal travelling companion. In the quiet of her family home would be the best place to read the contents of the buff envelope. As she crossed the tarmac and headed towards the bus stop, Kitty's bravado about not reading it left her and she put her suitcase on the ground and pulled out the telegram from her handbag. She stared at it, then ripped open the top. Taking a deep breath, she unfolded the contents.

[display text]

Back on home shores. Speak soon. Michael.

[display text ends]

Puzzled, Kitty reread the words. Was Michael back in Britain? Kitty heard the crunch of the bus gears as it wound its way towards the bus stop. She was torn between going home or staying in Cornwall for Michael to find her, and time was against her. Suddenly, the image of Michael's face, filled with disappointment because she wasn't where he thought her to be, made up her mind. She turned around and went inside to use the telephone.

Relieved her aunt understood why Kitty had delayed her trip home, she took time to consider where Michael might be and headed for her friend in the post room to ask after his son. After an hour and two cups of tea, Kitty was eventually informed Michael might be part of the Eighteenth Army group, newly created in February, some of whom had returned to Britain after its battle to force the enemy into surrender in Tunisia. Kitty's friend John told her there was word some of the soldiers had been allocated new units and sent back to Great Britain in connection with a top-secret mission.

'It sounds about right for Michael, John. Before he joined the Eighth he was part of a top-secret unit. I found him in Scotland by chance when I was based there at Drymen – Buchanan Castle. I wonder where they have sent him now?' Kitty said and sat frustrated that her fiancé was home and she could not contact him.

'Are you going to sit and wait it out around here?' John asked.

Kitty gave a semi-frown. 'To be honest, I'm at a loss as to what to do,' she said.

John looked behind him and around. 'All I can say is this: visit your friend with the pub and have a little break there. I'm not one hundred per cent, but let's say there's a lot going on with the Americans along the coastline. The Eighth joined the Eighteenth some time back; it was a mix of British and American units. Your chap could be with a new unit on this secret business. If he's done it before, well, who knows.'

An excited tingle ran around Kitty's body, and she pressed her hands together in pretend prayer. 'I wonder if he is. I wasn't aware he merged with the Eighteenth; our letters are so hit and miss. I wonder about going to The Stargazy, though.' Kitty leaned forward and lowered her voice. 'The so-called friend with a pub is in prison. Caught spying and helping the Italian POWs escape. Can you believe it? A Red Cross girl, too!'

John stared back at her. 'You are joking! Really? Well, well. You girls surprise us men during wartime with your skills, but spying for the enemy? That's treason.'

'I know, she shocked me. It was hard reporting what we suspected, but it had to be done,' Kitty said, still keeping her voice low.

John arched his eyebrows and gave her a shocked stare. 'You caught her at it?' he asked.

Kitty pinched her lips together and gave a slow, sad nod. She placed her finger across her lips and John nodded a silent agreement to keep it quiet.

'My friend worked for her and approached me with her

suspicions. I also had another person on my mind from our days back in Birmingham. A con man and crook in army uniform. It appears we were both right and they were eventually tracked down. Her parents were in on it too, and the chap had deserted his unit to go on the run with them. Word has it they were caught trying to leave the country via my hometown, for Holland. No doubt heading for Germany. It was like something from a novel!' Kitty gave a giggle, then corrected herself. 'It's no laughing matter, to be honest. Belle might lose her life; she's already lost her freedom, and rightly so. The pub is closed at the moment, but I am still able to visit my friends who are keeping it safe. Now you've said what you have, it connects what Belle did, and I have little doubt there's something secret going on down there – something big to finally rid us of the enemy.' She raised her eyebrows at John. 'We mustn't talk about it anymore – eyes and ears are about,' she said, looking around at the servicemen and women milling around the entrance, all hopeful for post.

'Trust me, Kitty. Your secret's safe with me. I just find it incredible she chose to support the Germans. There must be a reason. A family connection,' he said.

'Knowing Belle, it would be for material things and status should we be invaded. Thanks for the hints about Michael. I think I need to pay our friends in the pub a visit. I might glean news of his whereabouts. Meryn will enjoy a visit, too. I'm grateful to you, John. I'll knit that son of yours an outfit for the winter as a thank you.'

John broke out into a wide grin. 'Make it large, the boy has shot up recently. He's going to be tall like me,' he said, and Kitty could hear the pride in his voice. 'Leave your man a message and, if he turns up, I'll make sure he gets it.'

Kitty took his pen and paper and scribbled a note for Michael.

Gone to Sturguzy. Back Oct. 2. KX

Chapter Twenty-Eight

H ooking her kitbag onto her bicycle, Kitty rode to Tom and Maude's. She found Meryn sitting in the garden reading and strolled over to stand in front of her, blocking the light.

'Hello, Meryn. Fancy a trip to The Stargazy?'

Meryn jumped to her feet and nodded with enthusiasm.

'We've got to leave by the next bus if you do, so go pack a bag. I'll explain on the way.'

Meryn ran inside. Kitty greeted Maude, sitting at the table peeling potatoes. Kitty rarely visited when Maude wasn't peeling some kind of vegetable or another.

'Hello, Maude, here you are, working hard as usual while Tom plays in his shed,' Kitty said with a giggling lift to her voice.

Maude grinned back and pointed outside the window. 'You biked all that way with your kitbag on the handlebars? Be careful, my lovely. What are you doing here? I thought you'd be packing your case and heading home.'

'I'll not be making use of my suitcase yet, Maude. Something's happened. Keep it under your hat, but Michael might be in Cornwall, and, better still, at Mawnan Smith! I've telephoned and explained everything to my aunt and will get to see them next time around. Durham will wait but I'll go to visit Trix and Smithy once I've been to Mawnan Smith. I'll speak with Meryn, as I thought she would like to come with me to The Stargazy for a few days. I'll tell you about it when I return. We need to rush for the last bus.'

Meryn shoved her belongings in a bag and raced to the bus stop with Kitty. By early evening, the bus rolled into the village and pulled up outside the inn. The new route meant it was the last stop for the driver. As he parked up in the far corner of the yard, Kitty was surprised to see so many soldiers milling around and the pub doors open.

She and Meryn stepped inside to find Wenna and Pots working behind the bar. A steady stream of soldiers queued to receive their drinks. Kitty turned to Meryn and pointed to the area of the back entrance, and they made their way through the kitchen door. Once inside, they put down their bags. Meryn picked up a tray and cloth for them both and tilted her head to one side in question. Kitty nodded and took her tray. They walked through into the bar and Meryn immediately started clearing tables. Kitty slipped behind the bar and spoke with Wenna.

'What's going on?' she asked.

'Instructions from Belle that we are now custodians of the inn and I'm in charge of keeping records and handing over the takings to the bank.'

Kitty nodded as she spoke.

'The latest news on Belle is she has been moved and is now incarcerated in Holloway prison in London, charged with treason and espionage. I'm not sure about Eddie, but the army won't treat him lightly, that's a fact,' Kitty said and Wenna frowned.

'I heard about Belle from the solicitor dealing with this place. He said her case was heard and she has received eighteen years' penal servitude. He also said Eddie will be dealt with by the army – and that will probably be a firing squad punishment. It seems unreal. I know he was always a bad 'un, but still… Pots and I are in shock,' she said.

Kitty covered her mouth to express her own shock, then flapped her hand with a dismissive gesture. 'I know, isn't it dreadful? We had to send written statements; thank goodness we didn't have to take the stand! Belle is going to suffer hard with what she's done. Can you imagine life inside prison? She's got eighteen years of hard labour to cope with – and she deserves it. I'm still not convinced she was the brains behind it all – come on, Belle? Eddie was army, his sentence is bound to be a harsh one; but given it is the death penalty, I wonder if he is an infiltrator and recruited Belle and family. We'll never know the true story, but what a story it is! Incredible. Unbelievable.'

Wenna let out a loud sigh and shook her head. 'I'm not sure we will, but Belle always manages to worm her way out of anything from what I've witnessed working here. Your theory seems credible – I'm inclined to agree, the soldier is probably the real leader – Belle's so gullible. The police watch this place, but since the arrests and the American forces arriving, it's been given the thumbs-up for reopening. As you can see.' She pointed around the room. 'You two have arrived just in time. I think the soldiers have had a busy day; they are thirsty. Bless her, Meryn's got stuck in already. I kept her room clean for her just in case it didn't work out with your friends,' Wenna said and nodded over at Meryn. Meryn looked up at them with a smile.

Wenna moved on to other customers and Kitty joined Meryn collecting glasses. Meryn and Kitty fended off the attention of the customers and by the end of the evening, both vowed to wear padding around their backsides because of the excessive buttock slapping they received.

'I have the same problem,' joked Pots. 'I must say I'm happy to see you both, we were running out of glasses.'

'The till is happy,' said Wenna as she bagged the last of the takings. 'Now it's quieter, as good as it is to see you, why the sudden visit?'

'Something is going on in this area; I heard something through the grapevine. My Michael is back in the country and my friend wonders if he is here – the reason for my visit – oh, and to see you, too,' Kitty added hastily, her voice low.

Meryn came in from outside with the last of the glasses, and, behind her, carrying a tray, was the soldier Eli.

'That's the last, ma'am,' he said to Wenna, and Kitty watched as his face creased into a beaming smile. He was a handsome man and as Kitty dried the glasses Meryn washed, she noticed the girl barely took her eyes off him.

'Thanks, Eli. Close the door and you can leave out the back – but not before you have that pint you've earned. Take a seat while you have it,' Pots said.

Eli made his way to the living quarters, Meryn following.

'Just as well you are taking her back with you. Those two were friendly before she left. Not that I dislike the lad, I just wonder what sort of future is in their relationship,' Wenna said.

Kitty listened in amazement. She had no clue Eli and Meryn had struck up a strong friendship and Meryn showed no sign of missing a boyfriend when staying at Maude and Tom's place.

'He's quite a loner, and I was surprised to see her staring at him like a lovesick pup. She's never said a word about him to me. I'll have to find out more and what she intends to do with her life. It's difficult as she has no guardian as such, only you, Pots. The father figure.'

'She's not got anyone legal on her side. I can't do anything if she sets her mind to it – got a stubborn streak, that one,' Pots said between puffs on his pipe. 'I never thought of adopting her, with me being a man on my own. I felt it was not the proper thing to do, but the village accepted our situation and she's never asked for anything different of me.'

'I'm only a few years older than her, but see her as much younger and in need of protecting. Sometimes I think she hides homesickness for this place. We can talk with her tomorrow and find out where she wants to live, and what she thinks her future might be from now on,' Kitty said, and the others agreed.

'Walk you home, Wenna?'

Wenna picked up her wicker basket and lifted out a half

loaf of bread. 'I was going to take this home,' she said to Kitty, 'but you'll need something in the morning. Butter and milk are in the cooler as usual. I do my baking here. If you can persuade that girl to make her pasties tomorrow, I'll be grateful. I don't know what she left out of that recipe, but mine don't taste the same as hers did.

'Right, my lover, let's make a move before I fall asleep where I'm standing,' Wenna said to Pots.

Kitty smiled at them both; they had fallen into a comfortable friendship.

Chapter Twenty-Nine

Whilst waiting for Pots to return, Kitty sat and composed a letter to her friend Sarah, in Scotland. In earlier letters to Kitty, Sarah always wrote of how busy the hospital was, and how she had several new friends thanks to Kitty's introduction when she worked at Drymen. In her latest letter, Sarah's tone was more subdued. She wrote of the sadness she felt about family members who tried to escape Germany at the start of the Jewish persecution, and of her parents and brother in fear of the enemy who'd invaded Guernsey. Kitty read more and more about both situations in newspapers and tried her best to understand the reasons for such persecution, but could never work it out.

Dear Sarah,

I'm so sorry to hear of your family troubles. I do know the Red Cross will watch the situation closely, it always amazes me how quickly they react to situations and the care offered as soon as the service is available. Do try and remain positive and if there is any way I can find out news for you, I will do so. I have their names and will approach one of my seniors to ask if there is anything they can do to get news to you. You might consider leaving your current position to join the Red Cross. It might be possible then to see if you can find out more in an indirect way. What a sad, dreadful situation.

On a lighter note, your description of keeping up with the girls on an army hike kept me giggling for a week. I can see why you are wary of long grass and cowpats – I would be too!

Oh, and the shock of being chased by the herd must have made your heart race, but I do apologise for, once again, laughing out loud at your expense. At least you weren't alone. I am thrilled your friendships have remained strong and you no longer feel alone. We only had a brief time working together, but I know we would have enjoyed each other's company the more we got to know each other. I am a bit tougher than I was when you first met me, I'm no longer timid. War has taught me I needed to grow up fast and learn more about life other than what was happening in my small street back home.

Michael is well so far as I am aware; thank you for asking after him. I received a telegram telling me he is back on home shores and am assuming he means England and not Canada. Although if he was in Canada, I'd be happy as he would be safer.

I should imagine the most used words since the war started have been 'stay safe', and that's what I want you to do, Sarah, stay safe and try not to get too distressed. I am pleased you asked to be removed from the POW ward. Nursing Germans is not what you need right now. I truly understand, so do not feel guilty as you mentioned in your letter. I am pleased you still *receive your monthly news and gifts from your your grandmother, and that she is still active within the WI in Norfolk. It must give you some comfort she is safe.*

I must sign off now as I am about to head to bed. My leave is short and sweet, but much needed. Take care of yourself and, hopefully, one day we will meet again but for now, know your pen pal friendship is much appreciated.

With my very best wishes,

Kitty

When Pots returned with a reluctant, moody Meryn, who stood with her head down, he turned away from her. 'She's been up to no good. Flirting in the dark with someone. I warned him off.' Agitated and annoyed, he slapped a chair and a startled Kitty watched Meryn sit down at the table. 'I think we need to put our thinking caps on about the girl. I'll away and fetch Wenna back. She's an expert when it comes to young daughters. I'll explain it when we are all together. Don't let her leave,' he said pointing to Meryn, who glared at him in return.

The atmosphere in the room was tense. Wenna adjusted her bosom beneath her apron, and straightened her shoulders. Kitty knew Wenna had put her concerned mother hat on; she had seen it with Wenna's own daughter several times.

'You were seen canoodling, young lady.'

Kitty watched as Meryn's face flushed red. She dropped her gaze to the table.

'We can't be having you kissing and cuddling—'

'Wenna, she can't hear you. She's not looking at you,' Kitty interrupted.

Wenna tapped her finger under Meryn's chin and turned her head to face her.

'No you don't, madam. You do not blank me like that. What you did was wrong, and I think it is safe to say you will not be seeing him again. You'll go back to Tom and Maude's tomorrow. It's for the best,' she said, and Kitty thought if Meryn could not understand all the words, she would have had a clear idea Wenna was not happy with her behaviour from the look on her face.

She refrained from adding her own input to the conversation, leaving Wenna and Pots to offer up their thoughts on the matter. They were older and wiser, and Wenna had more experience with a daughter in need of guidance.

Meryn wiped the slate clean and scribbled down words at a furious pace

I want to stay here.

He is a good man. He's Eli's friend, Bobby. We love each other. He wants to marry me.

She looked at Kitty as she handed her the slate. Kitty read it and passed it onto Wenna, who in turn gave it to Pots. All three made disapproving noises and shared their concern on their faces with frowns and downturned mouths.

'Eli's friend? Eli's been covering for you?' Kitty asked.

Meryn nodded.

'It is far too early in your friendship for you to be in

love. Or do anything other than walk out when you visit Wenna and Pots. Understand?' Kitty said.

Again, Meryn lowered her head and this time it was Kitty who gently tilted it back to face her. 'I think we have to come to some sort of understanding, Meryn. You need to let us say our piece, no matter how embarrassed or annoyed you are with us.' Kitty kept her hand beneath Meryn's chin. 'We realise we are not your family, but we are the closest you've had for years. Pots had a hand in raising you. We are concerned for you. How about Bobby comes here and one of us acts as chaperone for a while when you visit again. Help us to find out more about him and his life in America. He'll tell you what you want to hear; with us he might be more open – honest.' Kitty turned to Wenna and Pots for their confirmation, and both nodded with enthusiasm.

Meryn wrote on the slate in front of her and slid it, with a determined look on her face, towards Kitty.

It's up to me. Not you.

She stared into her face, challenging Kitty to disagree, and it hurt Kitty to see anger in her eyes.

'We're worried about you, and somebody has to advise you, Meryn,' said Kitty.

Meryn banged her fist on the table, making them all jump. She pushed back her chair and ran outside.

'Well, that worked out fine,' Pots said and took another long draw on his pipe and leaned back in his chair.

Wenna gave him a clip around the ear.

'Enough of the sarcasm. This is a serious situation,' she said, and Kitty heard the annoyance in her friend's voice. Not wanting everyone to fall out and knowing she needed their support, she tutted and tapped her fingers on the tabletop as she took a moment to think.

'We can't leave her to her own devices, but we can't let her run loose; she's too vulnerable and her reputation – well, she won't have a decent one, that's for certain. Who is this Bobby? She didn't deny he was an American, so at least we have that information to work with.' Kitty shook her head with deep concern.

'She'll be run out of the village. Belle has already caused a scandal around here,' Wenna said, 'we don't need Meryn bringing trouble to the door as well. The police will have the place shut down. I'm surprised they agreed with Belle's request that the licence was transferred over to Pots and myself, but, as a widow, I am grateful for the income.'

Kitty sat listening and nodded politely. The situation was more than a misbehaving young girl, and it needed to be stopped. Wenna needed the support if Meryn returned to the inn and Kitty moved away; it was not fair of her to walk away from a responsibility of her own making.

'I might go to the camp and find out who this Bobby is and explain the concerns we have for her welfare. If he genuinely cares for her, he will listen to our fears and behave himself. She's got no one in her life and we have a responsibility of care,' Kitty said.

Pots grunted and bashed his pipe against the ashtray in front of him. 'What I saw shows he has no respect for her, and we need to speak to his company commander or someone high up. They won't put up with his behaviour and I'll make sure this Bobby get his punishment.' He replenished his pipe with fresh tobacco and lit it, puffing furiously before he exhaled the smoke with a loud hiss of disapproval. Wenna gave a tongue click and Kitty recognised the sound as the one used on her children when they misbehaved, or her mother annoyed her. Pots was not going to get his way.

'Do *not* go in with your guns popping. I think we need to warn him off and let him know we will go higher if he doesn't respect what we have to say. We will speak to the man first,' Wenna said.

Kitty watched Pots' face flush with annoyance.

'*We will*, will we? he said with deep sarcasm and Kitty heard the annoyed tone.

'Let's do as Wenna says and if he is still trouble, we'll support you, Pots. That way he's had fair warning and if he doesn't listen then he is no good for Meryn. We don't want her doing anything rash either. She's embarrassed and upset, we don't want her running away,' Kitty said.

Chapter Thirty

After further discussions and eventually Pots agreeing to hold back on his anger, the friends finished chatting for the evening.

'We'll leave you to it and see you in the morning,' Wenna said as she and Pots left.

Kitty decided to check on Meryn and entered her room. Meryn lay on the bed, her body shaking, and Kitty guessed she was sobbing into her pillow. Kitty took a moment, wondering whether to leave, but she decided Meryn needed to know she wasn't alone and that she understood what it was like to be in love and wanting to feel loving arms around you. She could empathise with Meryn and knew she needed to handle the situation with care.

She touched Meryn's shoulder, but the girl made no attempt to move. Kitty chose to stay; Meryn hadn't shrugged her off. She sat on the edge of her bed, leaving her hand on Meryn's shoulder as a source of comfort. The silent sobs subsided after a minute or so and Kitty removed her hand as Meryn slowly curled onto her side. Kitty reached out and dabbed her face dry with her handkerchief and tapped the end of her nose in affection.

'You can't hide from what you've done with this man Bobby, but it's more than kissing, I can tell,' she said, using what she hoped was a more sisterly approach to see exactly how far Meryn had allowed the man's affections to go.

With a move which startled Kitty, Meryn flung herself into Kitty's arms and buried her head into her shoulder. Kitty had her answer and let out a sigh; now she had to ask more questions.

She manoeuvred Meryn into a position where she could read Kitty's lips.

'More than once?' Kitty asked.

Meryn lowered her head and Kitty knew it was in shame rather than avoiding Kitty's questions. She tapped Meryn's chin for her to lift her face. Meryn slowly lifted her hand and showed five fingers. Another sigh escaped Kitty.

'I won't tell the others,' she said to gain Meryn's trust, 'but it has to end, do you understand?'

Meryn gave a flick of her eyes to show she did but wasn't happy.

Kitty tilted her head and frowned at her. 'Meet with Bobby in our company, but no more sneaking around. You hardly know him.' Kitty decided to be open with Meryn. 'I'm engaged, and we've only kissed. Michael loves and respects me.'

Meryn eased herself from the bed and walked to the door; she gestured for Kitty to leave. As she walked past her, Kitty gave her a reassuring smile and was rewarded with a brief hug before Meryn returned to soothe her heart under the eiderdown.

Kitty settled down in the guest room and listened to the distant hum of noises and the flicker of lights searching the skies, creating shadows across her wall. Her mind spun with worry about Meryn as if she was her own flesh and blood, and she questioned herself as to how far she was prepared to take on such a huge responsibility.

She inwardly cursed Belle for the troubles she had created with not only her offences against king and country, but her inability to consider Meryn in any plans she had for bringing about disruption to the inn. Belle and the men had received their punishment, but in some ways so had Meryn. She must have felt cast aside in her own home, and frightened. Tom and Maude's home was a sanctuary, but, Kitty now realised, Mawnan Smith was where Meryn wanted to live.

Kitty was also worried Meryn would feel let down if Kitty was moved on to another posting. Sleep was hard to come by, but eventually she managed at least three hours in between tossing and turning. When she came to, she heard the boots of soldiers echoing down the road beside the inn and peeped from the window onto the street. More American soldiers arrived and filled the village with their vehicles. She could not leave Meryn here alone, it wasn't safe. Amongst the gentlemen of any serving force there was always a rogue and Meryn would be an easy target. The new man in Meryn's life had proved that already with his disrespect.

She washed and dressed, then raced downstairs, ready

to prevent Meryn from leaving to find the mysterious Bobby, but when she searched around for her, Kitty realised she was too late.

The soldiers blocked many side roads, but Meryn had once shown Kitty a shortcut which led to the bay below. She scampered down the narrow track and stopped at the end to get her bearings. Barbed-wire barricades surrounded newly constructed concrete platforms and Kitty was surprised to see so many alterations since her last visit. It certainly looked a site of importance. At the right of the track, she saw it linked back onto the road and, not wanting to become embroiled in a confrontation with an alert guard, she slipped ahead of the soldiers heading her way. At the perimeter, she saw two guards and approached with a smile.

'Good morning. I wonder, have you seen a young girl walking this way? The young woman who sometimes clears the tables at the inn?'

One of the soldiers stepped forward. 'No, ma'am, and you are breaching the rules by being here. Turn around and head back to the village. I expect she'll soon want Mom to cook her up a feast,' he said, his voice firm and with authority.

Kitty, not ready to do as he asked, gave another weak smile. 'I'm concerned she's, well, become rather obsessed with one of your men, and I need to ensure she doesn't do anything silly. She's deaf, so she would not hear any warnings if she overstepped the boundary around here. His name is Bobby, possibly Robert – that's all we know about him. Please tell him she might be looking for him and to send her home if she comes visiting,' she said.

'Take yourself back to the village. We have a lot of Roberts and Bobbys here, but I'll put the word out for you,' the guard said and shifted his rifle as a reminder Kitty was on military property.

'Thank you,' she said and walked back to the village via the road. As she reached halfway, she spotted a Red Cross band on a soldier's arm. A medic. Remembering what John had said to her before she left, she approached him and called out.

'Excuse me. Have you come across a Canadian medic – a doctor with the British Army? Michael McCarthy? He was in Tunisia,' she said, breathless as she trotted beside him heading back down the road again.

'Part of the Eighteenth Army Group. He was with me. Yes. He's not here, I'm not sure where he was sent. I heard he was injured out, at one point,' he said. 'Wait there, I'll come back once we've offloaded this lot.'

Grateful she could catch her breath, Kitty was thankful she already knew about Michael's injury, so his words were not a shock. The medic returned, holding out a piece of paper.

'This place is where most of us were sent to. Some remained with the Eighth.' He tapped the paper. 'Others were assigned to another unit. He was with seriously injured patients due to fly back to Britain to join his new unit the last time I saw him. Some were sent to Canada, too. I can't say for sure he's still in Blighty, we are shipped out so fast nowadays. I really hope you find him and when you do, tell him Jed says hello.'

Kitty gave her thanks and watched him rush back down the hill. Once back at the inn, she gave the paper a quick glance.

21st *Army Group. Made up of British and Canadian (Second Army and 1st Canadian)*

Kitty decided when she returned to St Mawgan, she would ask John for help finding where the 21st group were based; in the meantime, she had to look for Meryn. Pots and Wenna were sitting chatting over a cup of tea in the kitchen when she walked through the door.

'Hello, you two. Have either of you seen her ladyship today?' she asked, as she poured herself a cup.

'Thought she was with you,' Pots replied.

'I went down to the beach where they are all headed,' Kitty pointed outside at the endless stream of soldiers still walking down the hill, 'and left a message for her to be sent back this way should she show up asking for Bobby.'

Kitty sat at the table and sliced a chunk of bread from the loaf sitting to one side.

'I'm starving. When I realised she had gone, I went straight out to look for her without eating breakfast.' She reached for the pot of blackberry jam and dropped a spoonful on top of the bread and smeared it across before taking a bite. She winced at its tartness. The days of sweet jam had disappeared with the harsh rationing of so many food items.

'She'll come back, I'm sure, when she realises she can't see him. We all know that's what she's trying to do, so let's go about our day and wait.' Wenna rose to her feet as she spoke. 'She'll soon get hungry.'

Both Kitty and Pots agreed and watched Wenna grab bags of flour down from a shelf. It was their cue to clear the table.

'I'll turn over the empty summer vegetable patch and drop a bit of compost around. Keep the windows shut, I've a good drop of steaming stuff from the ragman's horse today.' Pots laughed and grabbed a fresh scrubbed carrot from the pile on the table, putting his finger to his lips for Kitty to not let on to Wenna, who had her back to them preparing for the morning's baking.

'I'll go and see if I can find her in Trebah Gardens, Wenna. I think it's where I'd go if I wanted to think or have a good cry. I must try and persuade her to come back with me on the early bus tomorrow and wish me luck. I'm a bit uneasy about this Bobby business. Even Eli has not shown his face again. She was quite tearful last night – I did get a hug from her, though, so she's not overly angry with us,' Kitty said as she pulled on her coat and stepped outside again.

After an hour of searching the gardens, Kitty decided to give up and look elsewhere; she eventually found Meryn walking away from Blackberry Lane with her face flushed, suggesting it was more than pink from the cool wind.

She stopped in her tracks when she saw Kitty and hesitated. She gave her head a slight turn over her shoulder but swiftly faced front to Kitty, who, now fully aware Bobby must be nearby, stepped into her pathway and gave Meryn a soft smile to prevent her from running. She also spoke louder than necessary when she addressed Meryn, purely for the benefit of the man who she was convinced was hiding in the bushes.

'I think I can guess who you've been walking out with, Meryn. If he can hear me, he had better show his face as I am also sure walking out is a polite term for what he has in mind.'

Meryn stared at her with anger twisting her face. She waved her hands for Kitty to step aside, but Kitty stood her ground. She found it unbelievable she had the courage to fight for Meryn's honour. The Kitty who left home three years previously would have stepped to one side through lack of confidence and knowledge of what life can throw at you. For once, Kitty felt like the adult in the situation.

'No, Meryn. I will not leave. I think you are being led astray – understand? Please understand.'

Still waving her arms about, to stress Kitty's need to let her past, Meryn added a stomp of her right foot. Kitty pointed to the floor and shook her head. 'No. I will not respond to your tantrum, Meryn. You are not a babe wanting its own way. You are a young girl heading for trouble. And I am not prepared to let that happen." Again, Meryn waved her to one side.

'I will not move, Meryn. I will not allow you to ruin your life.'

A rustle to Kitty's right-hand side told her someone had moved closer and was trying to slide past them unnoticed.

'Bobby, I suggest you come out from there and speak

with me. I need to have a conversation about your intentions with Meryn. Do not think you can slink away.' Kitty kept her voice calm, but added a commanding tone. She kept steady eye contact with Meryn.

Meryn began to walk back where she came from, but Kitty stepped in her path and wagged her finger side to side.

'No. Stay here.' She ensured the words were a command, not a request, by following through with a deep frown and pushing her hands palm down with a forceful gesture towards the ground.

Meryn kicked at the ground in frustration and Kitty felt for her because words must have been flying around inside her head with no opportunity for release. Kitty stroked Meryn's tears away.

'Whoever it is taking advantage of you has to face up to this sneaking around. It's rude and disrespectful.' Kitty dried Meryn's tears and put her hand on her shoulder to try and calm her down.

They stood a while, but no one stepped out from the bushes, and, turning Meryn back to face the inn, Kitty encouraged her along the path. By the time they reached the kitchen door, Kitty felt as if she had stretched her arm muscles in a tug of war, Meryn had resisted and tried to run from her so many times.

As she pushed open the door, Meryn stepped inside first.

'Wenna, don't let her get to the bar door!' Kitty shouted when she felt a slight resistance from Meryn.

With pastry-covered hands, Wenna rushed to the door and stood in Meryn's way.

'Oh no you don't, young lady. I weren't born yesterday.' Wenna stood shaking her head and frowning at Meryn, who tried to tug her to one side.

Kitty went to her and moved her to a chair at the table. 'Sit.'

Meryn obliged and Kitty went to the back door.

'Pots! He's up the lane – it's Bobby, I'm sure of it. He's been sniffing around aga—' Before she could finish, Pots rushed past her carrying his gardening fork.

'Good God, what is the man doing?' Wenna cried out and rushed to the sink. She wiped her hands down her apron and looked over at Meryn. 'Stay there! Both of you!' she shouted and rushed out to follow Pots.

A bemused and frustrated Kitty looked across at Meryn, who had a defiant look on her face. Kitty knew then she planned to run from one door or the other.

'Don't do it, Meryn.'

She pushed the slate and chalk across to her.

'Were you with him all this time?' she asked, thankful Meryn continued to stare at her.

She snatched up the chalk and scribbled so hard it screeched against the slate and Kitty gritted her teeth.

He met me in the gardens. He's on duty.

'I think he's in a lot of trouble for deserting his post then, don't you?' Kitty took the slate and wiped it clean, then pushed it back to Meryn, who dashed out her response, again making the chalk squeal as she wrote.

Everybody thinks we are too young and shouldn't be together.

No one understands us; war made us meet, we can't help coming from different countries.

Kitty took in the words and her heart went out to Meryn. Bobby was like no one she had met before; he showed her attention. Loving someone was not a crime, but she had to ensure Meryn was not mistreated.

'We do understand, Meryn. It will work out in the end. Bobby needs to learn not to sneak about, and you must not give yourself to him so easily. You're not even sixteen. You are far too young – understand?

'We head back to Maude's tomorrow and a little time apart won't hurt you both.' Kitty watched as Meryn was about to write something on the slate and covered her hand with her own to regain her attention. 'If he continues down this path, he will end up in serious trouble, possibly prison, as you are, well, underage. Come back with me and write to him. We can visit again soon, I promise,' Kitty said and gave Meryn a soft smile of reassurance.

Chapter Thirty-One

Patient after patient flowed through the doors and Kitty's legs trembled from exhaustion. A colleague collapsed in tears as she tried to help a young soldier during his last moments. The war was taking a further toll on the medical staff. As much as she felt she should stay on and take on some of the extra workload, Kitty could not wait to finish her shift; she needed rest and food. Tom was picking her up from the camp and under Maude's instructions she was to eat and stay with them overnight.

Before she left, Kitty took a stroll to the post room before meeting Tom. John gave her a wide grin when she walked towards him, and he handed her a small batch of letters.

'I've a bit of news. I've heard there's a Canadian doctor training orderlies and other medics in Scotland; a place called Peebles. I'm waiting for confirmation, which my friend will bring with him tomorrow evening, and I'll leave you a message at the front gate.' He smiled with satisfaction when Kitty gave a whoop of delight. 'Now, I'm not saying it's your man, but it's the most positive news we've had so far, right?'

Kitty gave an enthusiastic nod. 'I'm so grateful to you, John. The last lead was a dead end, as you know, and I'm beyond being patient for Michael to turn up here. I'll be here waiting for news the minute I return, John. Brace yourself.' Kitty grinned as she put her post in her bag and walked towards the front entrance.

John gave a hearty laugh and waved her on her way.

When Kitty walked into Maude's kitchen, she sensed an atmosphere. Tom warned her there was a problem with Meryn and they'd had to collect her from the bus stop after she stormed out of the house. What surprised them was the fact that she was not going to Mawnan Smith, but waiting for the bus heading out of Cornwall.

'You look done in, girl, sit down and drink this. Nettle tea with a little honey. We've used our tea allowance for the week,' Maude said as Kitty put down her bags.

'Well, it's your lucky day, Maude. I've brought a few treats from grateful families. We shared them around the staff and patients. I'm the lucky recipient of a packet of tea, which is now yours, and...' Kitty placed the tea on the table along with a small, wrapped package – 'honey biscuits – eight of them.'

Maude clapped her hands together with sheer delight and pulled out a pretty plate to display four of the biscuits and sat them in the centre of the table.

'What a pretty picture they make – what a treat, thank you, Kitty.'

Tom joined them and tugged off his gardening boots. He

laid a lettuce, potatoes and a few radishes on the draining board. 'There's a few more potatoes but I'll leave them for another day. These will make a meal with the fish old Jack dropped off this morning. Ooh, what have we here?' he asked, eyeing up the biscuits.

'A present from Kitty – and tea!' Maude replied. 'And you will leave them well alone until Meryn comes downstairs.'

Maude rinsed the salad items in water and dried her hands on her pinafore when Meryn entered the room. Kitty looked up and gave the girl a smile, but did not receive one in return. Meryn slumped into a chair.

'As you can see, someone is not happy. She refuses to communicate, and we are at our wits' end. She's run off twice now and Tom can't use his petrol on a girl with a tantrum. He's going to have to donate his van to the ambulance service and use his bike again now he has retired and no longer gets a petrol allowance from his company,' Maude said, pouring Tom a fresh brew.

With no eye contact, Meryn reached out for a teacup and pushed it towards Maude. Her behaviour angered Kitty, and she snatched the cup away in the hope of gaining Meryn's attention, but Meryn pushed back her chair and left the room.

'What's got into her? She's never rude like this.'

'Been like this for a week. We can't keep running after her and Maude is finding it quite difficult, if I'm honest,' Tom said and bit into a biscuit Maude placed in front of him, grunting with pleasure.

'I'm grateful to you both, but she can't stay here and

treat you like this. Bear with me and I'll make arrangements for her to go back home. I'll head upstairs and find out what is going on with her, but I've a feeling it has something to do with a certain American soldier.'

Upstairs in the room opposite her own, Kitty heard drawers banging shut. She stepped into Meryn's room and saw her pushing her belongings into her suitcase. She looked up at Kitty with a face filled with defiance.

'Explain yourself, Meryn Tremayne! How dare you be so rude to them and treat such a lovely couple so badly. And why were you trying to leave Cornwall? I know you were, but am trying to work out why.' Kitty knew the volume in her voice was wasted on Meryn, but it felt right to express her anger.

Meryn made no attempt to respond to her and continued to pack her case.

Kitty slumped onto the bed and put her head in her hands. She was far too tired to deal with the situation and could no longer find a way to get through to Meryn. She sat contemplating her options and decided it was time for Meryn to go back to Mawnan Smith and lead whatever life she felt suited her and suffer the consequences.

A gentle tap on the back of her hand made her jump and she leaned back to see Meryn staring with concern. She opened her arms palms facing the ceiling and moved them from side to side, her face silently asking Kitty what the problem was.

Kitty sighed, stood up and smoothed the eiderdown straight again. She ignored Meryn in much the same way as Meryn had ignored them downstairs. She turned her back and walked out of the door and into her room. She lay down on the bed and allowed peace to creep into her mind. Meryn had to work out for herself the direction she was to take. Kitty needed sleep.

A knock at the door brought Kitty from the deep sleep she had enjoyed. She glanced at her watch and frowned. It had stopped at six o'clock, and she gave it a few twists to set it by the clock on her beside. It was, in fact, five minutes past seven.

'Come in,' she called out and peered outside the window. Daylight flooded the room and Kitty realised it wasn't the evening and she had in fact slept several hours.

A rattle of a cup and saucer told her she needed to help open the door. She placed her feet on the rug and, grabbing her cardigan from the chair, pulled the door open. To her surprise, Meryn stood on the other side with a tray in her hands. She gave Kitty a wan smile and walked to the dressing table, placing the tray on its surface.

Kitty stood with her head down so when Meryn turned around, she was faced with the same situation as Kitty the previous afternoon – disrespect. She was not going to let Meryn off lightly for her rudeness and bringing worries and troubles to Tom and Maude's door.

She felt the light touch of Meryn's hand under her chin and raised her head. Meryn blinked and Kitty spotted the hint of tears. Kitty went to the dresser, poured herself a cup of tea and sat on the chair nearby beside the window. She sipped her drink and placed the cup back on the tray. Still ignoring Meryn and waiting for her to make the first move, Kitty picked up her wash bag, went to the door and opened it, but she was prevented from leaving when Meryn's hand covered the handle, and she shook her head.

'I've had a good sleep. I do not want any more drama, Meryn. Do what you want, I'm past caring.' Kitty removed Meryn's hand from the door handle and waited for her to step to one side.

Another shake of Meryn's head irritated Kitty and she tugged the door wide open and went out into the hallway with the intention of using the bathroom, but Meryn tugged at her cardigan. Turning around, Kitty saw the distraught look on Meryn's face and softened the irritation on her own.

'It's not pleasant being ignored, is it? Not when you do it to hurt someone who wants to help.' She eased her way back into the room, facing Meryn.

Meryn shifted from one foot to another and Kitty gave her a puzzled frown and opened a hand to invite Meryn to explain. From her dress pocket, Meryn pulled out a pencil and paper. She hesitated, and Kitty waited patiently to read an apology. She was taken aback when Meryn threw down the paper and followed through by throwing the pencil forcefully across the room. Kitty glanced down as the missile hit the floor and then turned her attention back to Meryn. Tears cascaded down her friend's face and she made no attempt to stem the flow. Kitty refrained from rushing to her and taking her into her arms; it was time to show tough love. She waited until Meryn had dried her tears and looked at her again.

Kitty gave a terse nod. 'No more tears. You must apologise to Tom and Maude,' she said.

Meryn picked up the pad and pencil from where they

landed and walked to the dressing table, while Kitty waited once again for a written apology. Meryn handed her the paper and Kitty read her words. When she looked up from reading, Meryn was standing straight-backed with her arms to her side, her hands gripped into fists.

Kitty looked at the paper, then back to Meryn.

'Are you sure?' she whispered.

Meryn's head bobbed up and down before she covered her face with her hands.

I think I might be pregnant were the last words Kitty had expected to read, and her mind went blank. This was a serious situation and one she was not sure she could handle alone. Confiding in Wenna and Pots would bring embarrassment to Meryn once the village learned of the situation, and Meryn could not bring up a baby alone.

Uncovering Meryn's face, she asked her how many weeks and Meryn held up both hands, all fingers spread out.

'Ten weeks. Did anyone teach you about the dangers of getting pregnant so young?' Kitty asked her as she realised being brought up by Pots would not have involved a discussion about the birds and the bees.

[display text]

Belle told me I was to have a good time as life was short. I'm not married. I didn't think it could happen if you weren't married.

[display text ends]

Belle. Kitty cursed her name inwardly. She might well have offered advice to have fun, but it most certainly made a naive young girl curious. No doubt Belle made it all sound fun and glamorous, never outlining the consequences.

'Go back downstairs, let me wash and dress,' she said.

Giving herself time to think, Kitty had a strip-wash and sat by the window for a short time before heading downstairs. She could not imagine being nearly sixteen and pregnant. Or deaf with a child. Meryn's only income was pocket money from the inn, which Pots sent her each week, and he paid Tom and Maude for her keep. Kitty knew Meryn would find life hard with no husband to support her. She thought about ways in which she could get her friend help.

Kitty pondered on making up a story to gain compassionate leave and taking Meryn to her aunt for help, but decided it would be far too much of a burden to drop in their laps, and dishonest. She knew Wenna would protect Meryn, and they needed to find out the intentions of Bobby. Another serious discussion with Meryn was on the table and Kitty decided it was easier to work several heavy nursing shifts than face the next drama Meryn brought her way.

Keeping the conversation light in the house and asking Maude to give Meryn something to keep her occupied whilst Kitty took a walk, as she needed a little quiet time to herself, Kitty made a call to Wenna at the inn from the telephone box at the end of the village. She explained the situation, asking that Wenna said nothing to Pots. Once she had finished explaining, Wenna said she would collect Meryn the following morning, but agreed for the sake of her reputation she could not stay in the village. Both promised to think of a solution before she arrived.

The horrid atmosphere had left the small home by the time Kitty had returned, and she learned Meryn had apologised to Maude whilst preparing vegetables, and to Tom as she helped fork over a spare bit of ground for planting seed potatoes. During the afternoon Kitty was thrilled to hear Meryn had asked Maude to teach her how to knit. After a teatime meal of baked potato filled with beef dripping, the four sat down by the fire. At nine o'clock, Kitty noticed Meryn looking pale and suggested she had an early night. Neither of them had told their hosts about Meryn's condition.

Kitty followed Meryn upstairs and explained Wenna was coming to fetch her back to Mawnan Smith and she must remain out of sight from the soldiers and from Pots. Wenna was going to tell Pots Meryn had injured her foot and Meryn was to limp when she got off the bus. The story was concocted by Wenna and Kitty for two reasons, to keep Meryn from the bar and from walking around looking for Bobby. Wenna wanted to speak to him alone.

To Kitty's surprise, Meryn agreed to abide by what was asked of her with no arguments. Her face expressed her worries, and Kitty gave her a comforting hug of reassurance that she was not alone.

Kitty waved Meryn and Wenna off and returned to say her goodbyes to Tom and Maude. When she stepped down from the bus, she headed straight for John's hut, but the door was closed. Disappointed, she went to her room to unpack and prepare for duty the following hour. Taking a moment to brush up on a new procedure, Kitty sat on her bed. The words became a blur as her mind switched from Michael to Meryn. In a sudden moment of clarity, Kitty snatched up her pen and writing pad and set out a letter to Trix.

Chapter Thirty-Two

Dear Trix,

Thank you so much for your help. You and Smithy have given me great peace of mind knowing Meryn will have the kindness and support of you both and of your village. I recalled the kindness shown to the girl who moved in with her grandmother, and what with your expertise, I felt this was the right place for her to live, but would have understood if you were to have said no. Wenna and Pots have insisted her name remains on the employee list so she will receive income. They feel Belle underpaid her and overworked her so much that she is owed the salary anyway.

Meryn wrote to me after finding out Bobby was a married man and her words saddened me. She trusted him and allowed herself to love him, thinking she would become his wife. Her mind is troubled by shame, but I have reassured her neither of you are judgemental and she is in safe hands.

My next visit anywhere will have to be to see my aunt and uncle, it is not fair to put off seeing them, although I get the impression I will need an appointment, they are both so busy nowadays, and I'm pleased for them.

I've heard from Jo, and she sends her love. She is extremely happy driving a van filled with doughnuts for American servicemen – who would not be?! I believe she has introduced them to a good old cup of English tea, too!

Michael is still hiding from me, but it is suggested he could be in Peebles, Scotland. When I return from my aunt's, I hope there is more news but from him this time.

The skies have filled with planes recently, and there is a lot of activity all over the base, and a lot of optimism which has brought a bit of light here on my ward. I do not miss the dark days of crawling around the rubble searching for victims, that's for sure. Anyway, I digress, thank you again for offering support to Meryn and allowing me to continue my work without the worries she brought to my door. I feel guilty asking friends to help, but with my duties it is difficult. I truly am grateful.

Much love to you both and stay safe.

Kitty x

'Staff Nurse Pattison, it's good to see you back. How is your family?'

Kitty was taken aback by the friendly address from the senior ward sister when she arrived on duty. She straightened her back and waited for whatever reprimand she was to receive and gave a cautious reply.

'Morning, Sister, thank you and they are well. Extremely well, I'm pleased to say. I've been thoroughly spoiled and am now ready for work to bring me back to earth.'

The sister rose to her feet and clasped her hands in front

of her. Her actions unnerved Kitty and she made a play of adjusting her apron.

'Don't look so nervous, Pattison. I have news. Word got around the camp that you were enquiring after your fiancé, a doctor in the army.' She raised her hand when Kitty went to ask her how she knew. 'Anyway, I have a lot of friends at Peebles, where you thought he might be stationed, and he *is* there. However, he has not been well and suffered malaria – not a pleasant illness, which is why you have not heard from him since the telegram he asked for them to send once he started recovering. As I understand it, he is soon to be discharged ready for duty, so no doubt you will hear from him.'

Kitty put her hands to her mouth to stop her crying out. Michael had been ill, and she could not comfort him. She composed herself; she had seen her colleague dismiss weakness in another nurse and did not want to face a lecture on strength of character.

'Thank you for telling me, Sister. It was kind of you to join in the search, but I didn't realise it was so widely known I was trying to find him,' Kitty said with slight embarrassment, and, as she spoke, she saw the sister through new eyes. Underneath her tough, strict demeanour lay a caring woman who did not ignore the plight of her staff.

'My fiancé never made it back from El Alamein. It was the least I could do,' the sister said with sadness in her voice, dismissing a grateful Kitty with a gentle smile.

'I'll never forget you, John. Or the way you helped me

find Michael,' Kitty said as she sat enjoying a freshly brewed cup of tea with him.

John sat with a goofy grin wide across his face. 'Call me a romantic.'

Kitty laughed. 'Romantic fool.'

John tapped the pack of tea in front of him. 'I'm no fool, I'll do anything for a pack of the black stuff. So, this is the last one we'll enjoy together then?'

Kitty set down her tin mug.

'Probably. I've put in for a transfer to Peebles. My unusual road to becoming a staff nurse with the Red Cross has its rewards. I volunteered at a time when training was offered, I accepted and worked my way through an official training scheme but added to it all with what some would call varied adventures. I've a lot to offer after my rescue missions, too. I've worked on limbless patients and rehabilitation. Gosh, that sounds like rather a boastful statement,' she said and felt her neck flush with embarrassment.

'It's impressive and I hope they offer you a place, Kitty, I really do, but you will be missed,' John said. 'Can I give you a hug?'

Kitty stood up and accepted his embrace. 'I'll write, and you keep me informed about that beautiful son of yours, you hear?'

'Will do, and you take care. Now, go before I cry,' John teased.

Kitty walked away from him knowing with his leave pending and her probable posting, it would be the last time they spoke.

'I'm sorry it isn't Peebles, but at least you will be in Scotland – what, an hour away at the most?' The recruiting officer pulled an apologetic face at Kitty when she arrived with news of the new posting. It had been granted, but Kitty was to return to Buchanan Castle in Drymen. Her disappointment probably showed on her face, but she reminded herself to be grateful she was to be closer to Michael. It had been two weeks since she had heard where he was stationed, and she applied for her transfer the same day.

A call to her aunt and uncle was well received and although disappointed, they understood her dilemma. They made her promise both she and Michael would visit them together once they were able. A promise Kitty was happy to make. Now the guilt of not visiting them and the worries of Meryn were behind her, she could concentrate on Michael and her duties.

Chapter Thirty-Three

The biting November wind cut through Kitty's coat despite its thickness. Her face stung in the lashing rain, and she cursed the bus for being late. Her heart raced with excitement. Today, she and Michael were to meet at his hospital once he finished his final shift of the week. At last, she would feel his arms around her body and enjoy the comforting knowledge that, for now, he was safe. In his note he mentioned exceptional tiredness, but it was to be expected. Kitty wrote back and told him if he wanted to sleep in her arms all day, it was fine with her.

At last, the bus trundled uphill and soon they were on their way. After half an hour, Kitty decided she was on the slowest bus on the planet. The scenery distracted her, and she was in awe of how, even on a bleak day, Scotland looked incredibly beautiful with its breathtaking landscape. With no signposts to guide the enemy, Kitty had no clue where they were, but once the elegant building she was informed was the Peebles Hydro hospital – formerly a hotel

– finally came into view, all she cared about was that she and Michael were yards away from each other. The building was high above a central cascade of attractive garden steps, a magnificent setting, and Kitty imagined ladies in gowns being escorted to the lawn by dapper gents, in the old days.

She returned her focus to meeting Michael. He had instructed her to meet him beside a walled garden to the far right of the hospital grounds, and she made her way guided by his instructions with her heart pounding in anticipation of their first kiss of the day.

An impatient Kitty stood with her back to the wind, huddled against a wall, holding onto her hat with one hand and checking her watch every second with the other, praying Michael would not be late. They had four minutes to go, and her stomach began performing excited flips.

'There she is. There's the girl with a claim to my heart.'

Kitty swung around, all thoughts of holding onto her hat and bag forgotten the moment she heard Michael's voice. He was early and, going by his smile, as keen to see her as she was him. She ran into his arms. His lips came down hard on hers and it was a while before they parted, breathless with longing. They touched each other's faces, taking in the reality that after so long they were together again. Michael smelled just as she remembered, a clean, masculine aroma with hints of the outdoors, and of what she recognised as cigarettes and disinfectant. Nothing overpowering, simply the accumulation of Michael's world during wartime.

She held his face against her neck and guessed he was inhaling the rose perfume she had applied that morning.

Inhaling a memory to take away with him when he left again; she had done the same.

Kitty's stomach dipped at the thought, and she nudged it to the back of her mind as best she could – she could fret over that moment when it arrived. It was time to concentrate on the now. She moved her head as his hands guided her back to his lips for another memory-making moment.

The warmth of his cheeks next to hers brought about a deep sigh of satisfaction. Meryn might have taken the next step of intimacy, but Kitty enjoyed the simplicity and urgency she and Michael shared.

His finger was tracing her jawline and his smile was wide and only for her. The words whispered in her ear were melting her heart; these were tender moments upon which they were building their foundation of true love which Kitty treasured.

Eventually, they pulled apart and to Kitty's surprise the world was dull, grey and windy. When Michael held her, all she saw was bright happiness.

'How are you?' she whispered.

Michael took a step backwards and looked at her from head to toe. She stood still, unembarrassed by her thick coat and stockings. Michael only ever made her feel loved.

'All the better for seeing you again,' he replied.

His face was tired and thinner than when she saw him last, but Kitty only saw the handsome doctor she first met.

'Same here,' she said.

'You did a wonderful thing for me by transferring to Scotland,' Michael said as he picked up her bag.

Kitty linked her arm through his. 'I'd go to the end of the earth for you if I could, my love. But please, only in the summer,' she said with a laugh. 'Now, where can we get out of this wind? My lips will chap, and you won't want to kiss me anymore.'

Michael laughed. 'As if that will ever happen, sweetheart,' he said. He pulled her towards a small hut nearby. He pushed open the door and Kitty peered inside. It was a storage hut for items in need of repair. Michael stepped inside and pulled a bench closer to the entrance.

'Sit inside for a minute,' he instructed. He went outside, and Kitty heard him let out a piercing whistle.

After a while, Kitty heard the hint of a musical sound drifting across the field nearby, lifted on the wind towards them. Curiosity got the better of her and she jumped up from her seat. When Michael stepped in the doorway, he grabbed her hand and took her outside. He pointed towards a group of trees and Kitty could do nothing but stare in wonderment.

Walking towards them was a piper in full Scottish army uniform. His red-checked tartan kilt swung from side to side as he walked and played his bagpipes. Kitty's heart swelled at the scene unfolding before her, the pride in the piper's stance obvious as he came to a standstill and played through the last of the song, a beautiful, strong, haunting tune.

When he finished, he saluted and marched away upright and proud. Kitty had to blink twice to make sure what she had seen was real as he disappeared into the low cloud and mist. She turned to Michael.

'That was beautiful – incredible. He looked so smart. Thank you for arranging for him to play for me,' she said.

Michael kept his eyes focused on the disappearing image of the piper and saluted. Kitty saw the tears in his eyes and realised the piper's tune meant more.

'Tell me about it,' she encouraged with a soft voice.

Michael shook his head – a slow, sad shake.

'Memories. Not very good ones. We met in El Alamein when I relieved a medic in the 51st Highland Division. Mac was injured, but played his pipes to march them forward, until the second bullet put him out of action for weeks. His wounds became septic, and it was thought he would not survive. The troops were incredible in France; so brave. When I met them in North Africa, they had already been through so much, but were strong and determined men. I brought several home, but sadly most didn't survive. Mac did, and we've been friends ever since. He wrote the piece you just heard when he sat beside me through the dark days of malaria. Apparently, I kept calling out your name, and it inspired him. It's our song. He gave it the title "She Rests Within My Heart",' Michael replied, his voice distant and thoughtful.

Kitty sat in silence, allowing Michael's thoughts and feelings to seep from him until he leaned his head against her shoulder and closed his eyes in emotional exhaustion. She looked down at the frown lines burned into his brow and wished she could smooth them away. They had a piece of music, written when he couldn't reach out and touch her, but he'd made sure she felt his love with his gift today. The piper, Mac, received her silent thanks for using his talent and friendship to ensure that Michael's ramblings, during a frightening moment in his life, were a reminder of how strong their love was and that nothing could tear them apart. Michael's breath against her neck sent tender trembles through her body; they might only enjoy snatched hours in the near future, but this was their forever moment.

Chapter Thirty-Four

'I can't believe he did that for you, how romantic,' Sarah gushed as Kitty shared the thrill of seeing her first piper with Michael at her side, and that they had a piece of music dedicated to them both. Sarah was overjoyed when Kitty announced her arrival back in Drymen.

'It was quite something,' Kitty said as she folded linen and passed it to Sarah, who dutifully lined the shelves of the storage cupboard. A mundane job, but one which both were happy to carry out after a long and heart-wrenching shift.

Kitty and Michael were not due to see each other again for two weeks, due to shift patterns colliding, and each time Kitty needed reassurance that two weeks wasn't that long, she took her mind back to the bagpipes on the wind and found the memory soothing.

'Any more news on your family?' she asked Sarah. She realised dwelling on her own happiness or sadness was selfish considering the worrying situation Sarah and her family were dealing with, because of the persecution of the Jewish community.

Sarah sighed and perched on a set of wooden steps, wrapping her thin arms round her body.

'Nothing. Gran's not heard a thing, either. The Channel Isles are completely cut off from help and the situation in Germany for the Jewish people is – well, dire, as you are aware. I doubt my family there are still alive.' Sarah gave a sniff and cuffed away her tears. Kitty touched her arm in comfort and Sarah gave her a smile of thanks. 'I can only hope my extended family in Austria are safe. My transfer request to join the Red Cross was turned down, as you know, and now I'm stuck here – helpless,' she replied.

'Just keep writing to them all. Eventually, I'm sure your loved ones will get your letters. Oh, and keep nagging the Red Cross, they'll soon cotton on you want to join. I'll draft a note of recommendation for you. I'll do it tonight. Right, end of shift. I'm starving,' Kitty said as they stacked the rest of the linen. Once finished, they said their goodbyes to the rest of the staff and walked back to their quarters.

When Kitty worked at the castle previously, she'd nursed Hess when he flew into Scotland to attempt a secret negotiation to agree peace with Great Britain and crashed his plane nearby. Kitty had later learned the man she'd escorted to London was Hitler's right-hand man and often wondered what life might be like had he succeeded in his mission. That time she'd had her own bedroom with easy access to the kitchen, but this time she bunked down with the rest of the nurses. She hankered for the tiny room downstairs again, just for peace and quiet. Each day, regardless of the weather, Kitty and Sarah took a stroll around the grounds and they would often bump into other girls doing the same. The walk would end with long chats and debates, and new friendships formed, but Kitty missed the companionship of Jo. Kitty had written several letters, but not received any replies for a while.

When she wrote to Trix enquiring after Meryn, she had asked if Trix had heard from their friend, but Trix always replied in the negative. She did write uplifting letters about Meryn, about how she'd blossomed and been accepted by the people of the village, who were most excited about a new arrival to boost their community. She'd estimated Meryn's due month as April, and said Meryn was now making small pasties for the bakery. In her own letters to Kitty, Meryn also mentioned that she had been embraced by the community.

Once Kitty had received positive news from the other people in her life, all her worries were now of Jo. For the moment, Michael was within reach, Meryn was settled, as were Trix and Smithy. Her uncle was busy growing food and her aunt enjoyed fussing over her billeted soldiers.

A letter from her friend Stanley, received that morning, touched her heart. He wrote of missing Jenny and the sadness of them all having to leave Fell Hall. He spoke of Kitty's twenty-first birthday picnic and the dreadful bomb incident at Roker. She guessed he was in a melancholy mood when he wrote it and knew she could understand his offloading of emotions without going into a wild panic over him. They had that kind of relationship – a big-brother-and-sister style of caring for each other, no longer nurse and patient or employee, but friends for as long as they had life.

Inside the envelope was a note from the orphans she had cared for, Eric, Peter and David, and a few charcoal drawings of the farm and farm machinery. David showed the most talent out of the three. She missed their cheekiness and ability to hide from her when they all lived at Fell Hall. Her days supervising orphans felt like a lifetime away. She'd loved each child she'd held in her arms during their darkest moments, and some rewarded her with letters or drawings, but getting news from the lads was always a joy.

Dear Kitty,

We miss yoo. The farm is busy, and we arr happy. Stanley is a gud teacher; he comes when he is not finding ways of chasing the enemy by sending pilots to shoot them down. He teaches us to stay safe for attacks and how to help if there is a fire on the farm.

Our new parents are kind. We have a babby sista, Susan. She spits and cries. Sometimes she stinks. We have to be kwiet and mum tells us off if we aint. We have good food and all our vigtables are growin. David fell in a muddy ditch, and three men had to dig him out. He was up to his chin! He stank worser than our sista for days!

We've got six kitens and their mum is a great ratter. Peter keeps the tayls. Eric writ this.

We hope yoo are safe in Skotland.

Bye.

Eric, David, and Peter

Each boy had scribbled his name at the bottom of the letter. Kitty smiled at the scrawl across grubby paper, but knew it was a letter she would treasure for ever. They had come through the horrors of the Roker Beach bombings and had embraced a new life. It was all she had ever wanted for each child in her care. She chuckled over the tail-keeping when she recalled the mouse tail they had tormented her with when they first met. Their lack of schooling showed, but all three would become farmers and prove the enemy couldn't bring them down, regardless of having missed much of their education. Stanley had tried his best, but it was hit and miss lessons when he visited, and the new parents were feeding the country; their days ran into nights, much like her own. Bless them all, they strived forward and had formed a loving unit. Hitler had not banked on the likes of the Gaskin brothers and Eric or the kindness of strangers.

'Interesting?'

A shadow crossed the table and, to her surprise, Michael pulled out a chair opposite her. He leaned on his elbows, staring into her eyes. Being in the canteen meant they could not embrace, and she clamped her hand across her mouth to stop herself squealing with excitement.

'I only came in to see if someone could fetch you from the ward, and here you are, reading love letters,' Michael teased.

'Oh, darling, how wonderful to see you! I'm reading from three little folk I adore, and they have a little sister, Susan. Isn't it wonderful the boys have a new family?'

Michael reached across the table and placed his hand on

hers, then slowly withdrew it before it was noticed. 'Fancy a walk?' he asked, his voice soft and low. His lips were white and tight, his eyes tired and red with strain.

Something in the way he spoke jarred Kitty into a sense of fear. Her throat constricted and although the last dregs of her cup of tea looked inviting, she thought she might choke on them – Michael had new orders, she'd bet her supper on it!

As they walked to the special place they used to meet, behind the room she'd had when she worked at the castle before, the twilight gave it a romantic backdrop and the autumnal air of woodfires and pine trees added to the magical atmosphere, but still Kitty carried with her the sensation of disappointment pending.

'You're leaving, aren't you?' she whispered as she stared into his face, absorbing his features from chiselled jawline to neat eyebrows.

His silence spoke volumes and when he looked to the floor and kicked at a clump of grass, Kitty had her answer.

'When?' she asked, the damp air snatching at her words and sending them skyward on vapour.

'Two days.' Michael's breath joined hers.

'Forty-eight hours. Embarkation leave, I see. It would have been nice to have some notice so we could be together.' Kitty tried not to add bitterness to her words, but she could not hold back her hatred for the army at that point.

'I'm a nomad, just like you,' Michael joked, trying to make light of what he had just told her.

Kitty, at the risk of annoying him, raised her hand high.

'Don't. Don't try and make me feel better with silly jokes. Am I allowed to ask where or is this yet another of their top-secret events?' She bit her tongue when she failed to hold back the sarcasm.

Michael nodded and lifted his head to stare her in the face. Kitty could tell that he wanted to see her reaction to his reply.

'Canada. I'm being shipped over to help train new medics before they come to England. It appears I'm the best candidate. It must be something to do with the accent,' he said with a half-hearted laugh.

Kitty stood with her mouth open; the words she wanted to use would not come.

Eventually the large lump in her throat disappeared and she managed to speak.

'You're going home?' Kitty shivered as the words left her lips. This was it. Canada would seduce her man to stay where the soil touched his birth soul, and the air fed his veins. Home. Never to return to the country he adopted. He was going home.

In that split second, she wanted to despise Canada, to scream at the country for forging a divide between her and Michael, but then he looked at her and she restrained her jealousy. Michael had no say in the matter; it was the army's doing. But once there, if he chose to remain in the place where he was born, she had to accept his choice. Childish reactions and cold indifference were not what he needed right now. He had come with a heavy heart to tell her the news; she had known that from the moment he smiled at her in the canteen.

Trust. She had to trust their love. Not Michael, not herself and certainly not Canada. She had to trust love to find a way to tie them together in a silent victory over distance.

'I'm going to teach in Canada and then return to England when they see fit. We've done this before, Kitty, and we can do it again – until the end. Until we can make a life together.'

Kitty watched Michael as his face twisted with frustration that she might not understand his words, or she might think he was abandoning her. She read it in his eyes. Kitty saw the pleading and concern, the pain and worry, and knew she could not burden him with her fears and neediness.

'Ignore me, I'm jealous of Canada. You've told me so much about it, and I hope we'll get to go together one day.'

They stood there in the cold wind and, when it became too strong, Michael pulled her close. Tight into his chest, strong arms holding her, willing her to trust him.

'And we will. I can't say much, but something big is happening. When it does, it will mean I'll be back in England before next summer. It's a game-changer, or, in the present climate, a life-changing event. That's all I can share with you, sweetheart,' he said and held her tighter to his chest. 'We will have our day – we will, I promise,' he whispered.

'Don't make promises you can't keep. We can't promise each other anything apart from this moment, now. Just hold me, Michael. Take the fear of losing you away,' she begged.

'I have my own fears about losing you, but we have to

hold onto our love for one another. I'm no softie, but when I'm with you my heart melts and my words are only for you, but if I speak, I cannot do this...'

Their kisses became frantic when Michael heard the honk of a truck.

'That's my cue to leave. I'll drop by again tomorrow,' he said and kissed her lips before walking away.

Kitty found a dark corner out of the wind and let her angry tears fall. The war was cruel. She had been promised more of Michael and now he was to be torn away from her yet again. Absence might make the heart grow fonder, but it could not help with healing the pain of waiting for news twenty-four hours a day. The thought of going through it all again broke her. She even doubted that a haunting tune from a set of bagpipes would make her smile any time soon.

Chapter Thirty-Five

Christmas parties filled a gap in the winter months and the American guests were generous with their gifts. Kitty tried hard to enjoy the leisure time, but resented the fact Michael was so far away.

Scotland held beauty for her; freezing weather and a hint of loneliness, although there were so many people nearby. She sat wrapped in warm layers, a pair of fingerless gloves – a knitted gift from her aunt – and her overcoat, staring at an opened parcel from Michael on her bed. It was filled with sweet treats, jams, nylons and perfume. She traced her finger over words written in a loving message that filled Kitty's heart yet at the same time sent warning signals through her mind. Michael was unsettled.

M McCarthy (Medic)

My darling Kitty,

And as Bing Crosby would say, Happy Holiday! Or, in the truly British manner, Merry Christmas, my love.

Enjoy the gifts and know there are kisses packed inside, too. I miss you – miss you so much. My heart feels raw inside.

It's cold here, but the new recruits are willing to work harder in order to stay warm. After 15/16 hours of it, they are too tired to notice anyway.

It is satisfying to see them complete their training and take their place on the ships to Britain. I'm proud to be a Canadian, and get teased for being in the British Army, but it is well meant. I often ponder whether to apply for a transfer into the Canadian forces and be true to my heritage. Those men are heroes. Not that I want to become a hero, I just have a sense of belonging. Being back here has given me time to think about after the war, and I want you to consider starting married life here. We could marry with your family around and then honeymoon here. Food for thought. A few more months in Scotland and you will have adapted to a cold climate enough to cope with a winter in Canada.

I hope you hear from Jo soon. Give my regards to your aunt and uncle.

My love always and for ever.

Michael xx

Kitty reread the letter and let out a sigh.

'Trouble?' Sarah called over from her bed. Kitty smiled at her.

'Not really, it's Michael. I think he is considering finding a way to join the Canadian forces on the medical side, rather than remain in the British Army. The Canadians have kidnapped him,' she added lightly, despite the heaviness she felt inside. She recalled the time she once thought it would be best if Michael was in Canada for his safety, but, having read his letter, she retracted the thought. She wanted another bagpipe moment, another trip to Durham or an adventure to a new place to make memories. Michael in Canada was no longer a good thing in her eyes.

'Do you mean to remain living in Canada after the war? What about you?' Sarah asked, wide-eyed. The rollers in her hair bobbed as she raised herself higher on the bed and made Kitty giggle. However, the giggle threatened to become one she could not control, and she knew it would end in hysterical tears if she was not able to force herself to focus on something other than Michael remaining in Canada.

Taking a deep breath, Kitty responded with a shrug, 'I think he intends for me to join him, after we marry over here. I'm still not going to marry him until the end of this nightmare, so you're stuck with me, and, before you argue, I have chocolate – fancy a piece? But don't go telling the others or there'll be none for another night for you and me,' she said as she broke off a piece and passed it to Sarah, now perched on the end of Kitty's bed. Both savoured the square of creamy chocolate in silence. Once finished, Sarah gave a dramatic sigh. 'I think that was the best part of Christmas for me – that and the tiny slice of Christmas pudding. This war does nothing for a girl with a sweet tooth!'

'Nurse Pattison!'

Kitty looked up at the ward sister waving to attract her attention at the end of the ward. Patients had been arriving steadily all night since a small rescue fleet managed to bring them home from the shores of France.

Kitty washed the blood from her hands and dried them at great speed; the expression on the ward sister's face was one which expected speed and urgency as a response. Kitty wove her way amongst the wounded and the composed staff going about their business. As she moved the length of the Nissen hut, the fresher the air was around her and she took a few gulps before reaching the side of the senior nurse on duty. 'Someone's for it,' the nurse whispered with a wide grin, but before Kitty had the opportunity to give a witty retort, the ward sister called her name again.

'I'm here, Sister,' Kitty said and stood with her back straight and her arms by her side, awaiting instructions.

'Unfortunately, you are relieved of duty, Pattison. Compassionate leave for two weeks has been granted. I'm sorry to say, your uncle telephoned a message to say your aunt passed away this afternoon. Heart attack.'

The ward sister went to walk away, having issued her message, but Kitty broke all rules and grabbed at her arm. The manner in which the woman had delivered the news was dismissive and cold. In Kitty's opinion, the ward sister didn't deem an aunt dying a good enough reason for a nurse to leave her post.

'She was more than an aunt. My parents died when I was tiny. She stepped up as my mother – brought me up as her own,' Kitty replied sharply. All thoughts of breaking rules flew from her mind; the woman was thoughtless and indifferent, and Kitty did not want her to walk away thinking she had performed her duty to its highest standard. The sister turned around and took a moment to absorb Kitty's words.

'My condolences,' she muttered and walked away again.

Not wanting to waste time on someone who gave no thought to another person, Kitty ran to her room and packed her bag. Then she ran to the entrance and begged a lift from the next truck leaving the camp. Fortunately, it was transporting patients to London, and Kitty was able to catch the last train leaving for Colchester. From there she knew Colchester Barracks moved vehicles to and from Parkeston Quay and she would be guaranteed a lift home.

For the entire journey she beat herself up for not visiting sooner. She convinced herself she would have read the signs of her aunt's heart condition. By the time she'd pushed open the back door, her mind was a mess of 'what if's.

Inside the kitchen were two neighbours fussing over her uncle and Kitty dropped her bag, accepted their condolences, and went to him. She saw by the redness of his eyes he had cried, but seeing the four empty bottles of stout sitting next to a whiskey glass filled to the brim, she guessed some of the redness was alcohol induced.

'Uncle. I came as soon as I could,' she said as she put her arms around him.

He gave a grumbling sound in reply and pushed her away.

'She's gone,' he replied and gulped down the amber

liquid in his favourite crystal glass – a gift from Kitty when she earned her first week's wage.

His words hit home. Aunt Lil was gone. All the motherly love and advice Kitty would ever need no longer existed.

'I'm sorry I've not been home for so long,' she whispered, and she hugged him close again. This time he returned the embrace.

Kitty thanked the neighbours, who fussed over her and worried about everything that had landed on her shoulders. She promised them she would cope. They in turn promised to look in on them both in the morning.

Taking the glass from her now snoring uncle's hand, she covered him with a blanket. The house was cold, not as cold as her room in Scotland but enough for her to pull her coat around her. She moved around the house turning out lights and made her way into her old room. It took a while to register it was not the room she left behind. It was the room of a male, and she remembered her aunt's letters telling her of two billeted soldiers living under their roof. Seeing the evidence of hasty packing, she guessed the soldier had left out of respect. She crossed the hallway and noted the same mess and muddle in the other room. Inside her aunt and uncle's bedroom she hesitated; although her aunt was resting at the local undertaker's, Kitty felt her presence in the room. A tear slid down her cheek and she reached out for one of the neat white squares sitting on the dressing table. Fresh handkerchiefs, ironed to perfection, were something her aunt always insisted upon. Nothing had changed, except her aunt had not welcomed her home with loving arms.

'By the time last week was over, I'd cleared everything at his request. I understand his wanting to clear anything which reminds him, but it was a lot for me to do alone. I just hope I made the right choices,' Kitty said to Jo as they walked along the promenade.

Word had filtered through to Jo on her return from Suffolk that Kitty was asking after her and had also lost her aunt. Instead of returning to Bristol for her leave, when Jo found out she was only an hour away from her best friend, she caught the train to Parkeston. Her knock at the door transformed Kitty's miserable world, and within an hour of her being there it had become bearable.

Jo pulled Kitty closer to her side. 'I'm here now, and I will help you both get through the funeral. I noticed a steady flow of widows from the church bringing him food, so don't be getting yourself het up about his well-being,' she said, then called out to a soldier patrolling the beach, 'Is it safe to sit here?' She pointed to a protruding part of the sea wall not covered in barbed wire.

'Only there,' he called back, and both Jo and Kitty sat down with their feet dangling over the wall.

'I'm not sure how he'll cope, Jo. Lil did everything for him,' said Kitty with a sigh.

Jo gave a tut. 'He'll cope better than you think. He didn't have to do anything, but that doesn't mean he can't do for himself. Once he's finished his bottle of drink and has to return to work, he'll slip into a new life. You'll keep in touch with him and your neighbour friends, so if he needs help, they'll let you know.'

Jo jumped down from the wall onto the sand and received a telling-off from the soldier for her effort.

'Climb up the steps, over there,' Kitty said and pointed to a recess where the steps were under the wire. She clambered down from the wall onto the promenade and met Jo at the steps.

'Thanks for coming to help me, Jo. I appreciate it, I truly do. You also made sense. Uncle Frank will find a way. His church companions will be a support, he has the allotment, and if any of the ladies in the street want to take him on, they are rising to a challenge. I'll not stop them.'

Jo picked up Frank's bicycle and made herself comfortable. 'We'll travel together, too. That way you won't have to walk away alone,' she said. 'Last one back makes dinner,' she called over her shoulder as she pedalled away.

'Don't forget I know the shortcuts, clever clogs!'

They cycled back to Parkeston from Dovercourt, and despite arriving at the door a fraction before Jo, Kitty prepared their lunch and extra for the journey back to London and then onto Drymen.

At her uncle's insistence, she accepted his gift of her aunt's few pieces of jewellery, which he must have held back before her arrival, plus Lillian's scarves, gloves and two warm cardigans, also folded and handed to her for her to pack. Frank muttered about making use of gifts he'd once bought his wife, and of how Kitty could do with warmer clothes. She looked at her own cardigans, now worn and slightly discoloured, and agreed with Jo she would be foolish not to accept them. She rolled and crammed them into her kitbag.

Her farewell hug with her uncle lasted a while and when he released her with gentle prompting from Jo, he stared at her for a moment or two before stroking her cheek. A neighbour let herself in as planned, and after reassurances and promises were made, before Kitty knew it, she and Jo were on the train out of town. When they reached London, Kitty broke down and Jo listened to tales of when she was younger and her life with Lil as her aunt and then as her mother substitute. Somewhere on Liverpool Street Station, Kitty closed off a piece of her heart to protect her memories of her Aunt Lillian and prepared herself for the journey back to Scotland. When they were purchasing tickets, Jo insisted on accompanying her, ignoring the argument about where she would stay. Kitty caved in, too fragile to fight. It annoyed her the way her mind played with her ability to deal with whatever came her way. One minute it allowed her tremendous strength and courage – enough to scramble through the wreckage of a collapsed building; the next it brought her to her knees with the stress of worrying about loved ones.

The closer they got to Scotland, the more she realised just how much of a friendship she had with Jo. It went beyond the events which happened in their lives; this was a deeper connection. If ever she had been lucky enough to have a sister, all spats and arguments aside, she would have wanted one like Jo.

'Are you feeling all right? You've a weird look on your face,' Jo asked.

'I was just wondering if I'd thanked you for turning up and helping me – if I haven't then thank you, Jo,' Kitty said.

Jo's face flushed red, and she turned to look out of the soot-smothered window.

'That's what friends do, they look out for each other – and argue,' she replied and turned with a smile and a wink.

Chapter Thirty-Six

The snowfall failed to ease, and Kitty tugged her cardigan close. It was Valentine's Day and a month since her aunt passed. February was always a dismal month, but Kitty refused to be drawn into the miserable state she got herself into when Jo returned to duty. When she watched her friend walk away, a loneliness and a deep sense of foreboding caught up with her. She gave in to it for twenty-four hours before she found reading to patients in her spare time helped stop her mind from wandering.

Today, Kitty also learned Sarah had received the go-ahead for a transfer into the Red Cross and was to report for duty in London. Something she was extremely excited about, having never visited before. When she declared she wanted to see Buckingham Palace and wave to the King, no amount of explaining that the royal family did not walk around the grounds in full view of the public persuaded her that this would not be possible.

Although she would miss Sarah and her quirky ways,

Kitty could only wish her a successful time in the Red Cross and hope she would eventually find a way to reach out to her family. An impromptu send-off left Sarah in tears, and she walked away with more pen pals than she had ever imagined. Kitty recalled the friendless girl who swept the floors with old tealeaves on one of the original POW wards and was touched by how Sarah stepped out of her timid bubble and found the courage to mingle.

Jo wrote often and shared news of antics between her and the American girls she worked alongside. It was good to read something which made her laugh out loud without feeling disloyal to her late aunt. One of their longstanding neighbours telephoned Kitty at an arranged time and reassured her all was well before passing her over to speak with her uncle. He spoke loud and clear and told her all she wanted and needed to know – that he was adjusting and coping.

Trix wrote that she and Meryn were taking a trip to purchase whatever they could from the haberdashery to fashion baby clothes and nappies from a large donated bag of flannel and cotton sheets, and were also altering dresses for Meryn as she expanded rapidly in the latter stages of her pregnancy. Kitty thought of Meryn becoming a mother in approximately two months and of how she would cope. Trix wrote to say Smithy spent more time pulling splinters from his own hands than from those of patients. He was determined to convert an old drawer into a small rocking cradle as a gift for Meryn. Kitty felt a slight twinge of jealousy as she would have loved to be in the thick of the activities preparing Meryn for motherhood, but she could not wait to meet the little one and hand over the delicate shawl she had spent hours knitting from an unravelled cream jumper one of the girls donated to her wool stash, along with bootees, bonnets and pram coats.

Through late February and early March, Kitty's daily routine kept her busy and she had little time for socialising. She studied anything new within the medical world and gained credit for implementing new ideas to help both patient and nurse. Everything she did was to prevent her from overthinking about Michael in Canada.

During a shift she was approached by a junior nurse concerned about her patient, a young man recently returned to England from Italy. His wounds were healing, but his health was in rapid decline, and the young nurse had noticed a rash appearing on his back when she washed him that morning.

Kitty went over to his bed and took one look at the rash. 'Nurse, go and scrub your hands thoroughly then fetch the doctor. Tell him to meet me in the equipment hut. I need to fetch something to help the patient,' she said and ushered the girl away. Once the nurse left the tent, Kitty actioned an orderly to assist her with moving the patient to the end of the ward nearer the entrance and called all nurses around her outside of the tent.

'It appears we have a patient with smallpox. Please scrub and wash all equipment and your hands, then wash your patients before putting them back into fresh bedding. It's a highly contagious disease and we cannot afford for it to spread. I'm meeting the duty doctor and will trust you all to get to work while we make a decision. Any patient with pustule-like spots on the back or anywhere else on the body, move them alongside my patient at the front, please.'

Without waiting for questions, Kitty relied upon her staff to get on with the job in hand and rushed to the equipment storage hut, where a doctor and two orderlies were waiting for her.

'I'm pleased to see you have a few muscles with you,' she said cheerily, when she greeted the doctor.

'I assumed you needed a piece of equipment and my advice as to which sort,' the doctor said. Kitty had never been fond of this particular doctor's pompous manner, but did not have the time to resent his insinuation that she needed his help for something so simple.

'No, doctor, but I do think we will need this hut cleared. I have a case of smallpox.' She needed to get the patient separated from the others.

'I'll check him over before we rush into panic mode, Nurse,' the doctor said and Kitty wanted to swipe the cigarette from his mouth, but instead she inhaled and let out a breath.

'He is in the front bed, left side, hut six,' she said without moving. She was not prepared for him to try and belittle her on the ward, nor did she want to waste time, 'I do need the assistance of the orderlies for another matter, so, if it is all right with you, I'll get them to help whilst you make the diagnosis.'

With a grunt as a reply, the doctor walked away, leaving a trail of smoke as he puffed and walked.

Wasting no time, Kitty set the men to work transferring broken beds to another shed and gave orders for them to set up other beds. They did as she asked and more. They brought with them new recruits and one muttered that they trusted her judgement and understood the urgency.

'Once the doc has seen the patient, he'll rush back, dashing out orders as if he's the one made the find. He doesn't like nurses to make claims they've found something wrong with a patient. He's not a fan of women. He'll ignore you as best he can, I'm certain of it,' one orderly said and, to Kitty's fury, he was correct.

'You said one patient, but your staff informed me they'd noticed four others. I agreed with them and all five will be transferred out of here once the hut is suitable. I see my orderlies have used their initiative and got to work just in case my diagnosis was right, which it is: we have smallpox,' he said and bypassed Kitty without another glance as he barked out the same orders she'd given the men. One of them winked at her as he walked out with an old cabinet.

'We know the truth. Well spotted, nurse – excuse the pun,' he said, laughing as he loaded a truck with the unwanted furniture.

Kitty gave him a smile of thanks.

'It's the patients I'm more concerned about, not his overblown ego,' she replied.

By the end of the shift, Kitty and the doctor found a way to work alongside each other without conflict. At one point he surprised her with a compliment and her quick retort of 'That must have hurt' made him grin. When Matron and her deputies arrived to inspect the hastily put together ward, the final stages of infection control facilities were put in place.

A dedicated team, including Kitty, moved the infected patients into their new accommodation, and received an information lecture on containing the smallpox. Fortunately, no more cases were found in the month Kitty worked on the ward. It saddened her when one patient lost his life. His body had experienced enough with battle damage, so the infection took its toll on what little strength he had left. She was granted a rest day and enjoyed moving back to her sleeping quarters and sleeping on a bed more comfortable than the one she'd slept on for a month at the end of the ward, behind a screen.

As she ate breakfast in the canteen, someone handed her a note instructing her she was to report to the front gate to receive an incoming patient. With such an instruction, Kitty wondered if the smallpox ward was to become a main unit for any cases found outside the army base. She drained the last of her tea and put aside the thought that she might have enjoyed a second cup. She headed up the long driveway, hoping the patient was not too injured and could cope with the added burden of a deadly disease.

As she turned a bend, Kitty could not believe her eyes. Standing at the end of the driveway was Michael. His handsome face beamed back at her, and he held out a small posy. He looked smart in his new uniform. She fought the impulse to run into his arms, but her pace increased.

'So you're the reason I have to report to the front guard room, eh?' she asked with a sloppy salute and a beaming smile.

'I am. It's a fleeting trip to collect much-needed Canadian recruits from the forestry camp nearby, but I have good news,' Michael said as he pulled her into the empty guard room when the guard stepped out and pointed to the space.

They kissed long and hard out of sight before Michael let her go. 'They'll be back for me soon, but here's my news. When I reached Canada, I manoeuvred myself into a position which meant I *had* to return to Cornwall. It appears I'm valuable to a pending mission. As much as I love Canada, I could not bear knowing you were in England, and we were apart yet again. Sweetheart, if I can get you onto a unit – maybe a recovery team-leading post – would you consider it?'

Shock rendered her speechless for a few seconds, and she stared at him in disbelief. When she took in all he said, she was thrilled by his news and grabbed his hands. 'I certainly would!'

Michael gave her another lip-tingling kiss before speaking again.

'Your ability to remain calm is what will be needed for this particular plan. It won't be an easy task and it is one which will throw us both onto the frontline for short trips, but we will be together in some way. What do you think?'

'I think you need to kiss me again. I won't admit to being nervous about the idea of the frontline, but if we can grab more time together, count me in!' Kitty said and enjoyed the many kisses he bestowed on her before his transport arrived to whisk him away as quickly as he had arrived.

On her final day on the ward, Kitty smiled to herself. She had four days' leave and was to spend it with Michael at Trix and Smithy's home before returning to her new posting back in Cornwall. The timing could not have worked out better. Trix telephoned to tell Kitty the good news that Meryn had given birth to a little boy, whom she named Kedrick Gordon Tremayne. It turned out Kedrick was Pots' real name.

Leaving Scotland, Kitty wondered if she would ever return. It was a place which always brought Michael back to her and would have a space in her heart for ever.

Walking up the path to the back door, Kitty and Michael laughed when they heard the cries of a baby and saw Smithy rocking a pram to and fro.

'If either of you know how to get this young man off to sleep, I'd appreciate the help. Trix is assisting Meryn and decided this one need fresh air,' he said, moving the pram faster and faster.

Kitty rushed to peer into the pram and pulled back a blanket from around the Kedrick's mouth. 'He's hot,' she said, peeling away one of the four blankets she found covering him.

'I was instructed he was to be well wrapped against the elements,' Smithy replied, defensively.

'I'll get him out, and maybe he'll cool down a little. It's pleasant enough and not raining,' Kitty said, scooping up the bundle from inside the pram.

Michael laughed. 'As if you needed an excuse to cuddle him. Ah, you have the golden touch,' he said as the noise abated and he turned to Smithy to shake his hand. 'Good to see you, my friend.'

Smithy grinned. 'Likewise. I think I'll take your bag

inside, Kitty, and put the kettle on. You seem to have this baby under control. It's been a noisy household for several hours and my ears need a rest,' he said and beckoned Michael inside. They left Kitty enjoying the pleasurable moment of comforting a now calm Kedrick, suckling on a fist as his eyes drooped into a comfortable sleep.

Chapter Thirty-Seven

Tapping on the bedroom door, Kitty waited for Trix to respond. Kedric gave the first mews of hunger, and she dropped a kiss on his forehead. 'It's been a pleasure meeting you, Mr Kedrick, but cuddle time is over.'

When the door opened, Trix gave Kitty a beaming smile. 'Isn't he gorgeous?' she asked, and Kitty nodded.

'How's Meryn?' she asked as she handed over the now bawling babe.

'Tired. It wasn't an easy delivery, but she coped. It wasn't easy with her not being able to hear me, either. Her tears came when he screwed his little face up and cried. She wrote she wanted to hear him. I was tempted to say, no, she didn't, but refrained from being heartless. It is going to be difficult for her. Ah, she's awake. Go and say hello while I change this one's nappy,' Trix said and left the room.

Meryn greeted Kitty with a loving smile and held out her arms. After they hugged, she grabbed her pen and pad.

Kedrick, my handsome boy. I am lucky he came to me healthy.

'I love his name and, yes, he is a handsome boy. Trix is bustling around like a proud auntie,' Kitty said, holding Meryn's hand.

You are all his family. Our family.

'We are and Wenna is our mother hen,' Kitty said with a laugh.

Trix told me about your aunt. I am sorry for your loss.

'Thank you. Michael is here. He has returned from Canada, which is a wonderful surprise. He asked if he could pay you a visit after you have fed Kedrick,' Kitty said and smiled down at the nodding Meryn. 'I'm very proud of you, Meryn. With Trix's help you will have a happy life here.'

Kitty and Michael took advantage of the warm spring weather and walked Kedrick in his pram whenever they had the opportunity. It gave Smithy and Trix a break. On their second morning, Meryn, still confined to home for her post-delivery rest, pleaded with Trix to let her have a short walk that afternoon, so it was decided they would all venture out for a walk around the block to post letters and allow the village to fuss over her.

'She seems to be returning to good spirits, Trix. No more fretting over Kedrick's dad, I take it?' Kitty asked, nodding towards Meryn walking with Smithy ahead.

Trix manoeuvred the pram down a kerbstone as she shook her head. 'No, thank goodness. She's resigned herself to being a young single mother. Whether Kedrick ever finds out the truth is up to her. It won't come from any of us – on that I promised her,' she said.

'He'll not go without, and she is getting wonderful

support. Thank you so much for taking her in like you did. It was a lot to ask, but I had to house her where I could trust people to understand her needs,' Kitty said with feeling.

'Smithy loves Kedrick, and he looks on Meryn as a little sister, which is nice for them both as they are only children. It has worked out for the best,' Trix replied. 'Right, time for her to rest up again. Can't have her milk drying up. That one in there might look innocent enough, but he's a greedy guzzler,' said Trix, laughing.

Kitty finished cooking their mid-day meal and looked around the large family kitchen. Nappies and baby clothes hung on a wooden airer, Smithy and Michael worked together on a jigsaw depicting horses in a field at dawn, Meryn sat in a large, comfortable armchair darning socks and Trix ironed shirts and baby nightgowns. It was a peaceful scene and Kitty gave a contented sigh.

'Everything all right, old girl?' Smithy asked when he looked over at her. Kitty gave him a little smile, and a shake of her head. 'All is perfect, Smithy. Perfect.'

'Put her on the sofa in the front room. I'll check her blood pressure in there,' Smithy instructed Michael as he carried Trix in from the back garden where she had been draping sheets over the linen line with Kitty on their final day.

Hovering behind Michael, Kitty –anxious and concerned – offered her version of what happened. 'Just as we shook out the large sheet and lifted it, Trix bent down for the peg basket and as I turned to take one from her, her face went a dreadful shade of white and she fainted.'

Smithy lifted out the sphygmomanometer from his

medical bag and focused his attention on his wife. 'Normal,' he said, and Kitty passed him cushions to place under Trix's legs to elevate them.

'I think she's coming round,' Michael said and gave a gentle stroke of Kitty's arm when she walked past him to fetch a glass of water for her friend.

Meryn stood in the kitchen, looking bewildered. She looked to Kedrick's pram and back at Kitty.

'He's not crying. He is looking around and making baby bird noises,' Kitty said to Meryn. 'Watch over him; Trix fainted, and Smithy is with her. I'll take her water and come back,' said Kitty. Meryn gave her a frantic look, then to the front room door.

'She's worn out, but I'll take over and make her rest for a few days. And it is not your fault. Trix always pushes herself too hard,' Kitty reassured her.

Meryn pulled out her pad and pencil from her apron pocket and scribbled out a hasty message.

[display text]

I did the same when I was pregnant with Kedrick. Twice. Do you think Trix has fallen pregnant, too?

[display text ends]

Kitty gave a loud laugh and patted Meryn with her free hand. 'That's it! I bet she's expecting.'

Smithy and Michael turned to look at Kitty when she walked into the room. Trix was sitting with her head between her knees.

'Does the midwife need a diagnosis?' Kitty said with humour.

Trix looked up at her and gave a twisted smile.

'Trix?' Smithy stared at her, waiting for a response.

Kitty burst out laughing. 'Two doctors and a nurse and not one of us thought of it. Meryn made me realise. Did you know, Trix?'

Her friend looked up at her with a dewy look in her eyes, 'I guessed yesterday, but I was going to tell Gordon at the weekend to be on the safe side. I'm nine, ten weeks,' she said.

Smithy leaned down and kissed the top of her head. 'It doesn't matter when you told me, I would be just as overjoyed. Thank you, my darling wife.'

Kitty gave Michael a glance and he walked over to take her hand.

'Congratulations, you two,' he said. 'We will give you privacy.'

'Well done, you two,' whispered Kitty. She saw the love between her friends grow into something even stronger than before and told herself off for envying their future.

'By the time Christmas rolls around, you will have two babies in the house, Smithy. We're off and will leave you with that thought,' Michael joked with his best friend, slapping him on the back whilst Kitty gave Kedrick a last cuddle.

'It will be a lively household, for sure,' Trix said as she entered the room. With relief, Kitty noticed that over the past few days Trix no longer looked as sickly as she had, and Meryn fussed over her as much as Trix had done with her.

'Take care, Trix. Meryn is ready to take over on days when you can't, so don't overdo things. Smithy will keep contact with Michael and let me know how you are getting along. Send letters, but do not leave anything out. I'll miss you, but the moment I am able to get to see you again, I'll be here.'

She embraced her friend and they clung together for a while before Meryn tapped Kitty for her farewell hug.

Once on the train bound for Cornwall, Kitty kept reminding herself it *was* Michael seated in front of her. As soon as the soldier seated beside him asked to be let out into the aisle, Michael shifted to the window seat and Kitty slid into the seat beside him. He placed his arm behind her back, and she snuggled close. As the train chugged and stopped along the way, she wished it would travel for ever so they could share the peace and comfort of each other eternally. The excitement that they were to see each other more made her heart quiver with excitement. At last Kitty had had a weight lifted from her heart and knew she could move forward from her mourning period without feeling guilty. Her Aunt Lil would never have begrudged her a moment of happiness and would be angry if she thought Kitty was suppressing it because of her death.

Chapter Thirty-Eight

When Michael asked Kitty to join him and mentioned that a team of doctors and others in the medical field would also attend the meeting, she was curious and guessed he was going to set up a new rescue squad.

The thought excited her, as it would mean they would have more regular contact. The rescue teams trained together when new ideas or systems were put in place. She longed to join in with the rescues again; people needed and deserved their support when the bombs dropped and took away all they had.

She arrived at the large tent at the base of Trebah Gardens with minutes to spare. When she had received the instructions about where to attend, she had been surprised. The Americans were arriving by their hundreds with heavy equipment, and Kitty's curiosity grew into an understanding of a pending military operation with their allies. Where she came into the equation she was yet to find out. She peered inside the tent and saw Michael reading through papers at the end of the room. She gave him a wave.

'Kitty, you came.' Michael rushed towards her and glanced behind her. 'Quick, kiss me before anyone else arrives.'

With a giggle and a swift glance over her shoulder, Kitty moved into his arms and gave in to his lips without hesitation. A slight movement outside suggested people were heading their way and they ended their embrace and moved apart.

'Morning. At ease and listen carefully,' Michael addressed the room as people stood facing him, standing at attention. Kitty followed suit, although it was not expected of her.

'I have selected you all because of our connections within the medical world in the past. As some of you know, Nurse Kitty Pattison is my fiancée, but from now on I need you all to forget that and look on her as one of the toughest recovery emergency staff I've ever known.'

Kitty felt the eyes of the room upon her and cursed the burning sensation rising from the base of her neck to her forehead. She smiled, then looked at the floor in the hope they would turn their attention back to Michael. Fortunately, they did, and she remained with her head down listening to Michael instructing the group to work in fours. He requested Kitty to join him for special instructions relating to the Red Cross and this created a smattering of suggestive laughter around the room.

'Children, please!' Michael said and followed through with a loud laugh.

Kitty raised her head and joined in with the laughter and wagged her finger at a couple of medics she had worked with before.

In the room she counted twenty-eight people aside from her and Michael. Thirty people in separate teams meant they were to work as recovery staff for a big mission of some kind. She'd done this in the past and was fully aware of the required headcount.

'What's going on, Michael?' she whispered when they were out of earshot of the rest of the team. The room was noisy with chatter as the formations of four were organised.

'I can't tell you, but I do want you on the sidelines with me when we get our orders to go. It's France, that's all I can say. It's going to be tough training, with a PTI.'

Kitty frowned.

'Physical Training Instructor,' Michael explained. 'If you feel you cannot support the unit, don't sign up just for my sake. Leave now. If you do agree, it is a big risk for us both and we might not come out of it alive.'

Kitty's face must have expressed her horror and fear at his words, because Michael took a breath and gave her a soft smile, a smile filled with love, and his eyes stared into hers.

'Yes, I am asking a lot, but we could go under during a rescue, so it's no different, and those men moving into France are in desperate need of being rescued. I haven't a lot of time to explain, but our mission is imperative to assisting the men abroad,' Michael said hastily, glancing at the group awaiting further instruction.

A loud laugh rang out from the other recruits and they both turned their way. Once satisfied no one could hear them still, Kitty spoke. 'France? What on earth? Have the Red Cross approved this? Why me and not your nurses? I can't see any here – why me?' Kitty questioned him with urgency, keeping her voice low.

Michael nodded.

'Listen, Kitty. You are calm when faced with the worst situations. I need someone to help maintain an organised rescue. It's not going to be easy, and I know you will be the best coordinator for our needs once we are back on the water heading home,' he said.

'I don't look for the easy route, and if you feel I will be of use and not a hindrance – and the Red Cross has given its approval – I'll stay and listen.' Kitty rushed her words, knowing Michael needed to speak to the rest of the team.

'That's my girl. After we've done a bit of training, I'll ask you again before I put your name down on the permanent list. Go and join the others and we'll get started,' Michael said and gave her a soft smile.

Waiting for the training to begin, Kitty dropped her guard and allowed her mind to wander back to the day she lost her parents. They took a boat trip with her baby brother while she spent time with her friend at a church fête. She had already enjoyed a boat trip outing with them and asked to be excused knowing there would be other occasions to join them. Her parents loved the water and her father had borrowed a friend's sailing boat for the trips, always vowing to buy one of his own in the future. Kitty was not a fan of sailing so was delighted when they agreed she could join her friend and her parents for the day. When the news broke that she had lost her family when the sailing boat sank, Kitty avoided all journeys by water from that day onwards. Often dreams turned into nightmares in which she had taken the trip and her imagination became the centre for horrific dreams of drowning, only soothed by the loving reassurance of her Aunt Lil.

Hearing Michael's mission news frightened Kitty, but the biggest fear was of stepping onto the vessel and sailing towards their destination. She would opt out of the mission after the training, so that it looked as if she considered herself unable to do the task asked of her, rather than explain what really petrified her.

Michael handed her over to an army physical trainer and the man put her through her paces. Her uniform was replaced with regulation clothing from the British Army, and she was treated as one of the men. They were told the mission was dangerous, essential towards holding off the enemy and winning the war.

Chapter Thirty-Nine

'Tuck and roll – excellent. Now do it with your assigned equipment.'

Kitty groaned inwardly and picked up the large khaki backpack filled with bandages and other medical items. The bruises from three hours of safety training felt as if they had bruises of their own as she rolled with what she considered the elegance of a pig wallowing in mud. Maybe she should opt out before she could no longer move her limbs.

'Pattison, move it. This is not a waltz. Jones, roll forwards! You are a bunch of...'

Kitty shut her ears to whatever he thought they were a bunch of and concentrated on untangling her arms from the backpack and standing up straight without grimacing from the pain in her buttocks.

'Can't take the pace, Pattison?'

Kitty chose to ignore the man goading her to give in – she knew it was his aim and she was only prepared to back down to Michael, who would be more understanding as to her reason.

'No, sir. Just stretching,' she replied and settled into a crouch, slid her arms into the backpack and eased herself back into an upright position. One she sensed she might be in for some time to come, given the soreness of the bruises.

For the next hour every man in the room pushed themselves into achieving what was asked of them, and Kitty opted for no favours. When they were allocated a break she sought out Michael.

'Sir. A word?' she asked him.

Michael gave a brief nod and directed her away from the group he was talking with.

'Kitty, are you—'

'Pattison. K. British Red Cross. Sir,' she said in a firm, clipped voice and stood tall.

Michael gave a small smile.

'You're joining us I take it, K – Pattison,' he said.

Kitty gave a nod. 'Men and women all over the world are overcoming fears and obstacles to bring freedom and peace to Great Britain. I have overcome some of mine and must overcome the rest to become the best I can be. I understand the dangers but want to support you and your men and ensure they get the best care – especially pain relief for bruises,' she said, laughing as she rubbed the top of her thigh.

'Don't tempt me to offer my services to administer a soothing remedy,' Michael said with a saucy grin. 'By the way, can you meet me at The Stargazy tonight? Our instructions are to stay until further orders.'

'Really? Yes, I'm not on duty until tomorrow night. How wonderful. Oh, I think I heard my name yelled out by Sergeant Bullhead,' Kitty said and turned away from Michael to acknowledge the instructor.

'Buldred. His name is Buldred. Go and show them what you are made of, Nurse Pattison,' Michael whispered as she walked away.

Warm sea air caressed her shoulders and Kitty closed her eyes for a few seconds. She eased the war from her mind and imagined the moment in peacetime. Michael stood beside her and imagination took her to another level. Music, a soft romantic tune, filtered around them and rose perfume mingled with the salt of the sea. They were standing in front of the lighthouse along the promenade at Dovercourt Bay – not Cornwall: they were in her hometown. They were married and life was easy, filled with promises of a future family.

'Headache?'

Michael's voice crept into Kitty's dream, and she snapped open her eyes.

'Just thinking,' she said and slipped her hand into his. She'd let down her hair and worn the same peach outfit she had when they did stand by the old lighthouse, the day he surprised her on a home visit.

The comfortable silence cradled them once again and she allowed the moment to drape around her like soft velvet. She rested her head against his shoulder and ignored the voices and machinery on the beach below.

The imaginary music soothed her, and she clung onto Michael, reassured that he was still at her side and this was not a dream within a dream. Would peacetime be like this? Would they be able to shake off the horror of living through such dreadful times? Would they survive?

On the final thought, Kitty gave a small gasp. Michael turned to her and kissed her forehead.

'We'll make it, sweetheart. Together we'll make it,' he said, and it was then Kitty realised he had probably got swept into his own 'what if?' moment.

'Let's sit over there – in the shadows,' Kitty said and encouraged him towards a small mound beneath a tree. A private place for a private moment.

Chapter Forty

Operation Overlord was activated on the sixth of June. On the seventh, Kitty stood waiting in Southampton for instructions to embark on the secret mission she had trained for. While she waited, she ran over in her mind the preparations for extraction from a place they called La Rive Plage in Bernières-sur-Mer, Juno beach.

Her task was to identify fallen soldiers and assess their ability to be rescued. The last stage of the practice run with the Americans in Cornwall was over and now they were deposited onto the quayside of Southampton docks to wait for further orders.

Michael had insisted the rescue crew all had doughnuts before they left, and, as they stood in the queue, Kitty noticed the wording on the blackboard read 'donuts' and pointed it out. Michael explained that it was the American spelling and Kitty had to admit, it was easier to remember how to spell the word. Around them was the sound of upbeat dance music, which helped calm some of the nerves she was experiencing before embarking on what Kitty hoped, and was reassured by Michael, was their one and only trip across the water.

'Michael, there's Jo! Look, she's serving someone at the front,' Kitty exclaimed, pointing ahead of her and frantically waving to her friend while calling her name, but Jo was busy and with the noise around them, there was no chance of Kitty's voice being heard.

Michael put his fingers to his mouth, gave a piercing whistle and called out to Jo, who heard then peered down the queue. Her face beamed from behind the counter. She gave a loud shout of glee when she saw Michael point out that he was standing next to Kitty, and, offering a hasty explanation to her colleagues, she jumped down from the van and hugged them both.

'What a surprise! What are you doing here – in, well, in that get-up?' Jo addressed Kitty.

'Rescue crew with the medics, and I'll have you know my outfit is the latest fashion for my new Red Cross position. I'm heading into the thick of it; I've had training for weeks with the Canadians,' Kitty said. Michael made his excuses and left them chatting.

Kitty linked her arm through Jo's. 'Listen, while Michael's out of earshot, I'll admit to being a bit worried about fate and what it has in store for my future. I need you to hear me out.'

She went on to explain to Jo how nervous she was, not so much of the war raging across the waters, but of the fact that her parents and baby brother had drowned in a boating accident, and she was trying hard not to wonder if it was her destiny, too.

Jo poo-pooed the idea and insisted a doughnut or two would not be her last meal. She went back to the van and returned with a tray piled high with warm doughnuts, coffee and tea for the team, before climbing back on the van and cheering on the other servicemen and women.

The tea was tasty, sweet and hot and Kitty urged herself to stop thinking about what might happen in the next six hours and focus on sitting with Michael, who kept the crew upbeat and prepared. Voices rang out and the music created a strange party atmosphere around the four entertainment and supply trucks. They sat and chatted, walked, stretched their legs and laughed with Jo. Eventually the shout went out for them to leave. A group of American soldiers saluted her as they walked past to embark on their first journey across the water, and Michael said he guessed Jo was letting everyone know there was a Red Cross nurse beneath the black hat and grey blanket draped around her shoulders. Two Canadians took their chances and swooped past, dropping kisses on her cheeks for their good luck. Michael laughed as Kitty relaxed into the moment.

'Be brave, my lovely, and I'll see you when you get home,' Jo whispered into Kitty's ear before pulling away and saluting Michael.

'Bring her home in one piece, sir – and yourself,' she said in a tone Kitty guessed to be humour forced through an emotional barrier – Jo's style of sharing the love she had for them both.

Kitty and Michael walked to a darkened area out of

view and sealed their love with frantic kisses. As they took their places in a waiting landing craft, Michael whispered in her ear as he crouched behind her, 'I'll be right beside you, Kitty. Always. We will do this together and return home together. Just remember all you've been taught. I love you, sweetheart, truly love you.'

The journey across the water was far from pleasant. Landing was horrendous, an experience Kitty never wanted to repeat. The noise grew louder the closer they got, and Kitty watched men struggling in lines to regroup and push themselves forward inland. Michael pointed to the edge of the shoreline. 'We'll get let down as close as they can take us; it will be cold and wet. Make your way to the concrete posts over there and we'll wait it out – dry out. It's sheltered. Sundown is when we take over. Go!' he shouted and everyone did as he asked.

The boat lurched onto the sand beneath, and men scrabbled to the front of the transport. The back dropped down and they rushed forward, dodging enemy fire. Kitty felt the dryness in her throat and gave a small cough. A nudge in her back from Michael told her it was time to run. Her clothing absorbed the water and bogged her down, but she forced her legs to move. High-explosive shells screamed into the sea created fountains of water and soaked them from the head down. Kitty's stomach churned as she waded toward the shore and pushed her way through oil and blood. She could see the concrete posts on the beachhead and pushed her feet across the sand until she reached her destination. All but one of the crew joined them.

Michael had run to their left and she could see him

waving and pointing towards the land beyond the beach, whilst another man also pointed. Eventually, Michael returned to the team and others nearby waiting to assist in the evacuation and shared what he learned.

'By nightfall the majority of the men will have made for a town called Putot, where they will attempt to hold off the Germans heading this way. We'll have to get our patients across to that point over there.' He pointed to a sandier area near the shoreline. 'And carry them to the boat – pair up and plan your direction that way,' he said to a group and pointed to his left. 'The rest of you will attend to the right side. Kitty, Jim, Art and I will do what we've trained for and try and get to those nearer the dunes.'

A soldier stepped forward. 'Sir, I'll take her place. We've just realised she's just a girl, and it's a lot to ask of her, so we...'

Kitty held her breath when she saw Michael's back snap bolt upright and he moved to confront the man.

'Just a girl? I'll tell you now, she's as good as ten men and you're lucky she is on our side. She's a trained member of our team,' Michael snapped back at him.

Unsure whether it was the fading daylight or Michael's ticking off, Kitty noticed the soldier's face pale.

'Thank you for wanting to protect me, but I have had the same training as the rest of the rescue team and I won't hold you back if I can help it,' she said in a gentle tone. She felt for him, as all he wanted to do was protect her – as did Michael, but he wanted to protect her ability to do her job, and for that she loved him even more.

Chapter Forty-One

The wind whipped around the shoreline and darkness settled on the beach. Kitty preferred it to the sights she'd witnessed in daylight. At one point she questioned whether she could continue, but after a long discussion with Michael, all doubts left her mind. If she was to die, it would be for the freedom of Great Britain – if not, she would have succeeded in saving many lives.

The cries of men calling for help added to the hideous atmosphere and intensified Kitty's nerves. She shuddered; it was a place of chaos and death. Terrified yet determined, she crawled along the damp sand in a khaki siren suit with her hair stuffed inside a black knitted fisherman's hat. When Michael gave the command for them to move forward towards the dunes, shellfire lit their way and they scrambled to retrieve as many men as they could.

'See anything?' Michael whispered from her right.

'A black mound at eleven o'clock. I'm going over…'

Wiggling on her front and trying desperately to suppress

the fear raging around her body, she silently thanked Michael for not holding her back. He showed confidence in her and gave her professional ability respect. As she edged her way through the rough grass, Kitty flinched each time she heard a shot. Even the tough training alongside Michael and the rescue crew had not prepared her for the reality of war. Could anything?

Kitty and another member of the crew carried stretchers back and forth, whilst Michael and other medics tended to the wounded before giving the instruction to load them onto the waiting vessels.

When they neared enemy territory, the order was to go low to the ground and issue morphine to those unable to move without pain. Kitty counted out their supplies and estimated the number of patients they would be able to help through medication.

A noise caught her attention, and she recognised the cry for help. Michael arrived with a fresh batch of medical supplies and dropped to the ground beside her, and once they had identified where the sound was coming from, Kitty made her move. Not far from the black mound she had spotted, between her and Michael, Kitty stopped belly-crawling and moved onto her knees. The blood pounded in her ears, and she willed her body on; someone needed her help.

Satisfied the soldier was sedated enough for them to move him back across the dunes, Kitty and Michael moved as fast as the ground would allow. Enemy fire was relentless, and both were exhausted. Kitty could see the haze of dawn as the sun attempted to lift itself lazily above the clouds, and as it did it highlighted men's bodies and large pieces of machinery scattered around them.

Carnage.

The choppy water made loading patients hard and Kitty tried to register where on her body she didn't feel pain. When no one was looking, she allowed sadness to wash over her as they made headway back to England. Thousands of men still needed rescuing, but her time was done; she had to concentrate on those they had managed to save.

Kitty noted how much quieter it was on British soil compared to the ear-pounding sounds they'd left behind. The stench of smoke, oil, gunpowder, blood and guts stayed with her as she stripped off her clothing and took a brief washdown in a makeshift shower unit put together by the Americans. Her crew and Michael were already eating in the food marquee. She dried herself off and dressed, not wanting to miss a moment with Michael.

As she walked through the entrance, a round of applause was directed her way from the men she'd worked alongside, and she felt the blush burn her cheeks. Michael beamed at her from his seat. He no longer looked beaten down and filthy; his hair was groomed and sat neatly around his ears, his face clean-shaven, and she wanted to sit with him, hold hands and kiss their distress away. She was briefed for one rescue; he was to return that following afternoon. She had to nurse the men she had brought back with her, but now she knew what was happening on the other side, she wanted to return time and time again. She was fearful for Michael's safety, but had her orders. It was not her place to question them. Kitty also knew she could not show Michael how worried she was; he needed her to be strong to deal with treating his fellow Canadians.

'Hello, you,' she whispered. She discreetly brushed his hand, dangling beside his seat, as she walked behind his chair. Some of the men did not know their relationship and she wanted to show Michael the respect he deserved.

'Sir, how many did we manage to bring home?' she asked as she sat opposite him.

'We totted up a hundred and thirty-nine between us. One hundred and thirty-six survived the journey back,' Michael replied. He raised his glass of water as a toast to the table.

A soldier stood up and turned to Kitty. 'Sir, I'd like to retract my "just a girl" knee-jerk reaction. Nurse Pattison, I take my hat off and salute you for your actions out there.'

Kitty's blush burned as she smiled her thanks around the table.

'We had a job to do and did it. I'm proud of us all, but thank you for retracting the "just a girl" bit. I'm a Red Cross nurse who had her eyes opened and worked alongside an incredible crew. Now, if you will excuse me—' She stopped as they all stood up. 'I'm going to see an old friend and reassure her I'm in one piece. Sir, I also need to hand over my final patient,' Kitty said as she addressed Michael, hoping he would get the hint for him to follow.

He did, and they found a dark corner to embrace.

'It was hell,' she said, 'wanting you to hold me, wanting to comfort you when I saw you struggle, and wanting to carry as many as I could to bring them home – even the bodies. What a nightmare,' Kitty sobbed into Michael's shoulder as he held her tight.

'We have to get this war finished, Kitty. Those men do not deserve to die for nothing. I have to go back; you understand that, don't you, darling?' He spoke softly, but with determination.

'I do. I can't. No matter how I try to tell myself it is my duty, my job, I just need to be released, Michael. Put me on the receiving post, I'll give the men my best care from there,' Kitty begged.

'I'll sign you off, my love. I cannot put you through it again. I was – am – angry with myself for putting you through it and being selfish wanting you by my side. I did not expect that kind of attack, or I would never have suggested the move. Forgive me?' Michael asked.

'There's nothing to forgive. I agreed to the assignment. I understand the war is raging around the area but, like you, never expected to walk into hell on earth. Let's find Jo. I'm quite taken by those doughnuts, and a hot cup of tea with flavour is not to be missed,' Kitty said and planted a kiss on his lips.

'The great British cup of tea, where would we be without it?' Michael quipped.

'Crying in a cup of acorn coffee, no doubt,' Kitty said and laughed. Humour was their saviour in that moment, and they discreetly left their quiet corner and headed for Jo's van.

Chapter Forty-Two

A few hours later, Michael broke the news that he and the remainder of the rescue team were heading back to French shores.

The pain of him leaving, knowing what was on the other side, broke Kitty down into tears and she pleaded with him to find work elsewhere. She knew it was selfish of her, but the darkness of what they'd witnessed had brought a veil of helplessness and added fear of death to her door.

When Michael returned from his fourth rescue mission, it was no longer as an exhausted man demanding tea and discreet kisses away from prying eyes. Instead, he returned as a severely injured patient.

The shock Kitty felt when she heard her name called and was faced with Michael on a stretcher was soon pushed to one side. She moved into action, suppressing the urge to scoop him into her arms.

'Get him straight onto the table!' she called out to the

orderlies carrying him inside. Once he was on the table she opened his uniform where blood seeped through and was faced with severe bleeding from a bullet wound to the chest. She added compression bandages to stem the flow.

'He hit his head,' said one of his colleagues, standing nearby. Kitty gave him a swift glance of thanks and placed her hand near another pool of blood on the table.

A doctor came to her side when she called out for assistance. 'Hmm, not good. Nasty head injury. Bullet wound clean?' he said, his voice clipped and precise.

'Yes, Doctor.' Kitty's voice was barely a whisper.

'Speak up. Don't mumble,' the doctor grunted at her.

'I'm sorry. It's just that, well, he's my fiancé,' she said much louder and in a controlled voice. She could not let her emotions get the better of her and she needed to remain close to Michael. 'It was a shock at first, but I'm dealing with it, and yes, his chest wound is clear. I am concerned about his head though,' she replied.

'So you should be,' the doctor replied bluntly and motioned to the orderlies to turn Michael onto his front.

'The wound is deep – not good. Not good at all. Patch him up and keep regular observations going, nurse. Steel yourself for the worst. I'll give him ten hours maximum – his mind has switched itself off. Do your best but you realise his war is over don't you? Keep it professional.'

Kitty stared at the doctor's back in disbelief as he walked away. He made her so angry, not so much with his blunt manner – she knew he had to stay in control too – but more by the way he gave her the stark news Michael might not live, knowing he was her fiancé. Back on the ward, the orderlies had placed Michael in a corner bed with a screen around him. She was touched by their thoughtfulness.

Four of his colleagues arrived to check on him, and she learned Michael had saved them by distracting the enemy tucked into a concrete bunker in front of them on the dunes. He placed himself between them and the enemy, giving them time to run for the boats waiting on the shore. One of the men said he turned just in time to see Michael fall back onto the rocks. If he hadn't, Michael would still be lying on the beach.

'It's a good job you weren't there, Kitty. We know you well enough to know you would have put yourself in danger by going to him. He's in your care now, but in a better place. Keep us updated. We have to go – there are more like him out there,' one of his men said, and Kitty expressed her gratitude by embracing them.

'I wish I could help them all,' she whispered as they marched away.

Her remaining shift and the night were the longest she'd ever known. She spent hours whispering to him, willing him to live. Wiping his brow with a cool cloth, to alleviate a slight temperature, Kitty glanced at the clock. It was four in the morning; Michael had survived ten hours more than the doctor had anticipated.

'Come back to me, darling. Don't leave me. You've come so far, keep fighting.'

'He's a fighter, for sure,' one of the orderlies said as he handed her a cup of Bovril in the early hours of the morning.

'I hope he fights harder,' replied Kitty. 'I can't imagine

life without him – even when we are not together he's always on my mind.'

'Same for me and my missus. If Michael rallies round and is moved, just think of him fighting somewhere – make it normal. My June pretends I am visiting my family in Ireland – she's a funny thing, but if it helps her cope…'

Kitty gave him a smile, but she doubted she would ever be able to pretend Michael was well when he wasn't – plus, she didn't want to think about being apart. She gave his hand a squeeze.

'Come on, Michael, it's nearly dawn. Wake up, sleepyhead. Just wake up.'

Michael was unconscious for over a week, but when he came around Kitty understood the doctor's words when he said the war was over for Michael.

When they got him out of bed for the first time, Michael sat with no expression on his face, even when she spoke to him and reminded him who she was and what he meant to her. He was lifeless behind the eyes and Kitty's heart was torn in two.

Her workload with other patients ate away at her. She wanted to spend all her days at Michael's side, for she didn't know how long he had to live. Kitty was fortunate enough to be able to organise her work rotation to spend as many shifts as possible without tiring herself too much, but even on her time off she sat holding his hand. She spoke with his men and asked them as a favour to get in touch with Jo and let her know the news. A week later, Jo arrived on a forty-eight-hour compassionate leave, stating she'd claimed Michael was her brother.

'I'm so angry, Jo. I hate so many people right now it turns my stomach. I've become resentful of other patients taking up my time.'

'You are not a bitter person, Kitty. Don't let the enemy turn you into one. *Please*, calm down and focus on Michael. Get yourself transferred to care for him – pull strings and beg, but don't go down this road of self-destruction. You will collapse and be of no help. We're worried about you, my lovely. I spoke to Smithy and Trix and they've said the same. Your calls to them are upsetting. This is not you. Come back to us, Kitty,' Jo pleaded when Kitty fired every ounce of anger her way.

Eventually, Kitty found a moment of calm and heeded her friend's words. The love and kindness shown to her and Michael could not be disrespected with hostile actions and verbal tantrums. Neither would mend his injuries; only her actions and those of the medical team attending him could pull him through.

'He's looking well,' Jo said as Kitty passed Michael a newspaper. He didn't move to take it from her, but simply sat staring into the distance.

'It's going to be hard bringing him back, Jo. The doctor declared the shock of what Michael witnessed, then the traumatic head injury – it switched off Michael's mind and he appeared to have shut out the world – including me.'

'Just keep being you, Kitty, and find the fire in your belly. If anyone can bring him back from the brink, you can,' Jo said and gave Kitty a gentle pat on her shoulder.

'I hope you are right, Jo. It all feels helpless at the moment. *I* feel helpless.'

• • •

When the doctor gave the go-ahead for Michael to go home, and declared him a lucky man, a senior medic who'd stepped into Michael's role arranged for Kitty to escort him back to base. He wrote to the Red Cross that Michael needed consistency and a voice he would recognise to help return him to a healthy state. No one questioned his request, and Michael was allocated billeted quarters, with a room for Kitty, in a village not far from Mawnan Smith.

Wenna and Pots volunteered their support and Jo visited whenever she was able. Although the situation went against regimental regulations, the powers that be showed no sustained interest in an injured medic off base with a Red Cross nurse as his medical support.

Kitty telephoned Smithy and he promised to visit when he could. He reassured her all was well in his household, and she was not to worry. Her uncle said the same about his situation, hinting that he had a deepening friendship with their widowed neighbour.

'He's still not spoken and moves like a babe sleepwalking,' Kitty said to Jo as she laid a blanket across Michael's knees.

'The Red Cross came up trumps by agreeing to this; it must have taken a load off your mind,' said Jo, sitting down opposite Michael.

Kitty took the opportunity to sit for a while and nodded in agreement. 'I am lucky, although I am due a visit this afternoon. I think it is to check all is as it should be. We've got a plan to show them it is, though. Pots will sit with playing cards laid out in front of Michael, Wenna will close early and arrive with pasties as if it is a normal day, and I'll be washing out his bandages and hanging them on the airer. We need to show them Michael is in capable hands, and his environment is still beneficial to his medical needs. Which it is – in my humble opinion, anyway.'

Jo walked over to Michael and opened the newspaper. 'Oh, it's an old one. I thought it odd when I saw El Alamein on the front page,' she said, placing it back into Michael's lap.

Kitty gave a sigh. 'Pots dug it out for me. I daren't let him see the latest ones, but thought casting his mind back might help. I'm at a loss as to what else to do apart from pray he comes through this, and it is not permanent. It's heartbreaking, but I have to separate myself from my feelings for him as Michael and treat him with care and respect as an army medic. The same respect he showed me during my stint in Rescue,' she said and rose from her chair to straighten Michael's blanket.

'We're heading off in the morning. I'll let you know where we end up, but take care, Kitty. Make sure you rest, too,' Jo said, her voice gruff with emotion. 'All this moving about between us gets confusing, but so long as we find each other again, that's the important thing.'

'So, in three weeks has there been any change, Nurse Pattison?'

Michael's doctor had requested an appointment on base and one of the rescue crew picked them up and took them there. Kitty's stomach tied in knots and hoped Michael would not be taken to a rehabilitation unit somewhere across the country, especially when the Red Cross agreed she could continue with his care.

'He did show a hint of interest in a superhero Canadian comic one of the men brought him yesterday. I read some of the stories to him last night, and he gave a smile before falling asleep. Something registered. I kept telling him it was a Canadian one as opposed to a British one. He's also taken to holding a maple leaf embroidery I made for him. At first, I was keen on pushing anything Canadian his way due to the trauma, but I am now wondering if it is helping. All I need is a few weeks and I think he'll rally round,' Kitty said, rushing her words, not wanting to be interrupted as the doctor was often apt to do whenever she'd spoken to him in the past.

'I see. Well, we'll give the situation another two weeks, but after that if there is no improvement in the mind, he'll have to be retired out. Shame, he's a good doctor and his skills will go to waste thanks to this unforgiving war. I take it the RC are happy for you to continue on a one-to-one basis?' the doctor asked.

'No one has objecte and I'm not sure they can keep up with where they send me and what they ask of me, so I assume yes,' Kitty said with a slight shrug.

The doctor wrote something down in Michael's notes, and then looked up at her.

'Devotion to duty is an admirable thing. I heard what you both did over there, Pattison. I'll keep the recommended medical care going, as I said, for two weeks. We can't give up on the man,' he said.

Kitty adjusted Michael's wheelchair and turned it around, then turned back to the doctor.

'No, we can't – and I won't,' she replied.

Chapter Forty-Three

'Remember the cathedral, Michael? The days we spent relaxing together. Durham, it's our special place,' Kitty spoke encouragingly as she pointed to the map in front of her and Michael. 'The bed and breakfast was here, along this road.' She traced her finger along the line on the childlike map of England she'd drawn. As she did so, she lifted Michael's and placed his finger beside hers. 'We went together, remember? Here is Scotland – where you proposed. Look, my ring is on this chain,' Kitty lifted the pretty jade ring from its resting place. 'Canadian Jade. A family heirloom.'

Michael simply stared at the ring.

'Canada.'

The word hit Kitty hard; it was the first he had spoken since being shot.

'Yes, your home. One day we are going together, just like you promised,' she said and pulled out an encyclopaedia with a world map from the shelf. 'Here's Toronto and

Vancouver. You've mentioned them before. Remember when we met you told me there is a Harwich in Canada, and other English names connected to my hometown?'

Kitty folded her hand over his. Michael's was cold and Kitty turned hers over and clasped his hand. She looked deeply into his eyes and smiled. 'Do you remember Canada?' she asked, her voice trembling.

'I'm Kitty, Michael. Come back to me. It is safe now. You've rescued them and brought them home. We're alone, my love. Listen. It is so quiet.'

'Canada?' he repeated.

'No. England. Cornwall,' Kitty said and squeezed his hand. 'We will have visitors soon, and they will take you away from me, Michael. I need you to focus and not shut us out. The doctors have given me two weeks with you and then they are taking you away – they'll strip away your right to practise, too. Michael, it is important you understand. Tell me you understand,' Kitty pleaded with him.

Michael made no reaction. She dropped a kiss on his cheek, but he made no move to return one. Kitty refused to give up on him; her man was still inside a shell of shock, clinging onto a sliver of sanity, and she would do all it took to bring him out to see the sunshine once again.

'I'm grateful to you, Jo. I do need a short break,' Kitty said as she pushed her arms into her cardigan and picked up her handbag. It was the final few days before Michael's assessment and she needed to step away from the thought for a few hours.

A trip to Truro for toiletries and other necessary items

would not be easy with Michael. The queues were always long and slow, so leaving Michael unattended at home was not an option. When Jo offered a few hours, Kitty did not hesitate to say yes.

'Go. He'll be fine with me, you know that, so stop worrying,' Jo said and picked up a tray of tea and toast with a boiled egg, 'I'll give him his breakfast and then we'll walk around the garden and sit in the warmth for a bit. Go before you miss your bus.'

Once in Truro, Kitty took a deep breath and set her mind to enjoying the time to walk and talk with other people. It was good to be out of uniform and feel her hair flow free around her neck and cheeks. The dark circles under her eyes did nothing to flatter her dry, pale face, but she hoped a pot of face cream was still available in town. July was a few days away and with the weather was much warmer, Kitty stopped to remove her cardigan before joining the end of a long queue of chattering women and small children to enter a bakery. She hoped it wouldn't take all her time in Truro, and she wouldn't miss out on a short browse around the other shops, when suddenly it hit her; here she was, worried about browsing in shops for trivial things when men were lying dead or injured to secure her privilege to do so. Michael's mind had taken a beating and he might never recover, and his body was still broken from an enemy bullet. She rushed from the queue and across the street, keeping her head down with the shame of the tears falling and soaking the front of her dark-green dress, when she ran into someone coming the other way.

'Hey, lady, slow down.' A male in uniform with an

American accent grabbed the tops of her arms before she tipped forward.

Kitty looked up and stared into bright-blue eyes. The eyes twinkled back at her, and the man's smile was infectious. She smiled back. Her tears were drying on her cheeks and with impatience she brushed them away. No doubt the mascara she'd carefully applied that morning had left black streaks. She must look a mess to the smart soldier standing before her.

Michael was handsome, but this man could only be described as beautiful. His lashes were long and dark, a stark contrast to the white-blond hair on his head.

'I'm so sorry,' she said as she caught her breath.

'No apologies, ma'am. You looked pretty shook up – can I help?'

Kitty composed herself and gave a shy smile. 'Thank you. Unless you can shake off nightmares and flashbacks, then I'm sorry, no, you can't, but it was kind of you to ask,' she replied. Not really sure why she made such a statement.

The soldier stooped to pick up her cardigan, lying unnoticed by Kitty, and handed it to her.

'I'm deeply sorry you have worries, ma'am. I'm a good listener if it helps – oh, here, use mine,' he said and handed her a crisp white handkerchief folded into a neat square.

Feeling foolish about her tearful response to the unexpected kindness of a stranger, Kitty quickly dabbed her eyes and offered the handkerchief back to him, but he shook his head, so she tucked it into her dress pocket.

'Walk with me. Let's sit over there,' he said, pointing to a bench facing away from the shop fronts, 'as repayment for my kindness. And out of the prying eyes of the bread hunters,' he added with a laugh.

Without hesitation, Kitty did as he asked. Although he was a stranger, she needed to be with someone at that moment and his calm voice with its unusual laid-back drawl eased her into a more relaxed state. She fell in step beside him.

'I'm Sergeant Lewis Porter, US Army,' the soldier said as they sat down, one at either end of the seat.

'Pleased to meet you, Lewis. I'm Kitty Pattison, nurse with the British Red Cross, supporting the Canadians at the present time.' Kitty held out her hand as she spoke. His hand was warm and comforting, reminding her just how cold Michael's always were since his injuries.

'So, what drove you to tears? The price of a British loaf of bread?'

Kitty laughed at his attempt to make her smile.

'Almost right. Something made me think it was all too trivial.' She pointed at the queue still winding itself around the corner of one street into another. 'A selfish thought made me snap myself out of feeling sorry for myself – and all over a pot of face cream.' She gave a part laugh, part huff of disgust.

The soldier also gave a gentle laugh. 'I get that way when I can't find my favourite brand, too. Seriously, I know tears and can tell the difference between disappointment and distress, and you were in distress. Wanna tell me what happened?' Lewis asked, his voice low and encouraging.

Before she could talk herself out of chatting with a stranger, Kitty offloaded her story from the moment she landed on the beaches of Normandy to when she left that morning. Of how Michael was not the man he was, but she felt sure she could bring him around again. Of how Canada might be the key. Lewis listened without interrupting and when she had finished, she noted the sadness in his face, too.

'Were you there?' she asked.

He gave a gentle flick of his head. 'One of the lucky ones,' he replied. 'Injured on Omaha Beach. Shoulder took a bullet, then got infected. Waiting for the doc to sign me back as fit for duty and I'll be heading out again.'

'I know the kinds of wounds and infections some of you returned with. Dreadful. Heartbreaking place,' Kitty replied.

Lewis wiped his hands down his uniform trousers, and Kitty could see beneath his bravado that he also carried the horrors as a reminder to be grateful for escaping the beaches. He gave a light cough and flinched; Kitty knew his doctor would sign him off even though he was still in pain, and he would be shipped out to deal with another battle elsewhere in the world.

'Forgive me, but I am still trying to visualise a girl who looks like Ava Gardner crawling around like the rest of us in the sand. Incredible.'

'I'm surprised the Red Cross agreed to it, but Michael, my fiancé, was the creator and leader of the rescue crew and put across a good case about me and my past as part of an emergency team in a hospital I trained in, and they agreed.' Kitty took a breath and sighed. 'I did it, in part, to be closer to my fiancé. It's awful as now we are further apart than ever – not in the flesh, but in the silences and blank stares. The only thing he can say is the word "Canada". I wonder if that is where his mind will stay – in the place where he was born but left several years ago, before the war? Is it wrong to feel jealous of a country?'

Kitty let out another sigh.

'I think you have every right to feel angry and bitter. You have experienced a tremendous shock. Listen, I have to get back to base but I've time on my hands. Can I come visit your fiancé? Talk with him? I know Canada well. Let me help.'

Kitty thought about Lewis's request and decided his offer was genuine and could do no harm to Michael. She agreed and wrote down where they were staying. Lewis told her he would visit the following day. When he walked away, Kitty ventured to buy her face cream with a calmer mindset and wondered what fate had in mind when it sent Lewis Porter her way.

Chapter Forty-Four

'Stanley says the boys are doing well in their studies, and he received letters from four other orphans we cared for. Isn't that wonderful?' Kitty didn't wait any more for a reaction from Michael; there never was one.

She continued to read the letter out loud, including the part where Stanley enquired after Michael's health, but again, she received no reaction. Although he had shown signs of his memory returning, Kitty now accepted she had done all she could and settled into a routine of care. If anyone could help restore her fiancé to his former self, it wasn't going to be her or Jo.

Jo was arriving that day and Kitty wondered if Lewis Porter would make an appearance. Michael's doctor was due the following afternoon; Kitty squashed the thought of Michael being taken to a rehabilitation unit, but, deep down, knew it was inevitable. Since crying in Truro, tears no longer came. Kitty had sealed off her heart to protect it from the pain she knew would rip through her and reduce her to someone unable to cope with anything else.

'Sarah is still searching for her family. She writes to say she has written notes for each box she sends out in the hope that someone will write back to her with information. She did receive a letter from a young man, and they've written ever since. I'm not sure where he is, but obviously somewhere he can send letters. I hope they get to meet one day.'

Michael continued to stare ahead. His face was no longer tanned, but thinner and pale. Kitty wanted to shake him awake from his trance-like state.

'Tom and Maude send their regards. They have two airmen staying with them and have put my personal belongings aside for Wenna to collect. She is going to store them at The Stargazy. Belle's place. Remember Belle? All posh frocks and lipstick. Then turned out to be a spy.'

Giving up on the letter reading, Kitty sat and wrote her latest notes on Michael. His inability to wash and dress himself and the use of only one word. She hated every statement and looked to Michael for a sign of something more positive to write about, but he gave her nothing.

Jo's voice broke the heavy silence as she called through the kitchen and entered the parlour.

'Hello, you two. It's a hot one out there today. Want me to wheel Michael under the tree? It's my last trip over. We're moving out tomorrow. Transit camp duties. Is this fresh?' Jo dropped a paper bag onto the table and busied herself pouring a tea from the pot in front of Kitty as she spoke. 'Grab a doughnut while they're fresh.'

'Morning, Jo,' Kitty said with a laugh, her heart lifting at the sound of her friend's chatter and the sweet-tasting doughnut.

'What's the news?' Jo asked and tilted her head towards the letters on the table.

Kitty licked her lips and brushed sugar from her chin before replying. 'The Gaskin brothers and Eric have managed to repair an old tractor between them, can you believe it?' Kitty replied.

'Good lads! I wonder if I can get to see them if we head that way with the truck sometime. They can help me overhaul mine.' Jo laughed.

'Can you imagine what they'd have done to it when they were younger? It would have lost all its nuts and bolts and wheels. Little scamps.' Kitty giggled. 'I do miss them. I miss their cheeky smiles and the days filled with the unexpected,' she said wistfully.

A knock on the door interrupted their chatter and Kitty opened it to find Lewis Porter standing on the step.

'As promised, one lanky American come to talk all things Canadian with a fellow soldier. I hope I'm not imposing, Kitty,' he said and removed his cap.

'Not at all, it is good to see you again. Come in and meet my best friend, Jo. She drives doughnuts around and we have a fresh batch on the table. One has your name on it now!' Kitty ushered him inside and tried not to giggle as he bent his head to get indoors.

'Jo, meet Lewis Porter. He helped me in Truro and has volunteered the rest of his sick leave to sit with Michael.'

Jo stood up to shake Lewis's hand. 'Good grief, you're a target on legs with that hair and height,' she said.

'Jo! Sorry about her; no manners and a mouth which speaks before her brain thinks,' Kitty said, laughing, relieved to see Lewis chuckling too.

'Pleasure, Jo,' he said and moved towards Michael. He saluted.

'Sir, it's a hot day that reminds me of Seattle sunshine, or a surfing day at Tofino in your neck of the woods, Canada.'

He turned to Kitty when there was no response. 'If you girls want to go chatter in the fresh air, Michael and I will get along just fine.'

Once outside, Jo pulled Kitty away from the open window and led her further down the path.

'Where did you find him? He's a looker, and super tall,' she asked with excited curiosity.

'I had a bit of a panic and literally ran into him. He talked me through it, and my fears about Michael came out, so he volunteered to use the rest of his sick leave by helping him,' Kitty explained.

'So, you offered up your life story to him and he drove here in his jeep for a man he's never met?' Jo questioned her with her hands on her hips. 'I think not, Miss Kitty. I think *you* are the attraction.'

Kitty's laugh rang out as she processed what Jo had said. 'Jo, you always think the worst of people. He's here to help Michael. He knows a lot about Canada. He's kind. He was there – on the beaches. He understands.' Kitty's voice softened.

Jo linked her arm through Kitty's, and they took a moment to allow Kitty to reflect and remember.

'I think we'll agree to disagree. We'll leave it that you've found a new friend. We'll write to him and make sure he's rewarded for his kindness by offering friendship. I'm sorry I was an ass,' Jo said, breaking the silence.

'Yes, we will. Writing to him is a lovely idea, but only if he wants a couple of mad English pen pals,' Kitty chipped in. 'Let's go and find out.'

Back inside they could hear Lewis's voice encouraging Michael to look at something, and Kitty also heard the resignation in his voice that he was getting nowhere. She'd heard it in Jo's voice and her own. Perseverance and patience were needed, but sometimes acceptance was, too.

Jo made her excuses to leave, and she and Kitty hugged in farewell before Kitty returned her attention to Michael, still oblivious to the book Lewis was reading to him.

'What book is that? It sounds intriguing,' she asked as she walked back into the room.

Lewis stopped reading and closed the book. He held it out for her to see. '*Evil Under the Sun* by Agatha Christie. A detective novel courtesy of the US Army,' he said.

'I wonder if Michael enjoyed it,' Kitty said and removed the cups and plates from the table. 'Another cuppa?'

'You Brits and your tea. Thanks, but no, I've had my fill. Your friend Jo is quite something else,' Lewis said. 'You been friends long?'

'We met at the start of our training, September 1940. We're close.'

Lewis smiled. 'I can see that. She's fond of you, even

with her tough exterior. I lost my best buddy in the water. It's hard some days, which is why I understand this situation here,' he said.

'I'm sorry you lost your friend. We all need friends right now,' Kitty said and turned to look out of the window. She wanted to admit she had the urge to run and never stop, to enjoy the sunshine without worries; she also wanted to know how to lose the guilt of wanting those things. Her world was caving in on her and Kitty failed to see the way forward. Earlier in the garden, before they reached the back door, Jo, with her blunt advice, told Kitty to unburden herself of Michael and to allow the Canadian army to take over. Of course Kitty reminded her that Michael was not a burden, but she agreed that at some point she had to let go and allow them to bring him back to reality.

'It's okay, you know,' Lewis said, again using his soft, encouraging voice, 'you've done your best and then some,' he said.

'What is?' Kitty gave a questioning frown.

'To feel guilty, and want to give up,' Lewis replied.

Kitty shoved her hands into her dress pockets, giving her time to speak. She did not want to snap back at Lewis, but he had managed to hit a raw nerve.

'I do not want to give up, but I realise I might *have* to. There is a difference,' she said in a controlled, calm voice.

Chapter Forty-Five

'Thank you for coming to see him,' Kitty said to four of Michael's men who had arrived to visit him. 'His doctor is making his final decision this afternoon, and, as you can see, I think it will not be in Michael's favour.'

The men nodded and muttered. She could see each one was embarrassed by Michael's position. He was a man who had led them through difficult times and now they felt useless.

'I have to abide by his medical advice, and as you four are aware we are a couple; it won't be easy for me. I'll let you know where they send him. Promise me you will still visit. I have a feeling I'm to be moved on as soon as he has left. The Red Cross will have something lined up, be sure of it,' she said.

One of the men saluted Michael. 'See you around, sir,' he said, then turned to Kitty. 'We promise we'll make sure we rotate visits and try and get him back for you. We'll let ourselves out – and thank you for all you did for us and what you are doing now, but – well, be kind to yourself too. It's a short life in a war.'

Kitty nodded her goodbyes to the men and watched them walk away down the path to the street. As she went to move away, she saw Lewis walk across the road and hold back while the men disappeared around the corner.

Opening the door to let him in, Kitty saw the men drive away.

'I wasn't expecting to see you, Lewis. I saw you hiding from Michael's men,' she teased. 'They are quite harmless.'

He laughed. 'I was not hiding. I would have to do a lot of explaining as to why I'm here, and it would waste time I haven't got.'

Kitty looked up at him. 'Have you been signed fit for duty?' she asked.

'I have, but I'm to stay here in England for a while longer, then they'll ship me off to Europe,' Lewis replied.

After fifteen minutes of chatting, the doctor arrived, and Kitty's nerves jangled when he examined Michael. She and Lewis waited for him to reappear and offer his wisdom about Michael's future.

He entered the parlour and graciously accepted a cup of coffee and plate of biscuits, which Lewis had brought with him as a gift for Kitty.

They stood quietly as he scribbled notes at the table. Kitty twiddled her fingers nervously, and Lewis reached over and placed his hand across hers, giving her a reassuring smile.

'Nurse Pattison, I read through your notes, and I must say, you have carried out a thorough package of care. Sadly, my examination shows no improvement at all since I last saw Doctor McCarthy. You say the only word he has spoken is "Canada"?' The doctor looked up from his notes and directed his question with a puzzled frown.

Kitty gave a bob of her head. 'He last spoke several days ago, and it was the only word he said. There's been nothing since. Sergeant Porter knows a lot about Canada and on hearing about a Canadian doctor needing support, he volunteered his time to try and encourage Michael to find a way back to us,' Kitty said and she watched as the doctor turned to address Lewis.

'Did you get anywhere with him?' he asked.

'Sorry, sir, no. Nurse Pattison here has done nothing but her best. Some of his crew have not long left, and they found the same, as did Nurse Pattison's friend, another Red Cross nurse.'

Kitty sent him a grateful glance for offering a professional response.

'My decision is not one you will want to hear, Nurse. I am fully aware the doctor is your fiancé, but my advice is this: step away from the situation. Doctor McCarthy will be taken to one of our best hospitals in Canada, where he will either remain or recover—'

'But he has no one there!' Kitty burst out, unable to hold back her horror that they were shipping Michael off to Canada. She had accepted that a rehabilitation unit would be his home for some time, but, in her naivety, she had expected it to be in Britain.

'He is a Canadian within a Canadian army unit; there is no other alternative. This is not operational fatigue. My fear is the blow on the head has caused considerable brain damage. I have a colleague with considerable expertise in electrical therapy. It might be the treatment required.'

Kitty could barely breathe and struggled to get out her words. 'But I'll lose him. What if I marry him and give up my post? I can care for him then, can't I?' she asked, desperate for a positive reaction.

'I'm afraid you have to be realistic, Nurse… Kitty, he is not the man you prepared yourself to marry. My duty is to ensure my soldier is returned to his homeland and attended to in the proper manner, and as soon as I can arrange it – which, I warn you, will be within days, not weeks. I suggest you turn to your friends for support, but also get back to helping others, because, from what I've seen, you are a caring, capable nurse.'

Kitty barely heard the rest of his words, but was aware Lewis had taken over the conversation and saw the man off the premises. Kitty rose from her seat and went to Michael. She knelt down and laid her head in his lap, waiting for some kind of comfort. She did not move when Lewis went around the cottage drawing the curtains and lighting lamps and candles. Eventually, she pulled herself together. Michael needed to be attended to and she only had days left to offer him the best care she could. It was no time to allow her emotions to get the better of her – Michael needed her now more than ever.

Over two days Kitty and Lewis cut Michael's hair and nails and groomed him to be ready for his uniform. Kitty was adamant he was not leaving the house in his pyjamas. Lewis remained with him while she went to the village telephone box and explained the situation to Smithy. He promised to drive to see them the following day.

Settling Michael in bed, Kitty sat and read to him while Lewis prepared them something to eat from the meagre rations she had left. He offered to get news to Jo when he returned to base. By eight that evening, Kitty was left alone with Michael sleeping, completely oblivious to what was happening to him. She climbed onto the bed beside him and put her arms around him, absorbing final memories.

'As soon as I can get out to Canada, I will come to see you. I'm sorry I lost our battle to stay together. I'll never forget you, Michael. No matter what, I'll never forget our love, our journey through this hideous war. I hope I am in your heart somewhere safe and, one day, you will remember your English girl.'

Kitty placed kisses on his sleeping face, now wet with her tears, but it remained unchanged and, deep down, Kitty knew their time to part had come. Unsure how she would cope in her own mind, she imagined him in a happier place, somewhere he once described, where pine trees stood tall on snow-capped mountains, where trout leaped from streams, and the eagles soared carefree.

Chapter Forty-Six

'How are you doing, old girl? What a state of affairs this all is,' Smithy said as he settled Michael into a seat. Kitty sat writing a list of addresses for Michael, and notes, for anyone who cared to read them, about memories Michael had made with her in England. She had removed her chain from around her neck and placed it around Michael's underneath his uniform, with a note explaining what it was and meant to him. She had not stopped all night, burning a candle to nothing simply writing letter after letter and packing his bags. Smithy had arrived early the previous day just as the news Kitty dreaded had arrived. Michael's transfer was for the afternoon of 20th July at 1500 hours.

'I'm doing, Smithy. I'm doing.' Kitty hitched a choking sob from her throat as she recalled the peaceful scene in his home when she and Michael visited Meryn and Kedrick.

'I'm under instructions to take you to ours later when...'

Kitty laid down her pen and looked at Smithy. A friend

in distress trying his hardest to be a supportive doctor and friend at the same time.

'I'm going to stay with Wenna. My orders will come through soon and, if I'm truthful, Smithy, I won't cope seeing Trix and your home. Tell me you understand and tell Trix as soon as I am free to visit, in my mind and my duty rota, I will. I just need time.'

Smithy moved to her side and lifted her to her feet. He put his arms around her in a brotherly embrace and held her as her heart broke into a million pieces.

An hour later, Kitty removed her uniform and put on the outfit she wore when she and Michael met at Peebles. She pulled a chair in front of him and, as best as she could, hummed the tune the piper wrote for them. His hands were limp and cold and his face unseeing, but she did not stop until a tap at the door announced the arrival of his ambulance. She encouraged him to his feet and adjusted his uniform, then walked him outside. Smithy kept a grip on her arm as the ambulance drove away and her legs threatened to give out underneath her.

Once the ambulance turned the corner, she shrugged her shoulders back and stepped inside. 'I'd better pack my things now. Pop the kettle on, Smithy, there's a love,' she said as she climbed the stairs to her room. Once inside, she lay exhausted across the bed with the memory of a piper playing just for her and his song dancing on the wind towards her ears and settling within her heart. Unable to shut out the sound, she embraced it and allowed her mind to take her to dark corners and onwards, to picnics on the beach, to a proposal of marriage ... and back to dark corners. For her own sake, Kitty understood she could not shut out the thoughts. Michael existed, just no longer in her world. She would do her utmost to remain connected with him via letters but had to accept she would receive none in return. The war had taught her many things; one of them was acceptance and another was resilience. Neither would have a place in the room until she had released the pain of loss yet again.

Male voices woke her, and she noted Smithy had company. She squinted at the sunshine blazing across her bedroom. She peered at her watch and registered five-thirty. She recalled a moment when Meryn woke her, and she'd slept soundly. A male's laugh sounded out and her heart skipped a beat as, for one fleeting second, she thought of Michael. Clambering from her bed, and giving her hair a quick pat into place, she took a moment to repress her emotions. She needed to settle them until darkness when she knew they would return in full force. Confident that she could cope in the company of friends, she went downstairs, and as she reached the bottom step, she heard Lewis's voice encouraging Smithy to tell him more stories about when he and Michael were student doctors.

Pushing open the door she wafted away cigar smoke and smiled at them both as they shot to their feet. She saw two bottles of beer on the table beside them, half full, and nestled beside them was a posy of flowers and a bar of chocolate.

'This is nice,' she said with genuine truth. It *was* nice to see them enjoying each other's company and she had no doubt in her mind that Lewis was the bringer of the gifts;

his way of saying sorry about Michael. When she'd told him Michael's oldest friend was arriving, he'd brought her food and instant coffee, something she declared to be an acquired taste; she never admitted she actually enjoyed it.

She learned quickly that Lewis was a protector of hearts and minds and although she had not known him long, Kitty had a feeling he needed to fill the void of losing his best friend, but with so many others suffering the same, and being so far from home, he had no one to turn to, so when they met and she shared her sadness, he must have learned she was someone who would listen when the time was right. Kitty sensed they were new friends together battling through an old past, and their pathway forward had not come to a dead end with Michael's leaving.

Kitty fully intended to repay Lewis's kindness once she was stronger after the shock of Michael being ripped from her world. She would start by asking him more about his life and that of his friend, and, when she was ready, she would ask him what he knew about Canada so she could plan a trip once the war was over. But, for tonight, they would celebrate Michael, the man who had her heart but would no longer know it, the doctor who believed in her abilities as a Red Cross nurse and gave her the strength and courage to continue down a path to a yet-to-be-written future.

Chapter Forty-Seven

1944

Killy Pallison,
C/O The Stargazy Inn
Mawnan Smith
Cornwall
August '44

Dearest Michael,

    As the days tick by, my thoughts of you strengthen and memories of our days together never fade. I have moments when I feel I failed you, but I know I did my best and if you were able to express yourself, you would set me right.

    I miss us and our silly ways. I miss you and your devotion to me whenever I needed love and support. I truly hope whoever is reading this to you can get across my words in such a way they will find their way into your soul.

Right now, I feel Canada has taken you from me and it will be some time before I can forgive her, but I will for she is your birthplace, and anywhere connected to you is precious.

Life has to move forward for me as a nurse knee-deep in war, but I will come to you and hold you in my arms once again as soon as I am able.

Our friends send loving wishes and are willing you back to good health. We have a new friend, you and I. Sergeant Lewis Porter of the US Army saved me from my darkness and despair. He is guiding Jo and me through the process of reaching Canada, which we will attempt once the madness of war has fled and we are free to move around the world in peace. He has taken it on himself to seek out any members of your family, aunts, uncles, anyone who might find it in their hearts to visit you and write to me. I have explained you are orphaned, and your grandmother was the last of your relatives, but we can live in hope there might be distant relatives willing to help in your recovery. We always have hope.

Smithy is a great source of strength for me, and relays amusing stories of your time at college together.

My darling, please find your way back to me as I cannot imagine a future without you at my side. Listen for the bagpipes tucked inside your mind, let their song comfort you.

My love always,
Your sweetheart Kitty xx

Kitty read over the letter. Although her words seemed inadequate, they were all she could think of at the time. Michael's colleagues took it to ensure it reached the next postal flight over to Canada, and all Kitty could do was wait and see if there was a reply of sorts.

Jo had rushed to her side once she received news of Michael, and between them they organised a trip to Canada together the moment the war ended. Smithy asked to be considered part of the plan, and an early draft was tucked between the cover of a diary Kitty had taken to writing.

'Keep them closed,' Jo instructed Kitty as she guided her blindfolded along a path.

'I can smell doughnuts, so I guess we're near your van,' Kitty replied, treading carefully by tapping her foot in front of her before she took a step forward.

The sea breeze was warm and comfortable, and, for the first time for a long time, Kitty's shoulders felt burden-free.

Today, she turned twenty-four, and although she once had dreams of being mother to several babies by that age, she had come to terms with the fact they were no longer something for the near future. Jo had insisted they went to visit Wenna, but had a surprise first.

'Right, stand there – stand still, stop fidgeting,' Jo instructed.

'Bossy boots,' Kitty chimed back with a giggle.

'Ready? Remove the blindfold.'

Not fully trusting Jo's humour, Kitty tentatively eased away the scarf from her eyes. She blinked and looked around her in complete shock.

'Surprise!' a chorus of voices shouted out.

Standing in front of her were a cheering Smithy

alongside a round and glowing Trix, a smiling Meryn holding Kedrick, Wenna and her mother both waving Union Jack flags, Pots, Stanley and Jack his gardener, all lifting ginger beer bottles as a toast, and David and Peter Gaskin and Eric all looking splendid in paper hats.

Kitty clapped her hands in delight at seeing so many friends together.

'This is wonderful, thank you so much!' she said and ran to kiss each one in turn.

The boys made a play of running away and Stanley held her close without saying a word. Words were not needed in the moment, just friends and happy voices.

'Ah, here comes the man we have to thank for organising the spread under this cloth,' Jo said as she tapped the table. Kitty looked over at Lewis, striding towards them with something in his arms.

'Happy Birthday, Kitty,' he said as he settled a mound of material onto the ground.

'Here we go, guys. As Stanley said, chocks away.'

The boys rushed forward, and each pulled out a string from beneath the cloth and paper and to Kitty's amusement they ran the length of the grassy clifftop to show off their handmade kite with the words 'Happy Birthday Kitty' painted across it. The run was a success and the kite bobbed skyward for as far as the string attached allowed.

'Thank you, Lewis – everyone. What a wonderful surprise,' she shouted to them as the boys yelled and called out with glee.

Jo stepped forward. 'The surprises are not over yet, Kitty. We have one more.'

Jo turned her around, so she was looking out at sea when Stanley gave a short whistle.

'You can turn around now,' Jo said and Kitty turned to face her uncle, grinning from ear to ear.

'Uncle Frank! Oh, Uncle Frank!' Kitty flung herself into his arms and he patted her head just as he had when she was a child in distress.

'Everything is going to be all right, girl. It will be all right, I promise. Just live your life the best it can be, and it will all work out in the end. You have our love,' he said and kissed the top of her head. Kitty believed every word he said. He had taken her in his arms and said the same words the day she lost her parents; she had no reason to doubt him. He nurtured her through hard times, never failing to guide her in the right direction. He gently reminded her that, like him, she had to move forward and accept whatever came her way. His reassurance promised her that she would survive the traumatic time with Michael, but only if she accepted she had to make a new life guided by family and friends.

He begged her to believe what was meant to be would be, and she needed strength of body and mind to survive not just the war, but life itself.

Kitty agreed. No one could have predicted her past, but she had to put her trust in those who loved her; old friends and new to guide her into the future emotionally intact and of sound mind.

She lifted out the photograph of Michael that was nestled in her pocket. 'Without love there is no hope, and we have both, my darling. We will survive this – we are meant to be,' she whispered and kissed it before returning it to its safe place.

Kitty clung on to what her uncle said: to believe everything would work out for the best, that the love of others would guide her back from darkness into the sunlight.

Acknowledgments

Dear Reader,
This sequel to The Red Cross Orphans Book I was written before the invasion of Ukraine 2022, but some of Kitty's thoughts about WWII are poignant and possibly relevant for the present day.
I've used my artistic allowance in this novel, but there were so many secret missions during WWII who knows whether I've written a true story in error!

Dear Team OMC,
Thank you for bringing out the best in me!
Charlotte Ledger, my emails probably make you want to run and hide at times, but you never do! Thank you for believing in me and my work.

For my supportive writing friends,
Thank you for supporting my work and for, well, being my friend.

Dear Family and Friends,

You are not forgotten.

Thank you for your love and support. Also, your patience when I can't make it to a social event or am bashing your eardrums with new novel ideas.

Glynis

ONE MORE CHAPTER

One More Chapter is an
award-winning global
division of HarperCollins.

Sign up to our newsletter to get our
latest eBook deals and stay up to date
with our weekly Book Club!
<u>Subscribe here.</u>

Meet the team at
<u>www.onemorechapter.com</u>

Follow us!

 @OneMoreChapter_
 @OneMoreChapter
 @onemorechapterhc

Do you write unputdownable fiction?
We love to hear from new voices.
Find out how to submit your novel at
<u>www.onemorechapter.com/submissions</u>